JUST THE BEGINNING

HALFMOON QUAY BOOK ONE

SARAH BENNETT

B

First published in Great Britain in 2025 by Boldwood Books Ltd.

Copyright © Sarah Bennett, 2025

Cover Design by Alice Moore Design

Cover Images: Shutterstock

Interior Images: Sarah Bennett

A CIP catalogue record for this book is available from the British Library.

Paperback ISBN 978-1-83633-573-3

Large Print ISBN 978-1-83633-572-6

Hardback ISBN 978-1-83633-571-9

Ebook ISBN 978-1-83633-574-0

Kindle ISBN 978-1-83633-575-7

Audio CD ISBN 978-1-83633-566-5

MP3 CD ISBN 978-1-83633-567-2

Digital audio download ISBN 978-1-83633-570-2

This book is printed on certified sustainable paper. Boldwood Books is dedicated to putting sustainability at the heart of our business. For more information please visit https://www.boldwoodbooks.com/about-us/sustainability/

Boldwood Books Ltd, 23 Bowerdean Street, London, SW6 3TN

www.boldwoodbooks.com

For Vikki Chapman Moorhouse

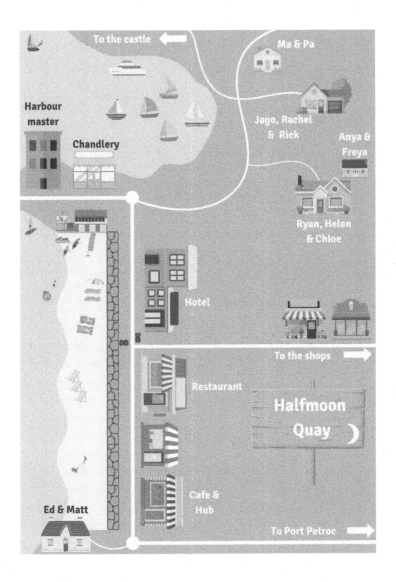

CHARACTER LIST

Ron Penrose – Patriarch of the family and retired boat builder.
Amy Penrose – Ron's wife.
Davy Penrose – Ron's brother – owner of the Penrose House Hotel.
Jago Penrose – Ron and Amy's elder son – the harbour master.
Rachel Penrose – Jago's wife – owns and runs the chandlery on the quayside.
Fitzwilliam 'Liam' Penrose – Jago and Rachel's eldest son. Lives and works in London doing something clever with numbers.
Frederick 'Rick' Penrose – Jago and Rachel's second son. Works with his mother in the chandlery and also owns The Hire Hut, a water sports hire company. Sits on the local parish council.
Henry 'Harry' Penrose – Jago and Rachel's third son and the eldest of the twins by a couple of minutes. A chef in a restaurant on the seafront.
Edward 'Ed' Penrose – Jago and Rachel's fourth son and the baby of the family. Training part time for a marine biology PhD

and working in a dead-end admin job to support himself. Shares a cottage with his cousin, Matt.

Ryan Penrose – Ron and Amy's younger son – self-employed joiner who works with his son, Matt.

Helen Penrose – Ryan's wife – works from home doing the accounts for Ryan's business and is a support worker at the local primary school during term time.

Matt Penrose – Ryan and Helen's son – works with his dad and shares a cottage with Ed which they are in the process of refurbishing.

Chloe Penrose – Ryan and Helen's daughter – works as a legal secretary at a local solicitor's office.

Anya Stokes – A widow who is very down on her luck. Helen's niece and cousin to Matt and Chloe.

Drew Stokes – Anya's deceased husband.

Freya Stokes – Anya and Drew's four-year-old daughter.

Lisa Maguire – Anya's mother and Helen Penrose's sister. Married to Bill; they are semi-retired and live in a villa in the Canary Islands.

Bill Maguire – Lisa's husband.

Issy Kernow – Close friend of Anya, Chloe and Kat – runs a café and oversees the Hub, a community space.

Maud Kernow – Issy's grandmother and a long-term resident at the Penrose House Hotel.

Kat Bailey – Close friend of Anya, Chloe and Issy – works for her father, who runs a café that is part of an international franchise. Also volunteers part time at the community library in the Hub.

Gavin Bailey – Kat's father – runs a Java Brava café franchise on the village high street.

Mr Hawthorn – A local newsagent.

Dr Ferguson – The village GP.

Caroline – Liam Penrose's girlfriend.

Lucinda – A friend of Caroline.

Tarquin Granby-Plungar – Lucinda's boyfriend.

Russ Armstrong – Renowned chef and owner of the restaurant where Harry works.

Steve – Night manager at the Penrose House Hotel.

Jim – The village postman.

Shelly Dean – An old classmate of Issy, Chloe and Kat's. Married with three small children.

Jason Dean – Shelly's husband.

Leo Dean – Shelly and Jason's son.

Poppy and Ella Dean – Shelly and Jason's twin baby daughters.

Morwenna Delaney – Head teacher of the village primary school.

Marie – Owner of Deliziosa an Italian restaurant in Port Petroc.

Phil – Barman at Deliziosa.

Kerry Wilson – Owner of the Curiosity Cave, a shop in the Quay.

Dr Hillman – ER doctor.

Jamie – ER nurse.

Nicky – ER nurse.

1

'What about these?'

Anya paused in the act of folding her daughter's clothes to glance over to where her cousin Chloe was holding up a set of picture books. A flood of memories of sitting in the antique rocking chair Drew had found for Freya's nursery as she'd read and reread those stories almost dropped Anya to her knees. The antique rocking chair had been loaded onto the back of the bailiffs' van the previous week along with pretty much everything else of value in the house. They'd left the beds, some kitchen basics and those personal effects not deemed valuable enough to auction off. Everything else had gone, including the designer labels and blingy jewellery Drew had insisted on showering Anya with. A very apologetic man had called only yesterday to ask her if she was aware that the majority of the stones were worthless reproductions. Anya had laughed to the point of hysterics, because wasn't that just the perfect representation of her life with Drew?

'Annie?'

Chloe's gentle question brought Anya back into the present.

'Sorry, um, let's take them. Freya's probably outgrown most of them but she'll need some familiar things around her. Let's pack all of her toys too.' There wasn't going to be a lot of space at her aunt and uncle's place, but her daughter had been through so much since that freezing early January night the previous year when the police had shattered their lives with a late-night knock at the door.

Chloe nodded. 'Good idea. We can look at replacing things gradually once she's settled in at home.'

Anya quirked her lips into her best semblance of a smile. There hadn't been anything to smile about since Drew's death, so it was a case of relying on muscle memory. Given she had the sum total of about thirty pounds in her purse, both she and Freya were going to have to make do with what they had for some considerable time to come. None of which was Chloe's fault. Her cousin was just doing her best to try and keep Anya's spirits up. Setting aside the pretty pink cardigan she'd been folding, Anya crossed the room to put her arms around Chloe. 'Thank you for doing this with me.'

Chloe's return hug was instantaneous. 'As if we would leave you to try and deal with this mess on your own.'

'I know, but it's not fair that we're turning all your lives upside down like this.'

Chloe leaned back so she could catch Anya's eye. 'Hey, listen. I wouldn't wish your circumstances on anyone, but I promise you that we are delighted that you and Freya are moving to Halfmoon Quay to be with us.'

Anya nodded. Growing up, she would've given everything in the world to live in Halfmoon Quay. The pretty village clinging to the edge of the Cornish coast had been a haven in comparison to the boring privet-hedged suburb she'd lived in on the outskirts of one of the many commuter towns that encircled

London. In a roundabout way, Anya had indeed given everything and now that childhood wish was coming true. Be careful what you wish for – wasn't that always the moral of fairy tales?

Her aunt Helen poked her head around the door. 'Matt's nipping to the shop to grab some sandwiches for lunch. What would you both like?' Her expression softened as she saw the cardigan Anya had been folding on the bed. Entering the room, she picked it up and brushed a hand over the pretty flowers stitched around the border. 'I remember when Freya wore this for your mum's wedding. Have you heard from her, recently?'

Anya shook her head. 'Not beyond the odd WhatsApp message.'

Lisa, Anya's mother and Helen's sister, had got married the previous autumn to a lovely man called Bill she'd met on a cruise. Lisa had wanted to postpone the wedding given it had less than a year since Drew's death, but Anya had urged her to go ahead. Her life had been lurching from bad to worse, the police having advised her they had questions about the car accident that had killed Drew. Knowing in her gut there was more trouble to come, Anya had wanted her mother to embrace her own happiness and hadn't breathed a word to anyone until she'd had no choice.

Over the course of the following few months, all Anya's worst fears – and several that had never even entered her head – had played out. First the police road traffic accident investigation unit had been unable to recreate a scenario that didn't involve Drew deliberately steering his car off the road and had submitted a report to the coroner stating that. As a result, the insurers had refused to pay out a penny, and as the unpaid bills piled up, Anya had learned the shocking truth about her husband's dodgy business dealings.

Still she'd kept quiet, unable to find the words to express not only her disbelief in what Drew had been up to, but the anger she felt towards herself for being so bloody naïve. While it was true that Drew had rebuffed even the smallest enquiry into their finances, Anya hadn't tried all that hard to dig deeper, content to live in her own little bubble. It was only when the bank had told her they were going to repossess the house that she'd had no choice but to admit to her family the full scale of the disaster Drew had left her to deal with.

By the time Anya had come clean, Lisa and Bill had relocated to a lovely little villa in the Canary Islands as part of their early retirement plans. Lisa had been furious with Anya for letting her go ahead, but what else had she been supposed to do? There was no way she was going to spoil her mother's happiness – or Bill's for that matter – because of what Drew had done. They'd worked their entire lives and had earned what they had. Anya's mum in particular had struggled to make ends meet after her dad walked out on them. Doing anything that would risk her hard-earned financial security was anathema to Anya. Unfortunately her refusal to take a penny from them had caused something of a rift and they were currently only communicating via WhatsApp messages. Though Anya missed talking to her mum, the distance was a relief compared to the fractious rows that had ended with them both in tears. She knew she could fix things tomorrow if she accepted their offer of financial help, but Anya was adamant. Drew had ruined enough lives with his schemes and lies; she would not add her own mother to the list.

Sheer desperation had forced her to accept her aunt and uncle's offer to move in with them. Matt, their son and Anya's cousin, had moved out recently to share a cottage with Ed, a cousin on his father's side of the family, and they'd converted the old summer house at the end of their garden into a studio apartment for Chloe. Without giving her the chance to refuse, Chloe had moved back into her old bedroom and told Anya the apartment was hers for as long as she needed it. Anya had accepted only because she literally had no other choice. Freya needed a roof over her head and Anya needed a job. With the summer season about to start she hoped she'd be able to pick something up. Anything would do as long as it brought in enough money to at least feed them.

It was her aunt Helen's turn to hug her. 'Give her time, lovely, and she'll come around.'

Anya nodded. 'I don't blame her.' There were only two people she blamed for the situation she found herself in: Drew for being a liar their entire life together and herself for letting him fool her so completely and utterly.

Helen hugged her again. 'I'd better get downstairs and finish up. I'll tell Matt to get a selection of sandwiches, okay?'

'Okay.' Anya didn't care what he got, because she'd lost her appetite weeks ago when the full horror of her situation had become clear. She still ate, but only because she needed to stay healthy for Freya's sake. At least she wasn't there to see them packing up what was left of the only home she'd ever known. Helen and Ryan had bought them train tickets and Anya had taken Freya down to Halfmoon Quay the previous weekend. She was staying with Chloe's grandparents while the rest of the family had piled into their cars and travelled back up to Surrey to collect the last of their belongings. Knowing the inevitable was coming, Anya had been thinning out for the past couple of weeks, selling what she could or donating it to charity shops, and recycling or dumping the rest. It had given her something to do in the evenings while Freya was asleep, and she'd found it somewhat cathartic.

Drew's stuff had gone first and it had been like a weight

lifting off her shoulders, giving her the boost she needed to tackle the rest. There was no trace of him left in the house other than in the photo albums Anya had tucked away in the bottom of a box. Her first instinct had been to toss the lot on a bonfire in the back garden, but Freya didn't know the truth about her father and Anya had sworn the rest of the family to secrecy. Anya knew how hard it was to grow up without a father, her own having left when she wasn't much older than Freya was now. She hadn't even had the illusion that he was a good man, having snuck downstairs when she should've been in bed and overheard her mum and Aunt Helen talking about what a bastard he was over a bottle of wine. She'd been too young to understand what the word meant, only that it was something bad, and had crept back to bed and cried herself to sleep. One day, when she was old enough, Anya would tell her daughter the truth if she asked about him, but for now, if looking at Drew's photo brought Freya comfort, she would hold her peace.

By the time Matt called up the stairs to let them know he was back, Anya and Chloe had finished the packing, and three suitcases and half a dozen cardboard boxes were stacked on the landing next to a couple of bags of things she'd decided not to keep after all. Anya sealed the top of the final box with tape and sighed. 'Not much to show for the past ten years, is it?'

Chloe put her arm around Anya's waist and hugged her. 'It's time to stop worrying about the past, Annie. What's done is done and from now on you have to focus on the future. On what's best for you and Freya.'

Anya nodded. 'Yes, you're right. At the end of the day, she's all that matters.'

Her uncle Ryan was coming back through the front door as they reached the bottom of the stairs. Giving Anya his most encouraging smile, he rubbed his hands together. 'Right, the kitchen is just about done and the boxes are on the trailer. There's just a few plates and mugs – and the kettle of course – but those will take five minutes to sort out. How are you getting on upstairs?'

'That's done as well. We've left everything at the top of the stairs.'

He nodded. 'Matt and I will grab it all after lunch.' He hesitated, his smile softening into something kinder. Anya's gut clenched, knowing what he was going to say. 'That just leaves your workshop.'

Anya swallowed around the lump in her throat. 'Everything in there can go.'

'Oh, Annie, no!'

Chloe's dismayed gasp was followed immediately by her uncle saying, 'But darling, your sewing machine means the world to you, and all that material you've collected over the years, it'd be a waste to just throw it all away. Surely you'll find some use for it?'

If Anya hadn't spent so much time hiding away in her workshop making clothes and furnishings for the house, perhaps she'd have noticed what Drew had been up to. Knowing she'd indulged in a little fantasy world while in the real world people had lost their jobs, their homes, their marriages to the string of failed businesses Drew had set up and abandoned made her feel sick inside. If she'd been able to sell some of the things she'd made, she might not have felt like she'd completely wasted her life on nothing more than an indulgent hobby. The evaluator from the bailiffs had killed that notion in a matter of minutes when, after a cursory flick through the contents of her workshop, he'd declared nothing in there worth the cost of storage. 'I don't have space.'

Ryan winked at her. 'Don't worry about that; we'll find room.

I was only thinking the other day that I haven't sorted out the sheds in a long time. I bet if I went through them I could empty one out and convert it into a workshop for you. I know it won't be the same as what you've got now, but it'd be something to tide you over.'

'That's a great idea, Dad,' Chloe chipped in.

Anya knew she meant well, they all did, but for a moment she wished she'd found another way to resolve her problems that hadn't involved turning to her family. It was an unkind thought and she regretted it immediately. She felt even more churlish when Chloe took her hand and squeezed it gently. 'Hey. Mum and I will sort out the workshop while you hoover around upstairs, okay?'

Anya closed her eyes against a sudden pricking of tears and she was simply too tired to argue about it. 'Okay.'

2

Anya's brave face held all the way through the long drive back to Halfmoon Quay. Perhaps sensing how close to the edge she was, Chloe hadn't argued when Anya had insisted on taking the back seat. She and Ryan had chatted quietly to each other, leaving Anya to stare out the window and brood. They'd just turned off the motorway and were waiting at a set of traffic lights when she felt someone's eyes on her. Turning her head, Anya met Ryan's gaze via the rear-view mirror.

'Everything okay back there?'

A small laugh escaped unbidden. 'Not so much.'

Ryan's responding chuckle was rueful. 'Sorry, stupid question. There's a services here if you want to stop and grab a coffee?'

Anya shook her head. 'No, I just want to get back h—' Her voice hitched and she swallowed the rest of the word. Halfmoon Quay meant a lot of things to her, but it had never felt like home. Though she'd always loved her visits over the years, and as much as her cousins had included her in everything, she'd still not truly been one of them. She didn't have the rock and sand of the village woven into her soul the way those that had lived there all their lives did. 'To Freya,' she amended.

'Sure thing.'

The lights changed and Ryan navigated around the busy roundabout towards the turn-off that would lead them to Half-moon Quay. Realising she'd been a little short with him, Anya loosened her belt and leaned forward to touch her uncle's shoulder. 'I appreciate everything you're doing for me.'

'It's all good, Annie. You just focus on looking after Freya,' Ryan said, keeping his eyes on the snaking queue of traffic ahead of them.

Chloe half-turned in her seat and smiled at her. 'You look after Freya, and we'll look after you.'

Unable to find the words to express her gratitude, Anya nodded then sank back against her seat, her gaze fixed once more on the familiar scenery. She knew every twist and turn of the road, every hill and landmark. There was the church steeple poking over the top of the trees. Here was the junction that always seemed to be a bottleneck whatever time of day or night she passed through it. On the right, the faded peeling paintwork and graffitied boarded windows of a once bustling coaching inn now long since closed down. Next came the long drag up the hill that had seemed to go on forever when she was younger while her tummy bubbled with excitement and she'd stretched and strained in eager anticipation of that first magical glimpse of the glittering silver-blue sea and the grey brooding walls of the castle standing watch on the promontory above the village.

For the first time in her life there was no excitement inside Anya as they crested the hill and the picturesque view of Half-moon Quay was laid out before her. The only emotion that gripped her insides was fear, accompanied by the never-ending drumbeat of words in her head that had been growing louder with each mile of their journey.

What am I going to do? What am I going to do?

Once they pulled up outside the sprawling whitewashed stone house with its grey slate roof there was no time to think as it was all hands on deck to unload the cars and hump all the boxes down to the end of the garden. Standing in the middle of the open-plan main living space of the summer house, Anya felt that familiar sense of panic rising again as she surveyed their piled-up belongings. Even though she thought she'd cut everything down to the bare minimum it still felt like they'd never find room for everything. Her aunt Helen came over and picked up a box. 'Why don't you let us sort this out while you go to Ma and Pa's and fetch Freya?'

Goodness, that sounded like a wonderful idea, but they'd already done so much for her it felt rude to leave them to sort out her mess – again. 'Oh, I couldn't do that.' She surveyed the stacks of boxes as she bit her lip. 'I suppose we should unpack the clothes first. Or maybe the kitchen stuff.' She cringed a little inside hearing the self-doubt in her own voice. She never used to be this indecisive. One of her great joys had been planning and designing the layout of their family home, and the compliments from guests about her eye for style had been a source of pride. Now they were a source of shame, knowing the money she'd spent on all those perfect accessories had been stolen from other people.

Chloe planted her hands on her hips, a steely glint Anya knew well in her eye. 'Yes, you can. Look, we'll just find and unpack a few essentials, make the beds up and everything else can go into the garage for now. That way you can take your time setting things up the way you want them over the coming days.'

Anya hesitated, still conscious of not taking advantage of them. 'I would like to go and make sure Freya's okay...'

Her cousin shooed her towards the door with a grin. 'Off you go then. Mum and I will be fine here, won't we?'

Helen nodded in agreement. 'I don't know why we didn't think of it in the first place. With Ryan and Matt's help it won't take long to move most of this out of the way. We should be sorted by the time you get back with Freya.'

'Thank you.' Anya didn't know how many times those two words had passed her lips today, but it wasn't enough, could never be enough, to express her gratitude. 'I won't be long.'

The walk from her aunt and uncle's house to the old stone cottage where Amy and Ron Penrose lived wasn't far, and after hours sitting in the car and then moving boxes she wanted to stretch her legs. Opting for a circuitous route, she headed not towards the castle but instead around the sweep of the crescent-shaped harbour that had given the village its name. There were one or two commercial trawlers moored up at the top of the quay nearest the open water, stacks of lobster pots and tangles of old fishing nets piled up beside them, but the vast majority of the vessels tied up were small pleasure boats. Their white hulls and shiny masts glittered in the sun. The quayside was a hive of activity even this early in the summer season. Most of the people she passed were working on their boats, washing decks or touching up woodwork with pots of varnish that filled her nostrils with a stinging scent when the breeze blew across her face. There were quite a few holidaymakers around, mostly older couples taking advantage of the nice weather before the schools broke up and the village was inundated with sunseekers. Here and there were families with very small children dressed up in bright T-shirts and floppy hats.

The shops and businesses lining the road facing the quay were a mix of traditional and new. She couldn't help but smile at the sight of Mr Hawthorn's newsagents with its rack of buckets, spades and fishing nets waiting to tempt the enthusiastic sandcastle builders and rock poolers. She paused beneath the striped awning, the blue almost bleached out to match the white, to cup her hands and peer through the window. Just as she remembered, the shelves behind the counter were stacked high with plastic jars full of penny sweets. Oh the agonising she, Chloe and Matt had done over what treats to buy with the shiny fifty pence pieces Ma and Pa would present them with. She'd have to bring Freya sometime and introduce her to the fizzy delights of sherbet spaceships and sticky strawberry laces.

Stepping back, she spotted the column of little white cards lining the far side of the window, noting the 'HELP WANTED' announcements on a few. She didn't have time now, but she'd have to come back and check them out because as soon as she'd got Freya settled in, the next thing on the top of her worry list was finding a job. Anything would do, because someone with her lack of both a bank balance and anything resembling a CV couldn't afford to be fussy. Tomorrow would be soon enough to start looking. Mind made up, she carried on along the road, past the faded glory of the old hotel with its peeling window frames and a pair of straggly hanging baskets framing the entrance door. It had always been the jewel of the seafront and it was sad to see it looking so neglected.

A few doors down, the sleek black paintwork and shining brass fixtures of one of the top-rated restaurants in the county provided an even starker contrast to the poor state of the other buildings, including a boarded-up shop next to it. Anya had vague memories of it being an old-fashioned dress shop, in every sense of the meaning. She'd never been in there, the dowdy frocks draped listlessly on headless display dummies enough to put off the trend-chasing teens she, Chloe and their friend Issy had once been. Thinking about Issy immediately drew her attention across the road to where her friend's pretty café stood. Like the restaurant, the outside was well-maintained, the collection of tables and chairs out front looking cheerful and welcoming with their little pots of sunny flowers that matched a pair of planters framing the door. A shiny black and white sign declared the extension next to the café as the home of the Halfmoon Quay Community Hub. There'd been talk of it the last time Anya had been down for a visit – goodness, was that really nearly three years ago? She was glad to see Issy and Rick had managed to get it off the ground. Promising herself she'd pop in and catch up with her friend soon, Anya walked to the end of the road and turned left onto the narrow street of old fishermen's cottages where Ma and Pa lived.

She'd barely lifted her finger off the bell when the front door opened and Ron Penrose greeted her with his familiar broad smile. 'Well, well, look what the cat dragged in.'

Anya grinned, no offence taken at the greeting, which was part of Pa's collection of quirky phrases. Leaning forward, she pecked a kiss on his wrinkled cheek. 'Hello, Pa, how are you?'

'I've got two knackered knees, an acid reflux problem that means my belly's a volcano. All the hair that used to be on my head has migrated to my nose and ears and my wife says I snore like the brass section of an orchestra. Apart from that, everything's fine and dandy.'

Anya mock-winced. 'I'm sorry I asked!'

Ron gave her a cheeky grin before his expression grew serious. 'I won't ask how you are, because I already know the answer. If that little shit wasn't already dead and buried I'd string him up by his guts and let the seagulls feast on him for what he's put you through.'

For all his once-strong frame was shrunken now, there was a fierce glint in Ron's eye that told Anya he was deadly serious. Such a bloodthirsty threat probably shouldn't be so comforting, but Ron had always been blunt and Anya appreciated he hadn't danced around the topic. 'God knows he deserved that and more, Pa, but it wouldn't have been worth the time. He's gone now and that's all that matters.' She placed a hand on his arm. 'I know everyone is angry about what Drew did but please, don't say anything in front of Freya, okay? She's been through enough and she's too little to understand anything other than the fact her daddy is gone.'

Ron held her gaze for a long moment before nodding once. 'I'll not say another word about him.' He stepped back and gestured. 'Come on in, girly girl, and have a cuppa. Freya's in the kitchen with Amy; they've been baking.'

'How has she been?' Anya asked, keeping her voice low as they headed down the narrow hall to the back of the cottage.

'As good as gold. It's been lovely having a little one about the place again, makes me feel less like an old codger. Six grand-children and not one of them showing so much as a hint of giving us any great-grandchildren to fuss over. Don't know what they've all been wasting their time with.' Ron shook his head but his wry grin was filled with pride. 'Any time you want us to look after Freya while you get straight, just say the word.'

'I appreciate that, Pa, but I'm sure I'll manage.' It was kind of him to offer, but she wasn't about to start abusing their good nature.

Ron stopped in his tracks and frowned at her. 'Don't cut

your nose off to spite your face, Annie. We wouldn't offer if we didn't want to help.'

Anya raised a hand to touch the heated blush on her cheek. 'Sorry, I didn't mean to be rude. Everyone's being so helpful and I don't want to take advantage.'

Ron pulled her into a hug that still carried the strength of a man who'd worked hard all his life. 'Nonsense. You're family – well, as good as.'

He was right. She needed to not let her pride, and her guilt, make life harder than it already was. Anya swallowed around the sudden lump in her throat. 'Thanks, Pa, that means a lot. I'm going to be busy job hunting, so if I can drop Freya off for an hour or two over the coming days, that would help me out a lot.'

'Whatever you need,' Ron assured her as he led her into the kitchen.

The back of the cottage had been extended years ago to create a bright airy kitchen-diner with bifold doors onto the narrow patch of the original cobbled yard that was filled with plant pots. The doors stood open, letting in a soft breeze and easing the heat created by the oven. Wire racks full of rock cakes, butterfly cakes and a square pan of what looked like Anya's favourite flapjack covered the round dining table, a testament to the morning's labours. Freya stood on a square red plastic stool that had been drawn up against the kitchen counter, stirring something in a large beige mixing bowl Amy was holding tightly in both hands. The moment she spotted Anya, Freya jumped down from the stool and ran over, still clutching the wooden spoon covered in cake mixture in one little hand. 'Mummy! Mummy! We're caking!'

Bending down, Anya scooped her up and propped her on one hip, doing her best to avoid the sticky spoon as she pressed a kiss to Freya's flour-covered cheek. 'So I see, darling. Have you had a good time?'

Freya nodded. 'Ma and Pa are fun! Pa said he'll take me to the beach tomorrow. Can I go, Mummy?'

Anya nodded. 'If you like, but you'll have to promise to be a good girl and listen to exactly what Ma and Pa say, okay?'

'Okay!' Freya flung her arms around Anya's neck. The urge to clutch her little girl tight was overwhelming for a second, but Anya made herself give Freya a quick hug before setting her back down. 'Come on then, show me what you've been making.'

They joined Amy back over by the counter while Ron made himself busy filling the kettle.

'Hello, love.' Amy leaned over and kissed Anya on the cheek before turning her attention to Freya. 'I think we're ready to spoon this mixture out, don't you?'

Anya leaned back against the counter, content to watch the pair of them fill the little paper cupcake liners. Freya got more on herself than in the cups, but Amy showed remarkable patience, rescuing the mess with a pallet knife and deftly filling the liners, all the while keeping up a merry stream of encouragement and praise. By the time they'd finished and Freya was over at the sink where Ron helped her to wash her hands, the little girl was glowing with happiness.

A soft touch on her hand drew Anya's gaze from her daughter to Amy's kind, concerned smile.

'Everything all right?'

Not sure she could go through it all again, Anya wrinkled her nose.

Amy patted her hand. 'You'll get there.'

Standing up straighter, Anya nodded. 'I will. I'm going to start job hunting tomorrow. Ron said the two of you wouldn't mind watching Freya for me?'

'Of course we don't mind, she's an absolute delight. We'll have her any time you like. In fact, why don't we have her every morning for the whole week?' she offered. 'It'll be better for Freya to have a routine and it'd also give you a decent bit of time to settle in and look around for something.'

It felt like too much, but the sooner Anya got things sorted, the better. 'If you're sure you don't mind?'

'Not a bit of it. It'll be our pleasure, won't it, Ron?' Amy called to her husband.

'What's that?'

'I was just saying to Anya we'd be happy to have Freya every morning for the coming week, to help her out.'

Ron's face lit up like he'd been offered a treat, not been roped into a full-time babysitting gig. 'Sounds good to me.' He glanced down at Freya. 'How about you, chicken? You want to spend lots of time with me and Ma next week?'

'Yes please!' Freya jumped up and down.

Ron beamed down at her. 'Well, looks like that's sorted. Now then, why don't we sample some of these lovely-looking cakes before your mummy takes you home?'

They returned home later than she'd been expecting, but Ma and Pa had been so lovely and time had quite run away with them all. Even after the gorgeous spread Ma had laid on for them, Anya hadn't been able to leave without a large Tupperware box full of cake. Worried about leaving the unpacking for so long, Anya walked as quickly as she could. Freya skipped along at her side, chattering away a mile a minute.

Ryan greeted them at the front door with a smile that widened considerably when Anya handed him the box. 'What have we got here?'

'Your mum and Freya have had a busy day baking lots of treats.'

'That sounds like the perfect excuse to put the kettle on.'

Anya smiled as she shook her head. 'You go ahead; we're already full of tea and cake. I'm sorry we took so long. I think I'll just get Freya ready for bed and sort the rest out in the morning.'

Ryan waved them through the house towards the back patio doors. 'Don't worry about it. We've moved all the boxes out the way and Helen and Chloe are just adding the last touches. I think you'll like what they've done.'

For the first time in months Anya felt her spirits lift. Taking Freya's hand, she led her across the garden just in time to meet her aunt and cousin, who were coming out of the summer house.

'Perfect timing!' Chloe said by way of greeting.

'Uncle Ryan tells me you've been busy.' Anya raised an eyebrow. 'What have you been up to?'

'You can see for yourself.' Chloe pushed the left-hand side of the double doors open. 'Welcome to your new home.'

Tears burned hot and sudden as Anya stepped inside and was greeted with a miracle. It was impossible to believe she was standing in the same place that had been a chaotic mess only a couple of hours earlier. The three-seater sofa Chloe had scavenged from a second-hand shop had been dressed with a soft cotton throw and plump cushions. A large pillar candle burned in the centre of the coffee table her cousin had bought for a few pounds through an online selling site. Familiar things from Anya's kitchen sat ready and waiting on the counter of the little kitchen area. A gauzy curtain covered in pretty flowers now hung at the end of the room, hiding the glass-panelled door that led to the bedroom area.

At the opposite end of the room the little chair and table from Freya's room sat in the middle of a pale pink fluffy rug, and a box of toys and a miniature bookcase filled with all her daughter's favourite books stood against the wall. A framed photo of the two of them sat on top of the bookcase, a smaller one of Drew tucked next to it. 'It's beautiful,' Anya murmured.

Her aunt put an arm around her waist and gave her a squeeze. 'It's enough to get you started,' Helen said. 'You can move things around as you want.'

Anya shook her head. 'No, it's perfect as it is.' She turned into her aunt's hold. 'Thank you.' She had to press her eyes tightly closed to stop the threatening tears from falling.

Behind them she heard Chloe asking Freya if she wanted to see the bedroom. Anya turned to watch her cousin slide back the curtain and push the door open before leading Freya by the hand into the other room. Her curiosity was piqued when she heard Freya squeal in delight, and Anya hurried over. She felt like squealing herself when she saw the bedroom. A single bed dressed with a quilt covered in Disney princesses had been pushed into the corner on the left-hand side. Fairy lights had been twined around the white headboard, and some of the pictures from Freya's old room had already been hung on the wall.

Freya was splayed on her back on the bed, waving her arms and legs. 'I've got a big girl bed!'

'That's because you're a big girl now!' Anya lay down beside her and pulled her into a hug. 'What do you think? Do you like your new room?'

'I love it.' Freya snuggled in next to her. 'And I like that I get to share it with you.'

Anya glanced across to where a small double bed had been tucked against the wall in the opposite corner. Unlike the bright cover beneath them, her bed had been dressed in cool tones of beige and white. With the wardrobe and a large chest of drawers, there wasn't a lot of floor space left but it was a miracle they'd managed this much. She reached out her hand to Chloe. 'You are amazing.'

Chloe's cheeks glowed pink. 'It's not much really, we just wanted to make you feel welcome.'

'You've done that and so much more.'

'It's not just a one-off, it's every week!' Gavin Bailey's face had been slowly turning red throughout his low-voiced diatribe and Rick Penrose wondered if the man had had his blood pressure checked recently. 'Every week!' Gavin continued, leaning closer until Rick could smell the stale coffee on his breath.

Resisting the urge to lean back, Rick held his body still. 'Have you tried speaking to them about it?' Gavin had always been a bit of a fusspot, but he seemed to take offence at everything these days. He was a regular feature at the Monday morning outreach sessions Rick ran here at the community hub. The notebook resting at Rick's elbow was testament to the man's endless list of complaints, from kids hanging around on the benches outside his coffee shop, to a delivery van for the clothing store next door over-running the loading zone restrictions by five minutes one morning. Rick wondered sometimes how Gavin got any work done, because his face must be pressed up against the window 90 per cent of the time.

The Hub was one of Rick's proudest achievements and he'd been over the moon when Issy had agreed to host it at The Cosy

Coffee Pot. He was sure it rankled Gavin that his direct rival had been chosen for the Hub, but it made sense to concentrate their limited resources under one roof, especially when Issy had already been doing the hard work. From weekly coffee mornings for new parents to her incredibly popular OAPs Friday lunch bargain, wherever she saw a gap in the community, Issy had done her best to fill it. With the support of the entire council, Rick had applied for a development grant from a government renewal scheme and they'd extended the Coffee Pot into a vacant premises next door to create the Hub.

'You think they don't know what they're doing? They don't care if their rubbish bags split open because Muggins here will clean it up!' Gavin jabbed a thumb into his own chest.

Rick could appreciate the man's frustration. The whole village had a seagull problem and the council had spent a considerable portion of their limited budget on installing spikes and other deterrent measures where they could. Not always easy when there was a balance to be struck with preserving the traditional look of the buildings that so appealed to visitors to the area. 'What exactly do you want me to do about it, Gavin?'

'Issue them with better bags instead of that cheap, thin rubbish!'

Rick clenched his jaw for a moment but managed to keep his voice even. 'We changed the bags to be biodegradable because that's what everyone wanted, remember?' Gavin had been the one behind the bloody petition because Java Brava, the international coffee chain he was the local franchisee for, had been on a green kick after customers had put pressure on them to improve their environmental credentials.

Gavin scowled. 'Well, that's because we expected you to do the right thing, but you've done it on the cheap, just like you do everything else around here.'

Rick left that bait well alone. 'I'll send an email to the business mailing list reminding people not to put their rubbish out too early and I'll arrange for the summer wardens to do an extra patrol to make sure everyone is complying.' Reaching for his notebook, Rick opened it and wrote down a reminder on his to-do list. When he'd finished, he capped his pen and set it down then made himself smile at the still-glaring man opposite. 'Is that everything for today?'

Gavin shoved his chair back with a snort. 'I don't know why I keep wasting my time, because it's not like you ever do anything useful, unless it's for one of your friends, of course.' He cast a significant look around the room they were in, his upper lip curled in a sneer of disgust that took In Issy, who was standing behind the counter, sharing a joke with her grandmother.

Determined to ignore the provocation, Rick stayed in his seat and held a neutral smile as Gavin rose. 'I'll make sure that email goes out today,' he said, but received only a brief glare before Gavin's attention was drawn elsewhere.

'Katrina! Come on, I need you back at the shop.'

Rick half-turned to see Gavin's daughter clutching a book to her chest, a deer-in-the-headlights expression widening her dark eyes.

'But it's my morning for volunteering here, Dad.'

One of the advantages of building the Hub was that they'd been able to create a small library. The grant had covered enough to provide a starter stock, which they supplemented with donations and fund-raising events, but there hadn't been enough to cover a salary. Issy had put her skills to work and recruited a team of volunteers to help her keep it running, including Kat, who was one of her closest friends.

Abandoning the café counter, Issy approached her friend

and took the book from her hands with a smile. 'It's fine, Kat. I can keep an eye on things here if your dad needs you.'

The small brunette cast a glance over to where her father was waiting, one hand holding the door open, his brows drawn down in an impatient glower. Rick didn't miss the brief hesitation, as though Kat considered standing her ground, but it was gone in a flash. Surrendering any thoughts of defiance, she bent down to gather her bag and cardigan. It was warm enough for most people to be in T-shirts or summer dresses, but Kat enveloped her small frame in the long woollen garment. 'I'll see you on Friday,' she promised Issy before hurrying towards the door. She hadn't reached it before Gavin released it and walked out, forcing her to make a grab for it before it shut in her face.

Clutching the saucer of a large cappuccino in two hands, Maud, Issy's eccentric, flamboyant grandmother, teetered across from the counter and took the seat opposite Rick. Her short, bobbed hair had been dyed a fetching shade of candy-floss pink that matched her sequin-covered T-shirt and cropped trousers. No one was ever going to miss Maud in a crowd, that was for sure. 'Well then,' she said, nodding behind her towards the door. 'What's he got his knickers in a twist about today?'

Rick bit the inside of his cheek to ward off a grin. 'Come on now, Maud, be nice.'

Maud snorted. 'I've wiped and powdered your backside more than once, Frederick Penrose, so don't come the high-handed Mr Councilman with me.'

The problem with growing up in a close community like Halfmoon Quay was everybody knew everything about each other. Deciding to fight fire with fire, Rick picked up his pen and tapped it idly on the cover of his notebook. 'So tell me, Maud, did you come over here just to remind me you're the same age as my granny, or did you have an issue that you wanted to raise?'

'Cheeky boy.' Maud's smile told him she had taken no insult. 'I want you to have a word with your uncle Davy. He's driving me to distraction with all his stupid rules.'

Rick sighed. Davy was actually his great-uncle, but he didn't think now was the time to give Maud another reminder of her age. He ran a hotel on Harbour Parade and accommodated a handful of full-time residents as well as regular holidaymakers. Privately, Rick thought it was all getting a bit much for Davy and he knew both his father, Jago, and his uncle Ryan had told him as much, but Davy wouldn't be a Penrose if he didn't have a stubborn streak. All he would say on the matter was that things were in hand and there was nothing to worry about. Still, whatever his private misgivings, Rick wouldn't be a Penrose either if he didn't back another member of his family to the hilt. 'Is this about the cats again?'

The way Maud bristled, Rick knew he'd hit the nail on the head. 'I can't stop them coming in my window now, can I?'

'But you could stop encouraging them by putting food out,' Rick pointed out, not at all unreasonably to his way of thinking.

'And let them starve?' Maud placed a hand over her heart, her voice rising to an almost theatrical tone of outrage.

And this was why he should mind his own business sometimes. Thankfully, Rick was saved by the appearance of Issy at her grandmother's back. 'Nan, you do realise you jumped the queue, don't you?'

Rick glanced over to where a couple of other residents were sitting on the comfortable chairs in the Hub and raised a hand in apology before turning back to Maud. 'You know I can't get in the middle of this. If you've got a problem with any of the rules at the hotel then you need to speak to Davy about it.'

Issy huffed a sigh before her grandmother could reply. 'Tell me this isn't about the bloody cats, Nan!'

Ignoring her, Maud fixed her fierce, electric-blue-eyeliner-enhanced gaze on Rick. 'I think you should speak to him.'

There was none of Maud's usual teasing or sass in her tone and Rick got the feeling the ongoing dispute between her and his great-uncle was merely an excuse. He nodded. 'I'll pop in later on my way home from work.'

Maud's cheery smile returned in an instant. 'Good boy.' She stood and picked up her cup before turning to her granddaughter. 'I need you to help me. I've seen the most amazing new nail polish on Instagram but I can't decide if sparkle fairy queen or va-va-vamp is more my colour.'

Putting an arm around Maud's waist, Issy laughed as the pair of them headed over to a table nearer the counter. 'Both sound perfect, Nan.'

Rick smiled briefly after them before his attention was drawn away by the next person taking their seat opposite him, and for the next couple of hours he didn't have time to dwell on Maud's cryptic message about visiting Davy.

He was just finishing up and packing his things away when Issy came over and handed him a paper bag and an insulated mug. 'What's this?' he asked with a smile.

'Lunch. Your usual.' He hadn't even thought about it, but the moment she said the word his stomach began to rumble. He reached into his back pocket and pulled out his wallet. Issy closed her hand over his before he could take out any money. 'No, it's on the house.'

He considered arguing with her but knew it was pointless. Issy could give them all a run for their money when it came to digging her heels in. 'You know it's possible to be too generous, right?' he grumbled as he tucked his wallet away.

She gave him a look that spoke volumes. 'Says the man who gives up more of his time than anyone else in Halfmoon Quay.'

God, she made him sound like a super hero when he was just doing what anyone else would in his situation. 'Maybe I should start wearing a cape or something.'

Issy laughed before her face grew serious. 'You shouldn't joke about it, Rick. What you do means a lot.' She pressed the bag and mug into his hands. 'Don't forget to pop in and see Davy. I know Nan can be a bit of a drama queen sometimes, but I don't think this is just her making a fuss.'

Rick winced, having forgotten about his promise to Maud. 'Did she tell you what the problem really is?'

'No, only that she's worried.'

He sighed. 'I was going to call in after work but I guess I should go over there now. Just let me give Mum a quick call and see if she'll hold the fort a bit longer.' His mother, Rachel, ran a chandlery shop on the quay, catering to the needs of the local sailors as well as the enthusiasts who packed the harbour with their pleasure boats every summer. Rick had started out working for her, but had slowly built up The Hire Hut, his water sports rental service, on the side. Though spending all day with your mother wasn't everyone's idea of a good time, both she and his father, who was the harbour master, were more like friends than parents these days and the arrangement worked well for both of them.

He transferred the sandwich bag into the hand also holding his coffee and took out his phone. As the call connected, the bell above the café door opened and, instead of greeting his mother, another name sprang unbidden to his lips. 'Anya.'

4

'Hello Rick. It's been a while.' Anya's slightly husky voice still had the same power to mesmerise him, almost as much as her beautiful, elfin face and smoky grey eyes. Her cheekbones were more pronounced than the last time he'd seen her and he couldn't miss the way her collarbones stood out beneath the wide straps of the pretty green and white striped dress she was wearing. Always petite, Anya now looked as if a stiff breeze might blow her away.

'Rick?' His mother's voice startled him and he realised he was still holding the phone to his ear as he stared like a goof at Anya.

'Sorry, Mum,' he said into the phone, holding a finger up to Anya asking her silently to wait one second. 'I'm just finished at the Hub but I need to call in on Uncle Davy on my way if you're okay on your own still.'

'Is everything all right?' His mother sounded concerned.

'Maud wants me to speak to him. I'm sure it's nothing. You know what those two are like for getting on each other's nerves.'

His mum laughed. 'It'll be about those bloody cats, no doubt. It's quiet here so take as long as you need.'

'Okay, thanks Mum. I'll be there as soon as I can.' Rick hung up and tucked his phone away. 'Sorry about that,' he said, smiling down at Anya, which was about the only thing he could do given he, like his brothers, topped out at six foot and she couldn't be much more than five foot two or three.

'It's fine, I didn't realise you were on the phone.'

They stared at each other for a long moment and Rick racked his brain for something to say. He wasn't normally short of words but Anya had been tying his tongue in knots since he'd first been old enough to decide that girls were interesting rather than an annoyance. What had she said to him just now? Remembering, he flashed her a smile of relief. 'Yes, it has been a long time since we last saw each other; it must be what, two years? How have you been?' The moment the words left his mouth he wanted the earth to open and swallow him whole. How had she been? *Christ, he was an idiot.* 'Sorry, I meant to ask how everything went with the move.'

Anya's mouth quirked in a vague semblance of a smile. 'About as well as can be expected under the circumstances.'

Her last two words dropped like a stone between them. He knew all about 'the circumstances' because they had been a constant topic of conversation between his mum and his aunt Helen ever since they'd learned the shocking news of Drew's death and the ugly aftermath.

When he'd found out what had happened, all Rick had wanted to do was rush up there and do whatever he could to help, but it hadn't been his place. Ever since they were teenagers he'd thought Anya hung the moon and stars, but to her he was just one of that pack of noisy Penrose boys she'd been forced to spend her summers with because her aunt was married to his uncle. When seventeen-year-old Rick had finally decided he was going to pluck up the courage and ask her out, she'd arrived in the Quay – as it was known to the locals – with a boyfriend in tow. A boyfriend she went on to marry. Knowing what they all knew now, Rick would like to have said he'd been able to see through Drew's bullshit from the start, but even though he had every reason to hate the man who had spoiled his romantic daydreams, Rick had been as susceptible to Drew's charms as everyone else. He supposed that was how he'd become such a successful conman.

Rick placed a hand on the back of his neck to massage the sudden tension in his spine. 'Yeah, of course, stupid question. Well, it's good to see you whatever the reason. If there's anything I can do to help you settle in, I have a lot of connections through my work on the council, so just let me know.' He fumbled in his pocket for one of the contact cards he'd had printed to hand out at his weekly hub sessions. Anya stared down at the card but didn't take it. *Cringe.* 'Or you can just ask Issy for my details, or pop in any Monday morning here at the Hub, whatever works for you.'

He was about to put the card away when she snagged it by the corner and tugged it from his fingers. 'That's very kind of you, Rick. What I need more than anything is a job. I don't suppose you know of anything that doesn't need any qualifications, or actual skills, do you?' She was smiling as she said it but he could sense the embarrassment behind the question.

'Not off the top of my head, but I'll keep an eye out. Have you tried the newsagents? They often have adverts stuck in the window, although I think it's mostly casual work. *The Halfmoon Horn* is out on Thursday and that has a pretty good jobs section.'

Anya's smile warmed to something a little less awkward.

'You really are a source of helpful information. I tried the newsagents just now but it's mostly babysitting or a couple of hours of cleaning. Not that I mind cleaning!' she added quickly, her cheeks colouring. 'I can't afford to be fussy; I'd just need something more than a couple of hours a week if I'm going to be able to make ends meet.'

'I understood what you meant.'

Anya nodded. 'Well, I'd better not keep you.'

Rick tried not to wince at the obvious dismissal. 'No, no, of course.' Realising he was blocking the entrance to the café, he stepped aside and pushed the door open for her. 'It was good to see you again.'

'You too.' Anya stepped past him and then turned back. 'Give my best to your uncle Davy when you see him, and I hope he's okay. He never minded when we used to run into the hotel and steal lollies from that jar on reception.'

He was suddenly ten years old, watching a triumphant Harry running out of the hotel with a fistful of lollies Ed had double-dared him to grab. Their great-uncle would grumble to their mum about them being ill-mannered brats but never turned up at the house without some treat or other for them. 'The jar's still there. If you pop in sometime he'll still let you help yourself to one.'

'I might just do that.'

'And don't worry about him. I'm sure it's nothing, probably just Maud up to her usual tricks.'

This time when Anya smiled there was no sign of any stress or tension in her face. 'Looks like some things in Halfmoon Quay never change.'

5
———

Rick spun his way through the revolving door entrance of the hotel a few minutes later to find the reception empty. The door to the little office behind the wide wooden desk was open, so he headed towards it. The jar of lollies was in its usual place on the reception desk, just as he'd told Anya it would be. With a grin, he helped himself to his favourite strawberries and cream flavour, unwrapped it and popped it into his mouth. The sweet stickiness brought dozens of memories flooding back, mostly of him fighting with his brothers over penny sweets and cheap plastic toys. He might be the second born, but he'd always been the tallest and had won more than his fair share of those silly scraps. On a whim, he reached back into the jar and pulled out three more lollies. He stared down at his palm for a moment before dropping one of them back in the jar. Even after all these years of Liam living away, he'd never got used to it. He slipped the other two treats into his pocket and called out his uncle's name as he circled around the desk towards the office.

Davy was in the office as expected. What he hadn't expected was the blood all over the front of his uncle's shirt, or the equally stained towel Davy was pressing to his head. 'My God, what happened?' Rick rushed around the desk.

'Don't start fussing,' Uncle Davy growled, fending him off with his free hand as Rick tried to lift the towel and take a look at the source of the blood. 'It's just a scratch.'

'Just a scratch? You're bleeding like a stuck pig.' Rick dodged his uncle's flailing hand and reached for the towel again. 'Stop it! Let me look, for goodness' sake, Davy.'

His uncle grumbled again, but this time he let Rick lift the edge of the towel. He winced at the sight of the ugly gash and quickly pressed the towel back down as fresh blood oozed from the wound. He placed his other hand on the back of Davy's head so he could apply proper pressure without pushing his uncle off balance. 'That looks really nasty. I think you're going to need a couple of stitches.'

'It'll be fine in a minute. You know what head wounds are like.'

Rick couldn't say that he did. 'I haven't got my car with me as I walked to the Hub this morning, but let me give Ed a call and see if he's around to give us a lift up to the doctor's.'

'No!' Davy jerked his head back so hard, Rick lost grip of the towel and it fell to the floor. He bent to pick it up, refolding it to find a clean spot before reaching for his uncle again. Davy snatched the towel from his hands and pressed it back against his forehead. 'I told you I was fine. Stop fussing.'

Although notoriously stubborn, it wasn't like Davy to be so belligerent. Wondering if he'd knocked his head when he cut it, Rick crouched down beside him and spoke to him in a soft voice. 'How did it happen?'

'I went to make myself a cup of tea and dropped the spoon on the floor. When I stood up I walloped my head on the edge of an open cupboard door.'

'How's your head apart from the cut? Do you have a headache? Is your vision okay?'

Davy rolled his eyes, then winced. 'Of course I've got a bloody headache; did you miss the bit where I whacked my head on the cupboard? And my vision is rubbish, but that's because I'm still waiting for my cataract to be sorted out. Any other questions, smart arse?'

Blowing out a breath, Rick sat on the floor and curled his arms loosely around his bent knees. 'Come on, Uncle D, stop giving me a hard time. I only want to help you.'

His great-uncle glared down at him. 'You can help by leaving me alone.'

'The quickest way to get me to go away is to let me help you.'

Davy snorted, then winced again. 'Persistent as well as a smart arse.'

Rick made no effort to hide his grin. 'Yeah, I wonder where I get it from, you stubborn old coot. Come on now, let's get you up to the doctor's and get you sorted out.'

'No! Not the doctor's. There's a first aid kit on the wall in the kitchen, just find me a plaster or something in there.'

Rick's amusement faded fast. It wasn't like Davy to make a big deal over something as trivial as this. A cold chill rippled down his spine. 'Why don't you want to go to the doctor?'

Davy pulled a face. 'You know what it'll be like up there: kids screaming, people coughing and spluttering all over the place. If you're not sick when you go in, you will be by the time you get out. I'll end up waiting for hours and then he'll make me do a load of tests that have nothing to do with a cut on my head and poke and prod me like a heifer at the market.'

That didn't sound like Doc Ferguson; then again, Rick couldn't remember the last time he'd had to go to the surgery. He supposed once you reached Davy's age there would be a lot more visits, but even so, it seemed like he was blowing things out of proportion. 'I know it's a pain in the bum, Davy, but you can't expect me to sit here and watch you slowly bleed to death. Come on, be reasonable.'

'Well it looks like you're going to have to, because I'm not going.' Davy's mouth closed in a tight, determined line. Oh yes, stubbornness ran in the Penrose family all right.

Rick closed his eyes for a second and willed himself to be patient. Something was very wrong for Davy to behave so unreasonably. Losing his temper would only cause the old man to put up even more barriers. He pulled out his phone and began fiddling with it.

'What are you doing? Who are you calling?' Davy snapped.

Rick turned the phone around so his uncle could see the screen full of cartoon fruits and vegetables. 'Seems like we're going to be here a while, so I thought I'd keep myself occupied.'

Davy scowled at him. 'Don't play games with me, boy.'

Rick turned the phone back to himself and began to swipe through the moves on the match-three game. 'It's single player only.'

'Smart arse.'

'Stubborn old coot.'

Rick carried on playing the game, his finger moving on autopilot, his eyes on the screen. He had no thought about actually trying to win the level because his focus was all on his uncle, who continued to sit in the chair, one elbow propped on the desk so he could keep the cloth pressed to his forehead. The handful of lives didn't last long and Rick closed the app and opened another one with different graphics, but the principle of the game was the same.

'You really going to sit there all day?' Davy's voice had lost some of its earlier anger.

Rick didn't look up. 'If I have to.'

His uncle grunted. 'Don't you have better things to do?'

Like get back to the shop and relieve his mum who'd been stuck on her own all morning. Or start tackling the list of calls and emails he needed to make and send to follow up on drop-ins at the Hub earlier. Or think about who might have a job that would suit Anya's limited skills and experience. 'Nope. Nothing that springs to mind.' He ran out of moves and pressed the replay button. 'We really going to sit here until you bleed to death?' he asked, keeping his voice light and casual.

'Good a way as any to go,' Davy muttered.

Rick's head shot up, the stupid game in his hands forgotten. 'What's that supposed to mean?'

His uncle's eyes flicked towards him then away. 'Just a joke.'

'Not the sort of thing you usually joke about.'

Davy sighed, the sound deep and low like it had been dragged from his boots. 'No, it isn't, is it.'

Setting aside his phone, Rick shifted onto his knees and placed a hand on the arm of his uncle's chair. 'What's going on, Davy? Why don't you want me to take you to the surgery?'

Davy turned to face him and, this close, Rick could see beyond the pattern of age lines and the general fatigue a man of his great-uncle's age was bound to experience. His eyes were red-rimmed, the skin at his neck looser, his cheekbones stark against skin that looked almost translucent. He looked... sick. Rick had to swallow twice before he could get his next words out. 'What is it?'

His uncle's mouth quirked up at the corner. 'You always were too smart for your own good, boy. Cancer.'

The news hit Rick like a punch to the gut. 'Where?'

'What does it matter? I've got it and that's all there is to it.'

'When—' Rick had to clear his throat. 'When did you find out?'

'A few weeks ago. I had to get one of my prescriptions renewed and the doc insisted on putting me through an MOT: blood tests, weight, a million questions.' Davy snorted. 'I told him it was a waste of money worrying about a clapped-out old banger like me. Wish he'd left me alone.'

'Surely it's better to know, because at least now you can do something about it.' A terrible doubt flooded through him. 'You are doing something about it?'

'I'm making the best use of my time by getting on with what's important.'

What could be more important that getting the treatment he needed? 'If you're worried about the hotel, we can help you with that.'

Davy barked a laugh. 'How? Who? You've all got your own lives to live and that's the way it should be. You've got better things to do than fuss around after an old fart like me, anyway.'

Rick reached for his uncle's hand. 'None of us are too busy to help you, Davy. We're family, we look after each other, that's just the way it is.'

Davy shook him off. 'And what if I don't want your help, eh? What if I want to be left in peace to live out whatever time I've got left?'

Rick's sense of disbelief grew. Things couldn't be as dire as his great-uncle was making out, could they? 'What can I do to help, Davy? Tell me what you need and I'll do it.'

Davy placed a hand on his cheek, a gentle smile spreading across his face. 'I don't want you to do anything other than promise you won't tell anyone else about this.'

Rick rocked backed on his heels. 'You can't be serious?'

'Oh, but I am.' The smile his uncle gave him held none of

the anger and pain he'd been showing since Rick had shown up in his office. 'I've lived a good life, my boy, and I want to end things on my terms.' When Rick opened his mouth to protest, Davy held up a hand. 'I don't want whatever time I have left to be spent in a hospital bed, or feeling too sick to do anything while the doctors pump one type of poison into my veins in the faint hope they can kill the other that's already inside me. I feel okay right now and I want my last summer to be as normal and as enjoyable as it can be. I'm so sorry you found out. If I'd have had my way none of you would be any the wiser until the end.'

Rick closed his eyes. 'You can't expect me to lie to everyone.'

He felt his uncle's fingers stroking his hair the way they had when he was a little boy. 'It's not a lie, it's an omission. You're a good man, Frederick Penrose, the very best there is. I am so glad I got to see you and your brothers grow into fine young men, and I couldn't love you all more if you were my own grand-children.'

Rick opened his eyes, unashamed of the tears washing down his cheeks. 'Uncle Davy, please...'

With a shaky thumb, his uncle did his best to brush the tears away. 'It'll be all right, lad. It'll all work out, you'll see.'

Rick scrubbed the back of his hand across his face as he sucked in a deep breath and swallowed the rest of his tears. It was clear that his uncle had made up his mind, but if he thought Rick was going to just go along with things, then he was about to find out who was the most stubborn of the Penrose clan. He needed time to work on a plan, a way to persuade his uncle that it wasn't too late. The doctor might have made a mistake, and if not, then there were always new treatments being developed. What he really needed was someone to keep an eye on Davy while he worked out the best way to talk him round. Someone who wouldn't rouse the family's suspicions, someone he trusted. When the solution hit him, it was so perfect he would've grinned if things weren't so serious. 'You won't be able to keep this a secret, not without help.'

'I don't need a babysitter!'

It would be easy to argue the point given Davy's current state, but Rick opted for a different tactic. 'What if I told you I know someone who can assist you with running this place without making it look like you're the one who needs help. It'll be the opposite, in fact. If you offer this person a job, no one will think twice about your motivation; they'll just assume you're doing it out of the goodness of your heart. It'll give you time to rest and make the most of the summer. Isn't that what you said you wanted?'

Davy narrowed his eyes at him. 'Do I have a choice in the matter?'

Rick rose to his feet. 'Sure you do. You can say yes and I'll go and fetch the first aid box and do my best to patch you up, or you can say no and I'll call Mum and she'll call Ma and Aunty Helen and you'll be sitting in Doc Ferguson's office faster than you can blink.'

His uncle sighed and nodded his head, because they both knew there was only one person more stubborn than a Penrose man and that was the remarkable women they married. 'Who do you have in mind?'

6

'Thank you again for lunch,' Anya said to Issy as she reached for the final bite of the chicken and salad sandwich her friend had made for her.

'It was my pleasure. I can't tell you how happy I am that you agreed to come and stay with Chloe and her folks for a while. I've missed you!'

'I missed you too. I wish I could've come sooner, but what with everything that's happened...'

Smiling, Issy reached across the table and touched her hand. 'Hey, I know how tough things have been. All that matters is you and Freya are here now.' The door opened and Issy slipped out of her seat to go and serve a couple of women who'd walked in.

Anya sipped her drink while she waited. They'd deliberately sat at the table closest to the counter so Issy could jump up and serve anyone who came in. It had meant their conversation was one of fits and starts, but Anya was happy to spend whatever time her friend could snatch between customers. Still, Amy and Ron hadn't agreed to babysit so she could sit around chatting.

Anya needed to get off her bum and get back to job hunting. There were plenty of shops around the village, and with the summer season fast approaching, surely someone would be looking for some help. She wiped her hands on her napkin then rose to gather their plates and mugs. Placing them on a clear spot on the counter, she waited for the two ladies to finish their order and head for a table by the window.

Issy frowned when she spotted her. 'You're not leaving are you?'

Anya nodded. 'You're busy and I need to get back on the job hunt.'

Issy moved away to the fancy coffee machine that took up a large part of the counter behind her. She placed a jug of milk under the steamer and turned one of the dials. Glancing back at Anya, she raised her voice over the hiss of the machine. 'You can't spare a few more minutes? Not even for a slice of caramel shortbread?'

Anya's willpower wavered at the mention of her favourite treat but she resisted. 'That's very tempting, but I really should go.'

Issy nodded as she moved to another part of the machine and began measuring out fresh ground coffee. 'Next time, then. Let me know how you get on, yeah?'

'I'll message you later if I have any news,' Anya promised, taking a step back from the counter.

'Message me anyway!' Issy called as she turned her attention back to the drinks she was preparing. Her mobile phone started vibrating on the counter. 'What now?'

'That's definitely my cue to leave!' With a smile and a wave Anya headed out the door.

She was waiting at the crossing for the lights to change when she heard Issy calling her name. Turning, she spotted her friend waving to her from the door of the café, one hand holding her phone in the air. She pointed to the open door and disappeared back inside. Curious, Anya retraced her steps and reached the counter in time to hear Issy saying, 'Here she is for you. You can tell her the good news yourself.' With a grin she thrust her phone at Anya. 'It's Rick.'

Anya took the phone. 'Hello?'

'Oh hey, Anya. I didn't mean for Issy to chase you down the street or anything; you could've called me later.' Rick sounded different, not his usual confident self.

'That's okay, I was only at the crossing. What's up?'

'So you know I told you I was coming to see my uncle Davy?'

Anya frowned, wondering where the conversation was going. 'I heard you saying something to your mum about Maud being worried about him. Is he okay?'

'Yes and no. He had a nasty encounter with the edge of a cupboard door and cut his head.'

'Oh, goodness, I hope he's okay.'

Rick exhaled hard. 'I have to tell you, when I walked into his office and saw the blood all over his shirt I feared the worst, but I've patched him up and given him a cup of tea and he seems fine. I'll give him a ring later and check up on him.'

'He's lucky he's got you to look out for him.' Anya raised her eyes to see Issy still smiling at her over the counter. Feeling a bit awkward, Anya turned away slightly and lowered her voice. 'Look, I'm glad to hear Davy is all right; I'm just not sure what him bumping his head has to do with me.'

'I'm getting to that bit. He's doing brilliantly for a man his age – hell, he's doing brilliantly for a man half his age – but managing the hotel is a lot. He's still sharp as a tack, but there's no getting around the fact he's slowing down a bit. I've had a chat with him and we've both agreed he could do with some help. And that's where you come in.'

A flash of hope leapt inside her, but she tamped it down. She'd meant what she said about turning her hand to most things, including cleaning, but she had zero experience when it came to being a personal carer for someone. 'That's very kind of you, but I'm not sure it's for me. I can look after a child, I have plenty of experience with that, but I wouldn't know where to start when it comes to someone older.'

Rick's deep laughter filled her ear, settling over her like a gorgeous cashmere blanket. 'Oh, God, sorry no that's not what I meant. Davy can look after himself just fine; what he needs is a personal assistant to help him with running the hotel.'

Warmth flooded her cheeks and she ducked her head even though he wasn't there to see her blush. 'Oh, I see! Well, again I'm not sure I'm any more qualified for that.'

'There's nothing that complicated, I promise. You'll be answering the phone, greeting guests and helping them out with stuff like restaurant bookings and ordering taxis, maybe running a few errands for Davy. There's a cleaning team that comes in and does the room changeovers, so you won't have to worry about that. Look, I know this is out of the blue but you'd be doing me a huge favour. It doesn't have to be forever, but it'd give you something to tide you over the summer while you find your feet and get Freya settled into life down here.'

'It sounds like you're the one doing me a huge favour.'

Rick chuckled. 'Consider us even, then. It's taken a lot for Davy to even contemplate it, and the fact you're practically one of the family will make it that bit easier. We haven't thrashed out all the details yet, I just told Davy I'd run the idea past you and see what you think. I'll sit down tonight and work out what the going rate is and put together a draft contract for you to review.'

Legs wobbling, Anya groped for the nearest chair and sank into it. A job for the summer, working with someone she knew and trusted. Money in her pocket and bit of breathing space to figure out what she was going to do in the longer term. 'I don't need a contract.'

There was a long silence, followed by a sigh. 'Okay. Well, look, I'll keep my ear to the ground and if I hear of anything else, I'll let you know.'

From the clear disappointment in Rick's voice, he'd obviously misunderstood. 'No, I meant I don't need you to send me a contract first, because I'd love to help Davy at the hotel. I mean, I *will* need a contract at some point, but I know you'll do right by me when it comes to salary and things.'

'Oh, thank God!' Rick burst out. 'Look, I'm sorry to drop all this on you but I really need to get to the shop before Mum kills me. Can I call you this evening and we can go through the details properly?'

'Of course.' She remembered the card he'd given her earlier. 'I'll text you my number, or better yet, why don't you come over and we can talk it through face to face? I'll make us a bite to eat. It won't be anything fancy: a bit of pasta—'

Rick cut her off. 'Anything would be fine, just tell me what time and I'll be there.'

'Oh great, umm, well I normally try and get Freya settled and in bed by seven. Why don't you aim for just after then, if that works for you.'

'Sounds perfect. I'll print off one of the standard contracts Davy uses for the hotel and we can go through that, work out hours and what have you. I'll see you later.' He ended the call before she even had a chance to say thank you, never mind goodbye.

Anya stared at the phone in her hand for a long moment before she looked up at Issy who was still grinning at her like the Cheshire cat.

'Well?'

Anya felt her own smile tugging at the corners of her mouth. 'Looks like I've got time for that slice of caramel shortbread after all.'

7

Rick handled closing time at the shop. It felt like the least he could do having left his mum to run the place for most of the morning. Not that she'd minded in the least. Rachel Penrose had greeted him with her usual smile and a kiss when he'd finally got his head together after leaving Davy with a half-dozen Steri-Strips sealing the cut on his head and a hot, strong cup of tea with extra sugar in it. He'd only agreed to leave because his uncle had threatened to renege on the whole deal, and having already told Anya he had a solution to her immediate financial situation, he couldn't bear the idea of having to let her down.

There'd only been a couple of customers in the last hour, which had given him time to download some sample contracts – one his uncle used for the hotel and the one they used in the shop for temporary workers. He and Anya could go through them after dinner and put something together that suited everyone. Davy had emailed over a list of the hourly rates he currently paid to the various employees at the hotel. Rick had done some poking around on a couple of the big national recruitment websites as well as the jobs section on the local paper's website and found half a dozen comparable salary ranges.

With a folder of information tucked under his arm, Rick locked up the shop and set the alarm. He pulled out his phone and called Davy as he started the short walk along the quay.

'No, I'm not dead yet,' his uncle snapped by way of greeting.

'Glad to hear it. How's your headache? Did you get that list of symptoms I texted to you?' In between all his other searches, Rick had popped on to the NHS website to check what to look for when it came to concussion.

'The only thing giving me a headache is you nagging at me,' Davy grumbled.

'Come on, Uncle D, humour me,' Rick pleaded.

His uncle sighed. 'I took a couple of tablets and it's a lot better.'

'And you read that list, right? No red flags from it?'

'None, I promise. No sickness or dizziness, no brain fog. Do I sound compos mentis?'

'You don't sound any more doolally than usual,' Rick said.

Davy snorted. 'Cheeky young whelp. Look I know I was a pain earlier, but I was still a bit shocked from the accident. Now you know everything, I've got no reason to give you the runaround, have I?'

'I guess not. Okay, well I'm going to leave you in peace.' A familiar voice called his name and Rick glanced round to see his father. He paused to wait for him to catch up. 'Promise to ring me if anything changes and just pop me a quick text before you go to bed.'

'Okay.' His uncle paused. 'Look, son, I'm sorry I dropped such a heavy weight on you earlier...'

'I'm not,' Rick assured him. 'Don't worry, we'll figure it out. Dad's here, so I'll speak to you in the morning.'

'I'll text you later.'

A warm hand rested in the small of his back and Rick immediately felt some of the tension he was carrying ease. Jago Penrose was a burly bear of a man and even though Rick was more than capable of taking care of himself, being around his father always made him feel better. 'Hey, Dad.'

'Hey, kiddo, busy day?' Jago patted his back before adjusting the weight of the backpack slung over his shoulder. 'Your mum said you've been out and about a lot.'

They began walking towards the steps that led from the quay to the top of the wall that had protected the village from the ravages of the sea for hundreds of years.

'It was my session at the Hub this morning and then I popped in to the hotel to drop off some lunch for Davy and he'd had a bit of an accident and banged his head.' Rick had been thinking about what he could say to his family and had decided to stick as close to the truth as possible. There was no hiding the injury Davy had sustained, and pretending he knew nothing about it would trip him up sooner or later.

'Bloody hell, is he all right?'

It was on the tip of his tongue to say Davy was fine, but that would be a lie. He'd promised to keep his uncle's secret for now, but he didn't have to feel good about it. 'It looked worse than it is; you know what scalp wounds are like for bleeding. Once I got him cleaned up, it only needed a couple of Steri-Strips and one of those gauze pads to keep it covered. That's who I was talking to just now, checking in.'

A frown creased his father's tanned brow. 'Do you think I should go and see him?'

Rick shook his head. 'He got the night manager to come in

early and he's planning a quiet evening. He's promised to text me before he goes to bed.'

Jago smiled. 'I should've known you'd have it all in hand, though how you managed to get him to cooperate like that is beyond me.'

'I threatened to set Mum, Ma and Aunt Helen on him if he didn't let me help.' Which was the truth, though again not the whole story. Rick swallowed, already hating the deception. He would have to work on Davy, get him to see it would be best if everyone knew about his health.

Best for who, though?

That stopped him short. He'd known about Davy's condition for all of half a day and it was already overwhelming; how must it have been for his uncle wrestling with it for however long he'd known about it? He had confided in Rick, and for better or worse it was his responsibility to try and do right by everyone. If things really were as dire as his uncle had suggested and this was his last summer, he would need help with putting his affairs in order. Had he even thought about a will? What would happen to the hotel? Rick started putting together a mental list of questions.

'Everything all right?'

His father's question shook Rick out of his introspection and he nodded. 'Sorry, I was just thinking about Davy. I... uh, I kind of took advantage of his accident to persuade him it was time to take on a bit more help at the hotel.'

Jago paused at the base of the steps, that disapproving frown once again darkening his brow. 'What do you mean you took advantage of him?'

Rick's insides shrank and suddenly he was back to those times in his youth when there'd been a call from school because of some scrape or nonsense one of the Penrose boys had started and somehow dragged in the rest of them. 'Nothing bad,' he protested, holding his hands up defensively. 'I suggested it might be time to take on an assistant at the hotel, that's all. The summer season will soon be in full swing, and as fit and active as he is, he's still getting on a bit.'

Jago nodded. 'Ryan and I have been talking about it for a while, but any time we try and bring it up, Davy's always told us that he has everything in hand and not to worry about it.'

Rick scuffed his shoe over a patch of damp moss that had formed near the base of the steps, making a mental note to speak to the maintenance team about it before the summer crowds arrived. The last thing they needed was someone slipping over. 'I'd just seen Anya at the café and it was clear she's pretty desperate to find a job. If Davy takes her on then it solves two problems at once.' He glanced down again at the moss. It would be dark soon. There were lights on the quayside, but it would be easy for someone to miss it in the shadows. Crouching, he pulled his keys out of his pocket and scraped the patch away.

It only took a minute, but when he straightened up it was to find his father smiling at him. 'You always have to be the one to fix everything, don't you?'

Rick dropped his gaze, uncomfortable at how often he'd heard the same accusation recently. 'I didn't want anyone to hurt themselves.'

Jago clapped a hand on his shoulder. 'It wasn't a criticism, my boy, far from it. And as for getting Anya to help Davy out, it sounds like the perfect solution.'

They headed up the steps, Jago leading the way. 'Your mum texted earlier saying she can't be bothered to cook, so I'm going to call in the chippy. Do you want anything?'

'No, thanks. I'm heading over to Anya's in about an hour.

She's going to make supper while we thrash out the details of her job. Davy told me I could sort it out because it was my smart idea.'

His dad chuckled. 'That sounds like him.' They reached the road, both pausing and glancing both ways on autopilot before heading across towards the bright lights of Good Cod! where there was a short queue already waiting. 'You don't have to wait with me,' Jago told Rick after they'd greeted everyone.

Rick pulled out his phone and checked the time. 'I've got an hour before I said I'd go to Anya's. It won't take me long to get showered and changed.'

Jago smiled and nudged Rick's shoulder with his own. 'It's nice to spend time with you, even if it's just a few minutes. It feels like we're ships that pass in the night at home.'

'Yeah, sorry, I've been working on a funding proposal and it's taking a lot longer than I expected.'

'Hey, you don't have to explain yourself to me. You know your mum and I love having you around the place, but we know you've got better things to do than hang around with a couple of old farts like us.'

'Hardly that, Dad.' His parents were both as fit and as active within the community as he was. In fact, he swore they had a better social life than he did. Being the only one of the four brothers who still lived at home sometimes felt a bit weird to Rick. Liam was off in London doing something complicated with numbers and enjoying the high life with his girlfriend. Harry had moved out years ago, going to live with their grandparents when he was still at school because he was off the rails and in danger of dragging his twin brother, Ed, with him. He'd eventually been diagnosed with severe dyslexia, but by then he'd developed such an aversion to school it had been almost impossible to get him to go. Their parents had paid a small fortune in fines from the local authority, but nothing could shift Harry from the safety of their grandfather's boat shed. Things hadn't got any better after school, and for a while it had looked like Harry might end up in jail, or worse. Rick could still remember the sound of their mother crying herself to sleep.

Harry had settled down now, thank God, and being away from his direct influence had helped Ed focus on his own studies. He'd moved out to go to university and never really settled back home afterwards, so it had been little surprise when he and their cousin Matt had decided to get a place together. The only thing that had been a surprise was the fact they'd been able to find anywhere to rent.

The rise of the short-term rental market and the popularity of holiday lets meant that properties had become a premium in the village, so it had suited Rick to stay put. With the others gone, their parents had let Rick convert one of the now spare bedrooms into a study and lounge for himself. It wasn't quite the same as having his own apartment, but he had enough space to do as he wished, and that was enough for now.

Rick waited until his father had placed his order and the pair of them wandered back outside to wait. 'I love spending time with you guys. My proposal needs a bit more work but the submission deadline is the 16th. Why don't I make supper for us the following Friday? I can see if the twins are free. Harry will probably be busy at the restaurant, but if we eat late he might make it for dessert or at least a drink, and unless Ed's got a date, he's never knowingly turned down a free meal.'

His father beamed. 'That would be lovely. It's been too long since we were all together.' His smile dimmed a little and Rick knew he was thinking about Liam. Thankfully, a voice called Jago's name from inside the chip shop, distracting him. Rick added another mental note to his seemingly never-ending list to

get in touch with his elder brother and see if there was any
chance of him coming home for at least a weekend over the
summer. He supposed he'd have to extend the invitation to
Caroline. A memory of overhearing his brother's girlfriend
mocking their mother's accent surfaced and he grimaced.
Maybe not. Why the two of them were a couple, Rick would
never know. Love did funny things to a man's brain, apparently.
Then again, at least Liam was in a settled relationship rather
than wasting years pining over a woman who had never wanted
to be anything other his friend.

8

'And the fairy princess and the blacksmith lived happily ever after.' Anya closed the book and set it on the floor by the bed. 'Lie down now,' she said, lifting up the top of Freya's quilt to encourage her daughter to do as she was told.

'But I'm not tired,' she protested, a telltale pout appearing.

Not tonight, please. She knew all the change must be unsettling, but sticking to a routine was vital. Everything had gone to pot after Drew's death, and Anya had needed the comfort as much as Freya had, but once the initial shock had passed, Anya had worked hard to establish a new normal for them both. If she backslid now it would make settling in that much harder. 'You will be once you lie down.'

'But—'

'This isn't a discussion, Freya. Now lie down, please.'

Freya's bottom lip worked like she still wanted to protest, but she did at least shuffle down in her bed until her head was resting on her pillow.

'That's my good girl.' Anya leaned forward and kissed her

forehead. 'How about I put your special light on and you can listen to one of your sleepy stories?'

'Yes, please.' Freya rolled on her side, tucking one hand beneath her cheek, and Anya could feel her watching her as she fumbled for the plug for the little lamp that cast coloured lights across the walls and ceiling. They'd seen it in the central aisle in Aldi, where in any given week you might find a slow cooker sitting in between a screwdriver set and a cuddly toy. It always reminded Anya a bit of the prizes conveyor belt they used to have at the end of *The Generation Game*. She flipped the power switch on and lines of soft pink and white light illuminated the room. Retrieving her tablet from her bedside table, Anya opened her relaxation app and scrolled through to the kids' stories section. She clicked on Freya's favourite playlist and set the volume low.

'How's that?'

'Thanks, Mummy.' Freya already sounded sleepy.

Anya stroked her hair and kissed her once more. 'I'll only be in the next room, okay?'

'Okay. Mummy?'

'Yes, darling?'

'Will Daddy still hear my prayers even though we live here now?'

Anya's heart lurched. A well-meaning relative on Drew's side had put the idea in Freya's head after the funeral. Anya wished she'd kept her mouth shut, because neither she nor Drew had any particular religious leanings and trying to explain the concept of God to a broken-hearted three-year-old had been the last thing Anya had needed. She'd finally settled on a simple message that Daddy would always watch over her and Freya could talk to him any time she wanted to and he would be listening. If there was an afterlife, Anya hoped the bit Drew was in was carpeted in Lego bricks that he was forced to step on, but she smiled as she knelt down beside the bed. 'Of course he will.' She touched a finger to Freya's cheek. 'Is there something in particular you wanted to talk to him about?'

Freya smiled. 'I wanted to tell him about our new house and caking with Ma and Pa.'

Anya kissed her cheek. 'I'm sure he'd love to hear all about that.' She rose and made her way towards the door.

'Mummy?'

Here we go... 'Yes, Freya?'

'Can I meet your friend when he comes?'

Anya glanced at her watch; it was nearly five to seven. Rick struck her as the kind of person who would show up on time, so the odds on her daughter being asleep when he arrived were very small. On the other hand, if Freya got up, the chances of getting her back to bed again were even smaller. She settled on the easiest solution. 'I'll bring him in to say goodnight, but only if you stay in bed like a good girl.'

'Okay.'

Leaving the door open a couple of inches, Anya hurried across the lounge to the kitchenette and crouched in front of the oven to check the pasta bake. The invitation to dinner had slipped out earlier before Anya had considered the logistics of her tiny kitchen, the limited food in her cupboards and the state of her bank balance. Freya loved pasta, so Anya had cooked extra when she'd been making her tea and chucked it in an oven dish with some frozen veg and a jar of sauce. Not exactly cordon bleu, but it would be tasty and filling and that was the best she could offer right now.

Everything was bubbling, so she turned it down. It would only be a case of sprinkling over a bit of grated cheese and whacking the temperature back up when they were ready to eat.

There was a soft rap and Anya turned to see Rick waving at her from the other side of the sliding glass doors. She beckoned for him to come in. 'I knew you'd be on time,' she said with a smile as he stepped inside and closed the door behind him.

His own smile faltered for a moment. 'I can come back a bit later if you're not ready.'

'Oh no, that's not what I meant at all and I'm exactly the same; in fact, I've been known to walk around the block because I've arrived somewhere too early.'

Rick's smile turned a little sheepish. 'I might have done a couple of laps of Ryan and Helen's garden before I knocked.'

His admission relaxed her more than anything else he could've said. 'You didn't need to do that.' She gestured towards the small lounge area. 'There's not a lot of room, so I'm afraid it'll be trays on knees. I should've thought about the logistics when I invited you to dinner.'

'A tray will be fine, honestly. It's just a treat to have someone else cook.' Rick unzipped the backpack he'd let slide to the crook of his arm. 'I've printed off a few bits and pieces for us to go over.' Reaching inside, he pulled out an A4 cardboard folder and offered it to her.

She placed it on the little coffee table. 'Great, thank you. Shall we look at it while we eat?'

'Sounds good to me.' The next thing he pulled out of the bag was a slender green bottle. 'I didn't want to turn up empty handed, but I also thought you might not want a drink during the week, so I bought this.'

She took the bottle when he handed it to her. It was a sparkling raspberry cordial with a label from a shop she'd never heard of. 'That's very thoughtful, thank you. I didn't know there was a deli in the village.'

He grinned. 'We've got all the fancy shops these days. It's

actually a new business, so I'm just doing my bit to shop local.' He dug in his front pocket. 'Last thing, I promise.'

She laughed with delight when he held out two pink and white lollipops. 'Oh, that's a blast from the past.'

'I thought Freya might want one too, though I wasn't sure on your policy on sweets.'

'She'll be thrilled to bits. I hope you don't mind but she was curious to meet you, so I said I'd take you in to say goodnight.'

'I don't mind at all. I was trying to think, earlier, the last time I might have seen her. She was still a baby, so it must be two or three years ago.'

'Three. Drew wanted to go to Spain the year after. Said it was quicker to fly there than drive down here.' She glanced away, not wanting to talk about him.

'Ah, well it's not surprising if Freya doesn't remember me, then.' Rick's smile was easy as he dropped his rucksack next to his feet and Anya was grateful for him not pursuing the subject.

'Let me just check if she's still awake.' Anya approached the bedroom door and nudged it open a little wider. 'Freya?' She kept her voice low.

Her daughter raised her head, her eyes heavy-lidded. 'Mummy?'

'Rick's here to wish you goodnight.' She stepped a little further into the room to make space for him at the door. He was so tall and broad, he made the little summer house seem even smaller.

'Hi, Freya.' Anya didn't miss the way he automatically matched her soft tone. 'Wow, I love your room, and especially the lights. It's so pretty and cosy.'

'Green is my favourite colour,' Freya said as the dancing lights shifted colour and the room transformed into an under-water world.

'It's my favourite too,' Rick replied, pointing to his bottle-green and white checked shirt. 'Well. I don't want to interrupt your story, I just wanted to wish you goodnight.'

'G'night.' The end of the word was swallowed in a big yawn.

'Sleep tight,' Anya said as she gestured for Rick to move back and the pair of them edged out of the room. 'I'm right here if you need anything.' She pulled the door almost closed and smiled at Rick.

'Thanks for that.'

'No worries.'

Once again she was surprised at how much space he seemed to take up. As though realising he was looming over her, Rick backed away towards the sofa.

'Dinner will be ready in a few minutes if you're ready to eat? Sorry it's not anything fancy, just a pasta bake.' Anya moved over to the fridge and pulled out the bag of grated cheese. She set it on the counter next to the oven then looked around for her oven gloves. She could've sworn she'd just had them...

'Looking for these?'

She turned to find Rick holding a cushion in one hand and the oven gloves in the other. *Way to look like a complete fool, Anya.* 'How on earth did they get over there?' She remembered putting the pasta in the oven then noticing the sofa was still a mess from where Freya had decided to build a den using the cushions and the throw Anya had draped over the back.

Dropping the cushion, Rick walked over, pausing at the table to pick up the bottle of cordial on his way past. 'Here.' He handed her the gloves. 'Shall I pour us both a drink?'

'Oh, yes, that would be great. There's glasses in the cupboard to your left, and if you wouldn't mind grabbing some cutlery from the drawer in front of you?'

'Of course not.'

While he did that, Anya opened the oven, leaning back to avoid the blast of fragrant steam.

'Smells good,' Rick said as she lifted out the bake and sprinkled the top with cheese.

She smiled at him, then hesitated with her hand in the bag. 'Enough, or a bit more?' she asked him.

'Is there even such a thing as too much cheese?'

How did he always manage to know exactly the right thing to say? She scooped out another large handful and added it to the top of the dish. 'A man after my own heart.'

9

A man after my own heart. Rick knew it was nothing more than a throwaway phrase used by thousands of people every day, but something about it struck home. Never a truer word spoken in jest was another one of those phrases, though surely Anya could have no idea he'd been nursing a crush on her for more years than was sensible. Of course she couldn't. There was no way she'd have invited him over if she had so much as a sneaking suspicion of his feelings.

Rick's hand shook a little and some of the cordial spilled on the counter. He quickly finished filling the glass then looked around for something to mop up the mess. A cloth rested on the corner of the sink and he wiped the counter and the base of the glass before rinsing the cloth under the tap and squeezing it out. 'I'll take these over to the table before I make any more mess,' he said, shooting an apologetic look at Anya as he gathered the glasses and cutlery and beat a quick retreat.

While she busied herself with plates and putting things back in the fridge, Rick grabbed the folder she'd left on the coffee table and pulled out the sheaf of paper he'd tucked inside and pretended to thumb through it. The only reason he was here was to sort out the details of her job. Everything else was just background noise, and as for these supposed feelings for her? What even were they other than the echoes of his lovelorn teenage self? He didn't know this Anya, not really. She seemed nice enough, but she had enough baggage to fill the hold of a bus. Not that any of it was her fault, but still, her life had been turned upside down in the worst possible way. What she needed was a friend, nothing more.

Personal pep talk over, Rick put the paper back in the folder and set it aside, raising his head to smile as Anya approached with a tray. 'Here you go.'

'Looks fantastic, thanks.' He rested the tray on his lap and waited until Anya had fetched her own and taken a seat in the chair opposite. Picking up the cutlery, he handed a fork and spoon to her then used the fork he'd kept to stir through the delicious-smelling pasta. He took a bite and his stomach gave a little growl of appreciation. 'This is great.'

Anya gave him a shy smile. 'It's nothing really, just whatever I had to hand. My, umm, my budget is a little compromised at the moment.'

'If this is what you can put together without trying, then I might need some tips. I've said I'll cook dinner for my folks and my brothers later this month.' He wasn't a bad cook, just a little lacking in imagination.

'I'd be happy to go through my recipe books after we've eaten. I'm sure we can find something that'll work. Do you have any particular preferences?'

Rick's expression turned rueful. 'I honestly haven't had time to think about it, it was kind of a spur of the moment suggestion. I've been busy lately and felt a bit like I was taking Mum and Dad's hospitality for granted.'

'You're still at home, then?'

'I haven't had a good reason to move out.' He couldn't help the defensiveness in his tone.

Anya rested her fork on the edge of her tray. 'I didn't mean anything by it. I'm living in a fancy shed at the bottom of my aunt's garden. I'm hardly in any position to pass judgement on someone else's circumstances.'

'Good point. It does feel a bit weird to be the only one still living at home, but I didn't want a house share and there's not much else around. It seemed a bit selfish to take on a family home when I don't need one, even if I could close a sale without getting gazumped by some buy-to-let out-of-towner looking to cash in.'

Anya nodded. 'I remember talking to Chloe about how difficult things were for her when she was looking to move out.' She glanced around the room. 'This was her little haven and she's given it all up for me.'

Rick leaned forward so he could catch her eye. 'Hey, it won't be forever.'

Her laugh was wry. 'That seems to be my new mantra.' She sighed. 'I don't mean to sound ungrateful, because honestly I can't think what kind of state I'd be in if Aunt Helen and everyone else hadn't stepped up. No. I need to stop feeling sorry for myself and focus on what I've got. Freya and I have a roof over our heads and that's all that matters for now.'

'How's she getting on with... everything?' As soon as he'd asked the question, Rick wished he could take it back. 'Sorry, I didn't mean to pry.'

Anya sighed again, though it didn't seem like an unhappy noise. 'She's remarkable, really. It feels like she's coping a lot better than I am most of the time. I've sheltered her as much as possible, so she has no idea about—'

'Of course,' Rick cut in, not wanting to make her go over old ground. He found himself wondering yet again how any man could do what Drew had done. Not just to all the poor people he'd cheated over the years, but to his own wife, his own child. To dig a hole so deep it almost buried them and then take the cowards' way out when it all got too much.

They ate in silence for a while and by the time Rick had cleared his bowl there was a heavy, satisfied feeling in his stomach. He set his tray on the coffee table and took a sip of his cordial. 'That was great.'

'There's more if you'd like some?' Anya set her own tray beside his and made as if to stand up.

'No, no, I've had plenty. If there's enough left, you might as well save it for another day.'

'Good point. I can't afford to let anything go to waste.'

His heart ached for her. 'It won't take long before you're back on your feet again.'

Anya seemed to slump a little before catching herself. Straightening her spine, she nodded decisively. 'No, you're right, it won't. It's all about a fresh start from here on in, and thanks to you sorting me out with a job so quickly, I'll soon be back on my feet.'

Rick shrugged. 'No thanks necessary. Besides,' he said with a grin. 'After a few days working for Uncle Davy you might be cursing me.'

Anya's laughter rang out for a second before she covered her mouth with a guilty glance towards the open bedroom door. 'Perhaps I shouldn't have agreed to this after all,' she said in a hushed voice. She stood up. 'Right, let's clear these plates and then we can go through the contract and then I'll try and find you a nice recipe for that dinner you want to make. How does that sound?'

'Great, thanks.'

Over a cup of coffee, Rick ran over the terms of the contract and what he thought her main duties would be. 'The job description can be tweaked once you've settled in a bit and you and Davy find a balance, but is there anything in the contract that you've got any questions or concerns about?'

Anya scanned over the printed pages in silence for a few minutes before she shook her head. 'It all looks okay to me, but I honestly wouldn't know one end of a contract from another.' She raised her hands to briefly cover her face before looking up at him, all trace of her earlier humour gone. 'I'm embarrassed to admit the only employment contract I've ever seen is when I had a Saturday job at school.'

It was another reminder of how little he knew her. 'Well, it's honestly not much different to whatever you would've had back then,' he said, trying to reassure her. 'But if you want to have someone look over it for you, then feel free.'

Anya shook her head. 'It's embarrassing enough having to admit this stuff to you. Who else would I talk to?'

Rick sat forward, his every instinct to offer her some kind of comfort, but he kept his hands locked on his knees. 'What about Chloe or Issy? They'd understand and wouldn't judge you.'

'That's true, I suppose.' She tilted her head and gave him a considering look. 'Wouldn't it bother you if I asked someone else to look over it?'

'Why would it bother me? I want you to feel you can trust me, Anya, but given everything you've been through, my ego is less important than your need to know it's all above board.'

She clasped her hands together so tightly the knuckles turned white. 'I don't really think you'd try and take advantage of me.'

God, if Drew Stokes was still alive, Rick would hunt the man down and... he sighed. Always the one to seek conciliation, violence had never been a part of his nature and he wasn't going to let the ghost of that bastard drag out a new ugly side of him. Swallowing the sudden rush of anger, he gave Anya what he hoped was a reassuring smile. 'Arming yourself with the right knowledge means you'll know for sure that I'm not. Trust is to be earned, Anya, not given away freely.'

She huffed out a breath. 'And where the hell were you ten years ago when that little nugget of wisdom would've been useful?'

I was right there, you just didn't notice me. Rick brushed the thought aside. 'Look, it's not like I know more than you, I simply know different things to you. I've had to learn about contracts because of my job and my role on the council. When we get planning applications through, half the time I can't make head nor tail of them, so I ask someone who understands, and each time I learn a little bit more. Not enough to be an expert, but enough to get by.'

'But that's the problem,' she burst out. 'I never *wanted* to learn! Things were so hard after Dad left. Mum did her best but we had to scrimp and scrape and I hated it. Hated not being able to go to the shops with my friends and buy the latest fashions or waste money on magazines and make-up. My Saturday job wasn't to earn pocket money, it was to help Mum make ends meet.'

Rick shook his head. 'I had no idea. You always seemed so sophisticated compared with the local girls. Always so stylish and put together. I can't say I was ever a connoisseur of high fashion, but your clothes always looked fantastic.'

A shocked gasp escaped her. 'You can't be serious?'

Rick shrugged. 'I was a teenage boy from the back of beyond, what did I know? But, yeah, I thought you had it all.'

'One of the only subjects I really enjoyed at school was textiles because I learned how to sew my own clothes. I would raid the charity shops and look for things I could adapt to fit me or pull apart and create a new outfit from scratch.' She sighed. 'When Drew came along, I guess I was all too willing to be swept off my feet. I liked being looked after, and though it shames me to admit it, I liked the idea of money being no object.'

'I can see why that would appeal.' He said it more out of politeness than any specific understanding of her experience. There'd been times when he was sure his parents must have struggled with feeding and clothing four voracious teenage boys who'd been on a permanent growth spurt, but Rick had never felt like they'd lacked for anything growing up. Sure, they didn't jet off on foreign holidays, but that was because his parents had always both worked and the summer was the busiest time in the Quay. And who needed Spain, anyway, when there were miles of golden sandy beaches on the doorstep? Rick had learned to swim and sail and there had always been endless places to explore. They'd built dens in the sand dunes, scrambled up and down the cliffs with no sense of personal danger, until Ed's accident at least. They'd gone from rock pooling to crabbing to deep sea fishing trips and loved them all.

'Can you? Because when I look back now, I wonder what on earth I was thinking.' She shook her head. 'Truth is I was only thinking about myself.'

Rick rubbed the back of his neck, not sure what to say. It was clear Anya was still wrestling with the demons of her past, and there was nothing he could do to help her with that. 'But things have changed and now you're thinking about Freya and what's best for her. Didn't you say before that she's all that matters?'

Anya nodded. 'Yes. Yes, you're right. Sorry, I shouldn't be dragging you into all my drama, you've already gone above and beyond, helping me find a job so quickly.'

Though he didn't like to hear her talking herself down, Rick couldn't deny he was relieved at the opportunity to turn the conversation back onto safer ground. 'Like I said to you on the phone, it's the best of both worlds. It gives you a bit of time to settle in and it helps Davy carry on working, which is what he wants to do.'

'I'm not sure I'll be much of a help, but I'll give it my best shot.' Not exactly a statement of confidence on her part, but at least she was willing to give it a go.

'Great. And don't worry about Uncle Davy; you'll find a way to handle him, I'm sure. Now, speaking of helping, shall we have a look at your cook books and see if you can find an idiot-proof recipe for me?'

10

Two weeks on the job and Anya was ready to quit. Rick's prediction that she'd find a way to handle Davy hadn't shown any sign of materialising so far, and she felt almost as out of her depth as she had when she'd had to learn the hard way how to manage all the accounts and bills at home after Drew died. It didn't help that Davy had very specific ways of doing things, some of which he'd clearly been doing since he'd opened the hotel in the years before computerisation.

Anya glared at the battered red leather ledger open in front of her. The post book, Davy had called it as he'd dropped it on the desk on her first day. Every item of post that arrived had to be logged in it and then she was required to sit with him while he decided what needed to be done and write down that instruction in one column and then update it when the action had been completed. On the opposite page to the post records, she was required to write down every phone call and every guest request and again update the action taken column when it had been dealt with. Steve, the night manager, had no truck with the book and left sticky notes on the inside edge of the desk with any messages, so it was Anya's first task of every day to transfer them to the book.

And then there was the diary that had to be filled in with any bookings she took, even though there was a perfectly adequate electronic system. Anya's second job of the day was to go through the computer and check to see if Steve had added any bookings overnight, or if anyone had booked directly via the internet.

When she'd suggested it seemed like a waste of effort to duplicate everything, Davy had given her a ten-minute lecture about a bad storm in the seventies that had left the Quay without power for a week. It had been on the tip of her tongue to point out that the grid would've been updated in the past fifty years and no one would want to stay in a hotel without any power anyway, but she'd decided to keep her mouth shut and do as she was told. She needed the job too much to start making waves and at least the repetition gave her something to do other than supply Davy with endless cups of tea, which appeared to be one of her other main duties.

The amount of fluid he consumed in a day was staggering; just thinking about it made Anya cross her legs. And, of course, Davy wasn't a dunk-a-bag-in-a-mug kind of tea drinker. He insisted on a pot being brewed with properly measured out loose tea. Fed up of getting a mouthful of bits in the dregs of her cup, Anya had brought in her own supply of tea bags and hidden them in the bottom drawer of the cabinet that Davy had allocated to her.

Right on cue the whoosh of the revolving door caught her attention and in came Jim the postman.

'Morning, Anya! Bloody filthy out there; you've got the right idea staying inside today!'

Jim had greeted her like a long-lost friend on her first morning, though she was pretty sure they'd never met before, and he wasn't the only one. Most of the people she passed in the street greeted her by name, even though she had no idea who half of them were. Obviously the local gossip network had been engaged and everyone knew about poor Ryan and Helen's niece. She shoved aside the thought; she had no time for a pity party. Moving to a small village had its ups and downs and, as she hadn't had any choice in the matter, there was no point getting her back up at the idea of everyone knowing her business. It was just the way things were in the Quay.

Turning her attention back to Jim, Anya finally registered what he'd said and frowned past him to see heavy rain battering the pavement outside. The large stone portico kept the front of the hotel sheltered so she hadn't noticed the change in the weather since she'd arrived an hour earlier. 'Goodness me, it's raining cats and dogs out there.'

'Joys of the English summer,' Jim said, chuckling like he'd told her the funniest joke in the world. 'Here you go, love, not too much today.' He plonked a small stack of envelopes on the top of the counter. 'How's his lordship this morning?' he asked, looking past her to the open door of the office where Davy was lurking, doing whatever it was he did to keep himself busy all day. The banter between him and Davy had a pattern to it and Jim had added Anya into the routine without hesitation.

'Grumpy,' she said, not bothering to keep her voice down.

'That's because you stewed the bloody tea again,' Davy growled. 'If you don't buck your ideas up, you'll be out on your ear.' It wasn't the first time he'd threatened her with the sack in her short employment, not even the second or the third. The first time he'd said it, she'd apologised so much he'd ended up telling her it was only a joke. Not exactly her idea of amusing, but she was starting to learn that Davy's bark was much worse than his bite and he actually seemed to like it when she pushed back.

'Give the poor girl a chance, Davy!' Jim protested. 'It's a miracle you've found someone who'll put up with you.' He winked at Anya. 'Right, best get on, no rest for the wicked and all that. See you later, Davy!' He called out the last bit in a louder voice.

'Not if I see you first!'

Beaming from ear to ear, Jim tugged up the hood of his bright red jacket and stomped off and out into the squally rain. His top half might be protected but his shorts-clad legs had been left to fend for themselves against the elements. Was there something in the post office contract that stated all postal workers were required to wear shorts whatever the weather, because it had been the same at home, though she'd never learned the name of the chap who'd delivered their post even though she'd given him an envelope every Christmas with a card and a twenty-pound note in it.

Speaking of contracts, she still hadn't signed hers yet. She'd arranged to have lunch with Chloe in the café and she and Issy were going to look over it with her. As Rick had predicted, they hadn't said anything other than of course they'd be happy to do it when she'd plucked up the courage to ask them via the What-sApp group Chloe had set up. They'd invited Kat to join them but she'd declined, saying one of the baristas had quit with no notice, so her dad was short-handed. If Gavin Bailey was anything like Anya remembered, he was short-tempered too. Which was probably why the barista had walked out.

Anya reached for the envelopes and sorted them so they were all face down before slitting each one open at the top using the ancient letter opener Davy had presented to her like he was bestowing some great honour. She pulled out each bit of post, stapling together any loose pages and paperclipping the envelopes to the back of each item. Davy had shown her exactly how he liked the post to be presented, and again it had been easier to go with the flow than raise any arguments. She eyed the dreaded ink pad, one thing she was determined to get rid of because it was impossible to use without getting red dye all over her fingers, then turned the dial on the date stamp and proceeded to stamp up each of the half-dozen letters. Most of them were bills and invoices. Once she'd written each one up in the book she'd have to go through the email inbox and see if anything had come in that way, print it off and add it to the book. She might not have much, if any, work experience but even she could organise an inbox better than what she'd seen so far. She would give it a few more weeks to really find her feet before making any suggestions. In the meantime she would get on with it and be grateful she had a job.

The storm had blown out as fast as it had blown in and bright blue sky greeted Anya when she left the hotel for her lunch appointment. There were plenty of people about, most in T-shirts but a few were still wearing lightweight waterproof jackets as though expecting to be caught out again. The ocean beyond the harbour walls spoke of the earlier winds, the tops of the waves still ruffles of white. Colourful sails stood out against the blue-green of the water and she could hear the faint zip of engines from a pair of jet skiers carving circular wakes.

As she strolled along the seafront, Anya spotted the deli Rick had bought the sparkling cordial from and she paused to have a nosey through the window. The beautiful display of cheeses, olives and meat made her nostalgic for the many parties she'd hosted when the wine had flowed and the house had been full of laughter and conversation. Parties where people had let their guard down and fallen for Drew's easy charms just like she had. Anya turned abruptly from the window, a sour twist in her stomach. Unwitting or not, she had played her part in his activities.

She crossed the road as though putting distance between herself and the deli would somehow give a similar distance to her memories – and her guilt. No chance of that.

'Watch where you're going!'

The harsh words in a strong local accent brought Anya up short, just inches from the front of a double-buggy being pushed by a scowling, blonde-haired woman who she recognised but couldn't place. In addition to the two babies strapped in the buggy, the woman was clutching the hand of a boy of maybe three of four.

'Sorry!' Anya pressed herself back against the wall to take up as little space as possible on the pavement. 'I was miles away.'

'Huh.' The woman looked her up and down. 'I heard you'd moved down here. How the mighty have fallen, eh?'

Anya's stomach twisted even more, the sour feeling beginning to bubble and burn up her oesophagus. She placed a hand on the centre of her chest as though she could soothe the rising acid. 'Again, I'm sorry I was in your way.'

The woman's sneer turned a shade uglier. 'You don't even recognise me, do you? Then again you always were a snobby cow. Don't bother with your airs and graces around me, we all know what that husband of yours did. He might have got away with it, but I'm surprised they let you walk free.'

It wasn't the first time she'd received this kind of comment, of course, but hearing it here, in the place she'd hoped would be a safe haven for her and Freya while she put the pieces of her life back together, was a horrible shock. There was one thing she'd learned over the past months, though, and that was not to let anyone know when they'd scored a blow. Adopting the cold, blank expression she'd developed as a protection mechanism, Anya straightened her spine and walked away.

'Nothing to say to defend yourself, eh?' the woman called after her. Anya could feel eyes on her, and she wanted to shrink in upon herself, but somehow she kept her head up and her gaze dead ahead. *Keep moving.* Every step would take her further from whoever that awful woman was and closer to the safety of Issy's café. Thankfully there were no footsteps on the pavement other than her own, so at least the woman had decided not to pursue it, having won whatever victory she had felt the need to score. The urge to hurry beat at Anya, but she fought it down. Running would only draw more attention, would make her look vulnerable and perhaps tempt others who heard and shared the gossip about her to toss in their two pennies' worth.

It felt like it took forever to reach the café, though in reality it couldn't be more than a couple of minutes. The smile of delight on Issy's face when she spotted her coming through the door was almost Anya's undoing, but she held it together enough to make it to the table where Chloe was already waiting. 'Don't hug me,' she warned her cousin through a smile threatening to wobble. 'I've had a run-in with someone and if you're too nice to me I might cry. I'll be damned if that's going to happen.'

Chloe's warm, friendly expression immediately darkened into a deep frown. 'With who? What happened?' Her gaze swivelled towards the door as though she expected a mob to be following at Anya's heels. Given the fierce glow in her eyes, Chloe would no doubt fight them all off if there was such a horde.

'It was nothing really, just let me sit for a minute and catch my breath and I'll tell you and Issy about it when she joins us.'

There was an older woman Anya didn't know also behind

the counter, so it wasn't long before Issy was sliding into one of the spare chairs holding two mugs, one of which she set in front of Anya. 'Hello, hello! How's work going? Has Davy driven you around the bend yet?' As though sensing the atmosphere, Issy's smile dimmed. 'What is it? What's happened?'

Feeling a bit more in control, Anya managed a smile and a casual shrug. 'Nothing really, just a run-in with some woman in the street who felt the need to tell me what she thought of me.'

'Oh my God!' Chloe exclaimed. 'Who the hell was it?'

Anya shook her head. 'I don't know. I mean, I think I recognised her but I couldn't place her. A blonde woman around our age with three kids, the youngest were twins, I think, though I didn't pay that much attention.'

Chloe's lip curled. 'Shelly Dean.'

The name triggered something in Anya's memory. Shelly had been part of the big gang who'd hung around together on the beach during her summers in the Quay. Part of the group, but not part of their inner circle, just one of the many classmates of her cousins and their cousins who'd gravitated towards their favoured spot on the beach. 'Yes, that's her.'

Issy reached across the table to cover her hand with a comforting gesture. 'What did she say, Annie?'

Anya screwed up her nose. 'The usual stuff about Drew and how I must've known what was going on.' She managed a wry smile. 'Oh and I got a side order of being called a snobby cow.'

Chloe rolled her eyes. 'She always was jealous of you.'

'Of me? What on earth for?'

Issy and Chloe exchanged a knowing look.

'Come on, guys, what am I missing here?'

It was Issy who spoke. 'All I can say is that if you weren't one of my best friends, I might have been a bit envious too of all the attention you received.'

When she looked between the two of them, no idea what Issy was talking about, Chloe tilted her head to one side, her expression a mixture of amusement and disbelief. 'Come on, Annie, you can't tell me you didn't know that you turned the head of half the boys in village!'

Anya raised a hand to her cheek. Was it hot in there, or was it just her? She supposed, if she thought back, there were one or two fumbling attempts to ask her out, but she'd been too shy to accept. Plus her mother had issued nothing but dire warnings about how men weren't to be trusted, so Anya had avoided them for the most part. Perhaps if she'd listened to her mother's advice things wouldn't have turned out the way they had. 'Oh, that. Come on, that was nothing, and if any of them did think they liked me it was only because I was something of a novelty. Look at the way they used to chase after the girls who were down here on holiday.'

Issy pursed her lips. 'If you say so.'

'You really have no idea of the effect you had, do you?' Chloe asked, shaking her head. 'The summer you turned up with Drew in tow, I'm surprised the local lads didn't all start wearing black armbands. Especially Rick.'

Anya scoffed. 'Now you're being ridiculous! Rick barely noticed I was alive. He, Liam and Matt always acted like being expected to look out for us was the biggest burden of their lives.'

Issy shrugged. 'Whether you were aware of it or not, back then Rick only ever had eyes for you, and plenty of the local girls knew it. Shelly had a big crush on him and she made a bit of a fool of herself asking him to the leavers' dance.'

'Surely she can't blame me for that?' Anya exclaimed.

Chloe frowned. 'No, I'm sure she doesn't blame you for Rick rejecting her, at least not directly, but seeing you probably brought back a lot of those teenage memories and she lashed out.'

'Well, I hope that's all it is because the Quay is too small for me to go tiptoeing around trying to avoid her.' She shook her head. Whatever Shelly's problem was, it was exactly that – *her* problem. As for what her friends had said about Rick liking her? They were surely mistaken, because he'd never shown so much of a hint of it. Not that she'd considered any of the Penrose brothers as anything other than an extended part of the family circle. Even if he had taken a shine to her back in the day, so much water had passed under that bridge.

11

'What can I do?' Rick's mother asked him as she peered around his arm to try and see what he was doing.

You can go away and let me get on with it. 'Nothing, Mum,' he assured her, keeping his eyes on the chicken browning in the pan. 'The whole point of me cooking this evening was so you and Dad could chill out a bit. Go and sit down and watch TV or something.'

'I don't want to watch the TV, not when I can be lending you a hand. Are you sure you don't need to turn the chicken? It looks a little dark on the edges.'

Rick turned his head and gave her a look. Amused, Rachel raised her hands and backed away but only as far as the kitchen table where she took a seat. 'So what are you making, anyway?'

'Chicken and chorizo ragu. I got the recipe from Anya and she promised me it was straightforward enough.' Rick flipped the chicken over with a spatula.

'How is she?'

Rick shot a quick glance at his mother. 'Anya? Okay I guess, I haven't seen her since I popped over to sort out her contract for the hotel.'

'Haven't seen who?' Ed Penrose swept into the kitchen like the force of nature he was, his limp barely noticeable these days. Twelve years previously, an accident had almost cost Ed his leg and it had taken months of physiotherapy and strength exercises before he could walk again. After bending over to peck a kiss on their mother's cheek, Ed came to lean against the counter next to Rick. 'Mmm something smells good, Freddie-boy,' he said, reaching into a bowl of sundried tomatoes and snagging a piece, which he chucked into his mouth. 'What's the special occasion?'

'Don't call me that,' Rick said, wishing for the umpteenth time that he hadn't come out the worst when it came to their mum's obsession with Jane Austen. She'd been pregnant with Liam when the BBC had shown a new adaptation of *Pride and Prejudice* and Rachel had been hooked from that moment on.

Bloody Colin Firth and his wet shirt had a lot to answer for.

It hadn't been so bad for the twins because Henry and Edward were pretty acceptable names as they stood, but being saddled with Frederick and Fitzwilliam had required a little more creative thinking from Rick and Liam to find acceptable diminutives.

Having finally read *Persuasion* a few years ago, Rick had come to accept his mum had meant it when she'd told him being named after Frederick Wentworth was a compliment because he was the best of the Austen heroes, but his younger self had found it an utter torment, which is why at thirteen he'd grandly announced he would no longer answer to Frederick or the utterly cringe-inducing Freddie and wanted to be known as Rick. Most people had accepted it without any fuss, though it had taken the family a bit longer to adjust. But this wasn't a slip of the tongue on Ed's part, just him being a brat. Rick raised the wooden spoon ready to smack the back of his brother's hand, which was edging towards the bowl again. 'Stop picking.'

'Leave your brother alone, darling, and come and help me set the table,' Rachel admonished Ed fondly. She said everything to him fondly, Rick thought, somewhat uncharitably, then immediately felt bad. Though Harry and Ed were identical twins and separated by a matter of minutes, Ed was definitely the baby of the family. Rick was just as bad as the rest of them when it came down to it, he acknowledged to himself as he fished out another piece of tomato and handed it to his brother before shooing him away. Given the months of worry they'd all gone through after his accident, it was no wonder he got spoiled.

Deciding the chicken was well done, Rick scraped it into the waiting casserole dish then chucked the chorizo into the hot frying pan, stirring it quickly before tossing in the diced onions and garlic. A fragrant hiss filled the kitchen and more than a little smoke, so he reached above his head and flipped on the extractor fan above the hob.

'Smells like something's on fire in here,' his dad said as he walked into the kitchen straight past everyone and pushed wider one of the windows Rick had already opened to let out some of the heat. 'So this is where everyone's hiding.'

'Not hiding, darling. I just came in to offer Rick a hand,' his mum said. 'But he's made it clear that I'm not needed.' Though she said it in a teasing manner, Rick could sense that she was a little hurt by his rejection of her offer to help.

He blew out a breath and wondered why he'd suggested making dinner in the first place. He loved his family, he truly did, but none of them were very good at taking a back seat. 'There's not really anything you can do here, Mum. I've done all the prep, so it's just a case of putting everything in the pot and that's really a one-person job. Besides, I thought you and Ed were going to set the table?'

'Yes, of course. Ed, get some plates down while I get the cutlery.'

They all set to work, including Jago, who opened the cabinet behind him and retrieved a set of wine glasses.

When his mum came to stand in front of the drawer next to him and began pulling out knives and forks, Rick gave her a gentle bump with his hip. 'Tell you what else you could do. There's a load of bits I picked up from the deli earlier; you can put a selection out for nibbles. I'll only be a few minutes and then we can all sit down together.'

'Leave it to me,' she said, giving him a sunny smile. 'What about drinks?'

'There's a bottle of white wine they recommended to go with it.' Rick was more of a lager drinker, but he wasn't averse to a nice glass of wine now and then, particularly on a warm Friday evening.

That was enough to distract them so Rick could finish up in peace. With all the ingredients added to the dish, he gave it one final stir before putting on the lid and placing it in the oven he'd set to preheat.

Taking his seat at the table, he accepted the wine his father had poured for him and raised his glass. 'Cheers.'

They all clinked and took a sip. 'Oh, this is a nice one,' his mum said, approvingly. 'Lovely and fresh. Make a note of the label, Jago, and we can pick some more up next week.'

'Yes, dear.' His father pulled at his fringe like an old-fashioned servant tugging at their forelock.

His mum picked up her napkin and swiped at her husband's head with it. 'Cheeky so-and-so.' But they were both smiling fondly as his dad picked up the bottle and took it over to the little blackboard they used to build a shopping list and made a note.

Resuming his seat, Jago swapped the bottle for his glass and raised it to Rick. 'Cheers again, son, and thanks for dinner.'

'You haven't tasted it yet!' Ed pointed out, earning a swat from their mother's napkin.

'Stop teasing your brother. Pay him no mind, Rick. I'm sure it'll taste wonderful. Anya gave you the recipe, you said?'

He nodded. 'Yes, when we had dinner I asked her for something foolproof.'

Ed whistled low through his teeth. 'Blimey, you're a fast worker.'

Rick shot him a shut-your-mouth glare. The last thing he needed was Ed stirring, especially when there was no cause for it. 'We were going through a contract because Anya's working for Uncle Davy over the summer. It was easier to do it at her place because she's got Freya to think about, *remember*?'

'Oh I remember lots of things,' Ed said, foolishly choosing to ignore Rick's warning look.

Time to change the subject fast, and Rick had the perfect distraction. You'd think after all these years Ed would've learned not to take him on because only one of them ever came out on top.

Rick rested his elbows on the table and made a point of leaning too close, as if studying Ed's face. 'You're looking a bit tired. Late night, little brother?'

Ed's eyes narrowed suspiciously. 'Not especially, why do you ask?'

'No reason.' Rick leaned back in his seat letting a slow smile spread across his mouth. 'I had a great sleep and woke up early. It was such a lovely morning that I went for a jog along the sea front, must've been about five-thirty. The air at that time is so refreshing, don't you think?' Ed had looked anything but refreshed when Rick had seen him climbing out the passenger seat of a little red sports car Rick hadn't recognised.

Ed's face flamed about the same shade as the paintwork had been. 'Bit early for me.'

'Uh huh.'

Their mother cast a considering look between them, clearly sensing the undercurrent but deciding to ignore it when she asked, 'So how is Anya getting on?'

Rick shrugged, taking a sip of his wine. 'I haven't seen her since she started the job. Thought it would be best to give her some space to find her feet.'

'Probably better to ask how Davy's getting on,' his father said with a gruff laugh. 'I'm still amazed you persuaded him to finally take on a bit of help.'

Rick stared into his glass, wishing he could just blurt out the truth. But he'd given Davy his word. 'That bump to his head must've finally knocked some sense into him, I guess.'

His dad smiled. 'Well, whatever it was, Pa's grateful you found a way. Seems like it's not only me and Ryan that have been worried about things. He said it's a weight off his mind knowing Davy's slowing down a bit. Mind you, he's a fine one to talk! You know him and Ma have taken on looking after young Freya while Anya's at work?'

Rick shook his head. 'I had no idea.' It hadn't occurred to him to ask her about childcare, which honestly should've been the first thing he'd thought about. It just wasn't something he was used to, because none of them had kids.

'Helen's doing a couple of afternoons a week. She offered to do more but Ma and Pa are loving having a little one around the place.' The slightly wistful tone in their mother's voice had both Rick and Ed shifting in their seats.

'Don't be getting broody on our behalf, Mum,' Ed warned her. 'Besides, you're too young to be a grandma.'

Rachel laughed. 'That's very flattering, darling, and I'm in no hurry. Not that I wouldn't mind at least one of you showing some sign that you might settle down.'

'Liam has a girlfriend,' Ed pointed out. A heavy silence fell over the table and Rick wished he liked his elder brother's choice of partner a bit better.

'What about you, son?' Jago asked Ed, in a not-so-subtle attempt to move the conversation on. 'Met anyone new lately?'

There was that hint of a blush again, Rick noticed. What was Ed up to, and more importantly, who was he up to it with?

'Who, me?' Ed shook his head just a fraction too quickly. 'Nothing to report, I'm afraid. Rick's your best bet for that kind of thing. Especially now.'

Their mother perked right up. 'Oh, have you got something to share with us?' she asked Rick.

'No. Ignore him, Mum, he's being a di—' It only took a raised eyebrow from his father for Rick to swallow the word. 'He thinks he's being funny.'

Ed held up his hands, his face the picture of innocence. 'What? I just assumed you'd be thrilled that Anya's back in the village given how often you wrote about her in your diary.'

If Anya caught wind of any of his nonsense, Rick would never forgive him. 'I was fourteen, for God's sake, just a stupid kid. I don't want to hear another word about it, understand?' he said in a dead-flat tone, and Ed winced as he finally got the message that Anya was one thing he was not prepared to be teased about. He knew his brother was only messing around, but there were times when he pushed a joke too far.

Ed held his hands up again, but his expression was serious this time. 'I was just mucking about, Freddie. I'm sorry.'

Rick nodded. 'Fair enough. Look, you can take the piss out of me as much as you like, but after everything Anya's been through, the last thing she needs is to be subjected to any more gossip, especially when there's no foundation for it. I helped Anya out because she's a part of this family now, that's all.'

It was too early to check on the ragu, but Rick got up and did it anyway, channelling his frustration with his brother's teasing into the wooden spoon until little flecks of tomato sauce spattered the top of the hob and more than a few landed on the front of his T-shirt. At least he'd chosen black, he thought, dabbing at the spots with a wet dishcloth after returning the pot to the oven. He could hear murmuring behind him, but whatever his father was saying it was too low for him to catch the words. Probably just as well.

By the time he returned to the table the conversation had turned and Jago was recounting a story about the lifeboat being called out from Port Petroc, the largest town along their part of the coast. 'A couple of blokes on paddle boards got taken out by the current near the Black Rocks,' his dad said, shaking his head. 'Didn't even have life jackets on, stupid fools. Thought they knew what they were doing because they've paddled around their local lake a few times.'

Rick frowned. 'What were they doing near the rocks?' The Black Rocks was a notorious outcrop about five miles south of Port Petroc with a nasty rip current that had caused more than a few boating disasters.

'They're down for the week with their wives and spotted *a pretty beach, a lovely quiet spot.*' Jago said the last bit in a sing-song voice, clearly quoting something that had been said. 'Didn't occur to them to wonder why no one else was sunbathing there, nor to read the massive warning signs in the car park, for that matter. Luckily one of the wives called for help as soon as she realised they were a lot further out than she expected, and the crew managed to get them off the rocks with the D class.'

'Were they all right?' Rachel asked, brows drawn down.

'A few scrapes and bruises, but other than that they're fine.'

'It's the start of the silly season,' Ed observed, plucking an olive from a bowl in front of him and popping it into his mouth.

Rick sighed, hoping very much it wasn't a sign of things to come. They'd all been raised to respect the sea, and not just because of their father's job. Every child at the village school was given safety lessons in the run-up to the summer holidays, and the council had a ring-fenced fund for lifeguards during the peak months of July and August. It was a big expense for a small village, but they all knew the grim truth – one disaster could ruin a season, and when so many of their livelihoods were bound up in the holiday trade, it was a price everyone deemed worth paying. 'Speaking of silly season, are you looking to pick up some hours at The Hire Hut again this year? I need to start recruiting, so I want to give you first dibs.' Ed was in the middle of a part-time marine biology PhD, dividing his time between his course and an administration job he hated but which paid him just enough to keep a roof over his head while studying.

That shifty look from earlier appeared on his brother's face. 'I, uh, I'm not sure yet.' Not meeting his gaze, Ed began forking bits of cheese and cold meat onto his plate.

Was he worried that Rick was mad at him because of his teasing about Anya? 'Well, I'll need to know one way or the other by the end of next week.'

Ed nodded. 'Sure. Look, I don't mean to mess you around,

there's just a chance I might be able to pick up some extra hours at work, and no offence, but it pays better.'

Rick supposed that made sense. 'Things improving at the office, I take it?' Normally Ed couldn't wait to get out of there.

His brother gave him a funny little smile. 'Yeah, you could say that.'

'I'm glad things are looking up for you. I mean, I'd always rather have you around but we've all got bills to pay, so I get it. I won't have any problems filling the job, so don't worry if you've got a better offer.'

'Yeah, cheers, like I said I'll let you know asap.'

Ed still looked a bit unsettled, but at least Rick had made it clear to him he was happy to have him. His phone buzzed and he pulled out and read the brief message from Harry.

Can't make it 2nite. Russ sick.

'Harry isn't coming,' he told the others as he typed a reply back. 'Russ is sick, so I guess he's taking charge tonight.'

U ok?

The only reply was a meme of a burning rubbish dumpster floating down a flooded street. Rick chuckled and set his phone back down. As long as Harry was joking, he was fine.

'Oh, that's a shame,' Rachel said. 'We hardly see him these days.'

'He has to work in the evenings, love,' Jago said, reaching for her hand. 'And the responsibility will do him good.'

She squeezed his hand. 'I know you're right, but sometimes I feel like we need to book a table at the restaurant to spend any time with him.'

Jago grinned. 'Now that sounds like an idea! It's Ma's birthday in August. Why don't we get the whole family together for a party at the restaurant?' He started counting on his fingers. 'With all of us, Ma, Pa and Davy, Ryan, Helen and the kids, plus Anya and Freya, of course, that'll be what? Thirteen? Fourteen?'

Rick ran a quick mental calculation through his head. 'I make it thirteen, unless you were counting a seat for Harry.'

'He might get a chance to grab a few minutes here and there.' Jago turned to Rachel. 'What do you reckon?'

She beamed at him. 'I think it sounds wonderful, but perhaps we should book for sixteen just in case Liam and Caroline can make it.'

'Don't get your hopes up about that, love,' Jago warned her.

'Well, we can at least ask them. It's not until next month so it's plenty of notice.'

'I'll give him a call over the weekend,' Rick offered. Not that he had much hope he'd be able to persuade his brother to come home for a visit, but at least he'd be able to soften their mum's disappointment when the invitation was inevitably rebuffed.

Rachel's expression brightened and her initial enthusiasm returned. 'Give him our love when you do speak to him. and in the meantime I'll text Helen and we can get the ball rolling.'

As she pulled her phone out, Ed leaned towards Rick and whispered, 'You know she'll find an excuse for them not to come.'

Rick nodded. 'Doesn't mean we stop inviting them, though. Liam is one of us.'

Ed gave him an I-don't-know-why-you-bother look then turned to their mum. 'I'll work on the seating plan, shall I?' Turning back to him, Ed gave Rick a wink and leaned in once more. 'Play your cards right and I'll fiddle the seating plan and put you next to Anya.'

'Dickhead,' Rick muttered under his breath, refusing to rise to the bait.

'Oh, darling, that's a lovely idea, thank you!' Rachel said, eyes on her phone, fingers flying, as she continued to text with Helen. 'We should go through the photo albums and put together some memories for Ma.'

Her enthusiasm was infectious and Rick could already picture his grandmother's delight, but even as he felt himself getting swept up with the idea of a big family celebration, a black cloud loomed heavy on the horizon. How was he going to sit and smile and enjoy the evening with Uncle Davy at the table and only the two of them knowing the truth?

12

'But it's going to be very hot today, sweetheart; you won't need a jumper on the beach,' Anya said, trying her best to keep her frustration to herself. 'Go and get changed into the things I left on your bed, please.' She checked her watch and swallowed a groan. They were already ten minutes overdue. Her aunt had suggested they take a picnic down to the beach and Anya had been happy to accept the invitation.

'No! No! No!' Freya's protest ended in a high-pitched scream as she burst into tears. She stomped her foot, not an easy task in a pair of too-small frog-faced wellies Anya could've sworn had gone into one of the charity donation bags when she'd been clearing out ready for their move. Teamed with her sparkling blue Elsa princess dress and a thick Nordic-style red jumper covered in a pattern of white snowflakes, her daughter cut quite the picture.

Anya stared at the tiny bundle of outrage in front of her and wondered if she should summon a priest to perform an exorcism. Freya was prone to the odd outburst, but nothing like this. Doing her best to keep her tone as calm as possible, she tried again. 'You won't be able to go swimming without your costume and you'll spoil your pretty dress if it gets covered in sand.'

All she got for her efforts was a fresh round of tears and another wailed, 'Nooooo!'

Give me bloody strength. Arguing the point was only making them later, so Anya took a deep breath and turned away to finish packing a large shop-for-life carrier bag with the endless paraphernalia any trip with a small child required. She'd just returned from fetching a packet of wet wipes from their tiny bathroom when Aunt Helen tapped and opened the door.

'I just came to see if you needed a hand,' she said, her bright smile fixed on Anya.

'Everything's fine, as you can see,' Anya replied, not sure whether to laugh or join Freya, whose screams had subsided slightly into funny little hiccup-sobs.

Helen's smile was full of sympathetic understanding. 'What can I do?'

'Persuade Freya to put something else on if you can. She won't listen to me, but perhaps you can talk some sense into her.' Anya folded up a couple of towels and added them to the bag, then headed to the fridge to grab a flask of juice she'd made up earlier.

'Why don't you let her wear what she has on?'

Anya returned to put the flask in the bag. *There was something else she was forgetting...*

She jerked her head up as her aunt's words registered. 'You have seen what she's wearing?'

Helen shrugged. 'She's old enough to learn that actions have consequences. Stick a change of clothes in the bag and once she realises she's made a mistake, she can get changed.'

Anya supposed that would be easier than arguing. 'And what if she doesn't admit she's made a mistake?'

Her aunt shrugged. 'Then she'll have to put up with being too hot.'

Anya sighed and shook her head. 'I just don't know what's got into her. She never normally makes a fuss about what to wear. She likes to pick things out for herself, but she usually listens to suggestions as well.' She frowned at Freya, whose tears were now little more than sniffs as she watched the two of them warily. Knowing the wrong word would set her off again, Anya decided to take her aunt's advice and admit defeat. 'Go and wash your face, please. It's time to go.'

Freya lit up like a Christmas tree, which Anya supposed was apt given her festive choice of jumper, and skipped off to the bathroom to do as she was told. Again Anya wondered how she managed to move so easily in those boots, but settled instead on retrieving the swimming costume, sundress, hat and sandals she'd laid out earlier. A couple of minutes later and they were out of the door and heading across the garden to meet the others, who were waiting patiently.

Anya was surprised to see her cousin Matt standing with the others. 'Hello! I didn't know you'd be joining us.'

Matt gave her an exasperated half-smile. 'Ed and I were supposed to be replacing the carpet in the dining room but he's had a better offer apparently and gone off somewhere for the weekend. I called round hoping to beg a bacon butty off Mum and instead got roped into making enough sandwiches to feed the five thousand.'

His dad handed him a large plastic cool box. 'Once you've helped us carry this lot to the beach you're welcome to push off again.'

Matt shook his head. 'And miss out on all those sandwiches I made? No chance!' With the cooler in one hand, he reached for a large rucksack and hooked it over his opposite shoulder.

'You'd think we were going on a polar trek, not five minutes down the road.'

'At least Freya's dressed for a polar trek,' Anya said, shaking her head as she watched her daughter skip down the path holding Helen's hand.

Her cousin's eyebrows almost hit his hairline as he surveyed Freya's outfit. 'Interesting fashion choice; must've inherited it from you.'

'Haha! Don't think I've forgotten that summer where you wore that floppy beanie constantly.'

Matt pulled a face at her. 'Bad enough having Chloe around to blow all my secrets; now I'm going to have to put up with two of you!'

Shooting her brother a triumphant grin, Chloe slung her arm around Anya's waist. 'Double trouble back together just the way it's meant to be.'

Anya returned the embrace, the old nickname for the pair of them bringing back a flood of happy memories. Whatever the circumstances that had brought her here, it was good to be back in the Quay with the people she loved.

It was only a few minutes to the beach and no one would've suspected that Freya had had a meltdown from the way she gambolled around between them, running ahead then racing back to point out something she'd spotted. She tripped once in her too-small boots but Ryan saved the day, dropping the large roll of mats he was carrying and grabbing Freya before she could face-plant on the pavement. He turned it into a game as he swung her into the air and up onto his back. Squealing with delight, Freya clung to his neck as he jogged down the steps and across the golden sand. Anya took the bag Chloe was carrying so her cousin could scoop up the mats and then they made their way down.

The beach was busy with both locals and weekenders but they found a spot not far from where several rows of water sports equipment had been neatly set out beneath a large green advertising flag emblazoned with the words *The Hire Hut*. As they dropped their bags, mats and other bits and pieces Anya spotted Rick nearby. He was wearing a baseball cap and a T-shirt the same lurid green as the beach flag, and a pair of long black shorts. He was talking to a couple wearing wetsuits and bright yellow life jackets. Rick held a two-bladed paddle between his hands, his wide shoulders dipping and rolling as he showed them the correct technique. As though sensing her watching him, Rick glanced over. Spotting Anya, he smiled and waved before turning his attention back to the couple.

'Fancy a paddle, do you?' Chloe said, pausing in her task of rolling out the straw mats to see what Anya was staring at. 'Or are you just admiring the view?'

'I don't know what you're talking about,' Anya said, snatching the mat her cousin was holding and shaking it out, making a point of turning her back on Rick in the process.

'My mistake.' Chloe's grin was so evil Anya was surprised she hadn't sprouted little horns on the top of her head.

While Ryan and Matt made a return trip to the house to fetch a windbreak and a couple of sun umbrellas, the three of them finished laying out the mats and towels. Freya squatted nearby, humming to herself as she dug a hole with a plastic spade. The blue net hem of her dress was already covered in sand but Anya told herself to channel Elsa and just 'Let it go'. If the worst came to the worst, she could rip out the skirt and replace it with something from one of the bags of material Ryan had stored in the shed for her. Perhaps it was time to think about getting her sewing machine out and finding space for it. Her evenings were quiet once Freya had gone to bed, so she could run up a few things and maybe try and sell them. Even if she only made a few pounds it would be better than nothing.

'Hello? Earth to Anya.'

Anya blinked as Chloe waved a hand in front of her face. 'Sorry, I was miles away.'

'Clearly.' Chloe shimmied out of her shorts and T-shirt to reveal a black fifties-style bikini with a halter-neck top and high-waisted bottoms. Anya coveted it immediately and told her so. 'Thanks,' Chloe said with a pleased grin as she settled on the towel next to her. 'So where were you just now? Anywhere nice?'

It took Anya a second to catch her meaning as she pulled off her own T-shirt to reveal an all-in-one swimsuit with a ruched waist detail that helped to disguise the softer bits around her middle that she hadn't been able to properly shift since being pregnant. 'Oh, no, not unless you count your dad's shed as nice. If Freya's dress survives a day on the beach it'll be a miracle, and that got me thinking about my sewing machine and making space in the house for it. I've got all that material just sitting around, I should do something with it, though I'm not sure what.'

Chloe gave her a big grin. 'I've been waiting for you to change your mind and I know exactly what you can do with it! You can make stuff for me and I'll sell it online. I've got a shop for some of my art – it doesn't earn me a fortune but I have plenty of repeat customers and I've even had a few commissions. I'm thinking about ramping it up a bit, designing some Christmas cards and making stocking and secret Santa gifts.'

Anya frowned at her. 'How come this is the first I've heard about this?'

Chloe shrugged then took some sun cream out of her bag and began to apply it liberally to her arms. 'I started it last year.

I didn't tell you because you had rather a lot on your plate. It's mostly been a hobby up until now while I've been figuring out how everything works. I'd like to make more of it, maybe even build it up to open a shop of my own one day.'

'I had no idea,' Anya said, shaking her head in wonder. 'All these dreams and ideas and you never said a word.' She reached out and touched Chloe's shoulder. 'I've been so in my head since...' Her cousin's understanding smile meant she didn't need to finish the thought. 'I've not paid enough attention to what's been going on with you.'

Putting aside the sun cream, Chloe leaned in and hugged her. 'Like I said, you've had a lot going on. It's no big deal.'

But it was. Chloe was more than a relative, she was supposed to be one of her closest friends and Anya had been so wrapped up in her own misery she'd neglected her. Issy too – and Kat. Just look at what Issy had achieved with the café and the Hub. And what about Kat? Was she really happy working for her dad? Anya doubted it but it was awful to realise she had no idea. 'If you're serious about making a change, then I'd love to be involved.'

Chloe's smile was as bright as the sun. 'Oh don't worry, I have big plans for us, Annie. I don't want to spend the rest of my days being a legal secretary and I'm pretty sure you never had being a hotel receptionist marked on your career card.'

'I never had a career card,' Anya admitted. 'I thought Drew would take care of me forever and I could live out my little fantasy life watching home decorating shows and playing house. I know I've only got this job with Davy because he probably feels sorry for me. I'm not qualified to *do* anything.'

'Bollocks,' Chloe said. 'The only person who is feeling sorry for you is you. You are brilliant at making stuff and your house wouldn't have looked out of place on any of those shows. You have a real eye for design, Annie, and I think between us we could do something special.'

'Like what?'

'Like open our own interior design business one day.'

Anya couldn't believe her ears. 'You can't be serious!'

Chloe looked her square in the eye. 'I'm deadly serious. Maybe not today, but certainly in the next couple of years. I deal with all the house sales in this area, remember. I see the people who are buying up places left, right and centre. All those rich London folks looking to snap up a holiday home by the sea but with no time to do it up when they're only down a couple of weekends a month. I've already put a load of business Dad and Matt's way for the repair works. There's a gap in the market, and I reckon we could fill it.'

Anya shook her head. 'But where would we even start? Between working at the hotel and looking after Freya I don't have time. I mean, I can make a few bits and pieces – cushions and throws and that kind of stuff – but that would just be the odd hour here and there in the evenings.'

'Like I said, I'm not looking to rush into anything, but I'm also not going to spend the rest of my life working for someone else, not if I can help it. We focus on the website for now and see where that takes us and in the meantime we can make plans.'

It all sounded completely mad to Anya, but Chloe had given up so much for her. It can't have been easy for her to move back in with her parents, even if that move had only been from the summer house at the bottom of the garden. She'd taken so much from everyone; now it was time to start giving back. 'Your dad did mention something about converting one of his old sheds into a workshop for me. We could speak to him about it and share it, if you like.'

'That's a great idea!' Chloe leaned in to hug her again. 'Penrose Stokes Design starts today!'

Anya shook her head. 'Not Stokes. I don't want anything to do with Drew tainting this. I've been seriously thinking about going back to Duncan.'

Chloe tilted her head as she considered it. 'Penrose Duncan Design... I like it! What about Freya?'

Anya glanced over to where Matt was helping her daughter build sandcastles. Though the pair of them looked completely absorbed, she kept her voice low as she said, 'It'd be easier if we both had the same name, but I'm not sure how she will feel about it in the future.'

Chloe tugged her legs up and curled her arms around them as she rested her chin on her knees. 'Hmm, that's a tricky one. I agree it'd be more straightforward if you both had the same name, and if you're going to change it, better to do it now before she goes to school in September. I don't see any harm in it, and we can sort the paperwork out for you at the firm. I don't blame you for not wanting to be associated with him any more.'

'That's an understatement,' Anya said, shooting her cousin a wry grin. It felt good to talk about it, to even make a little joke, something she never would've believed possible. Changing their names would be another step along the path to taking control of her life. 'I'll give it some serious thought and let you know. I've already decided to be completely honest with Freya about everything once she's of an age to understand. If I do go ahead and change both our names, I'll give her the choice to change it back if she wishes. Whatever happened, Drew was Freya's father and I won't deny her a connection to him.'

She knew what it was like to grow up with questions. After what she'd been through, Anya had much more sympathy with her mum over the decision not to have any contact with Anya's dad after he'd walked out on them. Or maybe it hadn't been her decision and her father hadn't tried to keep in touch. She simply had no idea. Lisa had refused to speak about him and Anya had never found the courage to ask. She wouldn't put Freya in the same position, regardless of her own feelings on the matter.

'All I can say is you're a better person than me,' Chloe said, stretching her legs out as she closed her eyes and turned her face up to the sun like a flower opening in bloom. 'If I was in your shoes I'd erase everything about that arsehole and pretend he never existed.'

Anya shook her head but didn't say anything. Chloe was far more generous and thoughtful than her, but Anya was determined to change. She'd been selfish and self-absorbed, cocooning herself away from the world, caring only about her little gang of three. But this was a fresh start, an opportunity to make the best of everything, including herself. She'd been someone's daughter, then someone's wife, and now someone's mother. Who was Anya Duncan without any of those labels?

She had no idea, but it was high time she found out.

13

By the time he'd packed everything away and headed home for the day, Rick was ready for nothing more than a hot shower, the takeaway he'd just picked up and an early night. The forecast for Sunday was even better, so he could expect another busy day. Not that he was complaining, far from it. Given this was only the start of the season, with any luck it might be their best year yet. He paused by the back door to wash the sand off his feet with the garden hose. It was a futile task trying to keep the floors completely clean, but they all did their bit to minimise the mess.

Leaving the bag with his dinner on the side, Rick headed upstairs and stood under the pounding hot water until the ache in his back and arms eased. He'd just reheated his food and was carrying it up to his sitting room when the front door opened and his parents walked in.

'Oh, you're not coming out tonight, then?' his mum asked by way of greeting.

Rick frowned. 'I didn't know we had plans.'

'There's a band on at the Smuggler's Den, I mentioned it to you earlier.'

So she had. 'Sorry, it completely slipped my mind. You guys go and have a good time, I'm going to eat this and have an early night.' He was also going to try and get hold of Liam and invite him and Caroline for Ma's birthday meal, but he decided to keep that to himself for now. He didn't want Mum getting her hopes up.

'All right, love.' She turned to Jago, who had shut the door and was toeing off his work boots. 'Do you want the shower first, or shall I go up?'

Jago slid an arm around her waist. 'We could always share one, good for the environment and all that.'

'Well that's definitely my cue to leave,' Rick said with a laugh as he ascended the stairs. 'Just try not to flood the en suite like you did last time!' he called to them over his shoulder.

'There was a blockage in the drain, and you know it, Frederick Penrose!' his mother exclaimed in a tart voice.

'If you say so!' Rick stepped onto the landing and hurried quickly to the peace of his sitting room at the far end. He adored his parents and he was glad they were still clearly in love with each other. He did wonder sometimes if the reason he and the twins were all so resolutely single was because the example their parents had set them was such a high one. It was something to ponder on as he forked chicken fried rice into his mouth with one hand and flicked through his various streaming subscriptions with the other. He settled on a new action film on Netflix, which looked interesting enough without needing much in the way of concentration to follow it, put his feet up and ate.

Forty minutes later the protagonist was in all kinds of trouble and Rick was already anticipating how he'd manage to turn the tables on the bad guys. Though it was tempting to watch through to the end, he paused the film and reached for his phone to call Liam. It rang half a dozen times and Rick was just about to hang up when his brother answered. 'Hey, stranger!'

'Hey, yourself. How's things?'

'Fine, fine. Everything's fine. To what do I owe the pleasure?'

'I was just calling about Ma's birthday in August. She's going to be eighty.'

'Bloody hell, is she really? Oh, hold on a sec.' Liam's voice sounded further away when he spoke next. 'It's Rick.' Pause. 'No, no, I won't be long.' Another Pause. 'Sorry about that.' His brother's easy tone had vanished.

'Everything all right? If I'm interrupting I can call back another time.'

Liam sighed. 'Just another one of Caroline's interminable dinner parties. Don't worry about it; the guests aren't due for another half an hour and it won't take me that long to open a couple of bottles of wine.'

'As long as you're sure?'

Before he could continue, Caroline's voice interrupted them again, much closer this time. 'Unless someone's dying I need you to come downstairs and help me.'

'To do what? All you've got to do is peel the covers off a couple of trays; the caterers have done all the hard work.' There was no mistaking the note of irritation in his brother's voice.

'I need you to do it because I've had my nails done. God, Liam, why do you have to be so bloody awkward about everything?'

Rick cringed. This sounded like an ongoing argument and not something he wanted to get in the middle of. 'Hey, bro. It's cool. I'll send you a text and we can catch up in the week, okay?'

Liam sighed again. 'Yeah, okay. Sorry.' He hung up without saying goodbye.

He knew it wasn't his fault, but Rick still felt rubbish about spoiling their evening. He quickly tapped out a brief explanation for his call, including the details about the planned dinner, sent it off and flicked his film back on.

An hour later and the hero had delivered vengeance on the bad guys in various creative ways. Rick let the what-to-watch-next recommendations pop up, but nothing caught his eye. When a huge yawn almost cracked his jaw he reminded himself he was going to have an early night. He hauled himself up off the sofa, turned off the TV and picked up his phone. A text had come through about five minutes earlier; he must've missed it with all the action on screen. It was a reply from Liam.

> Sorry about earlier. Things a bit tricky. I'll call in morning.

Rick sighed as he tucked his phone in his pocket and ambled across the landing towards his bedroom. He'd had a feeling it wasn't plain sailing for his brother at home. They were in the habit of speaking every couple of weeks but things had gone quiet at Liam's end over the past few months and it had got to the point where Rick had felt like he was intruding. Maybe it was time to stop ignoring his instincts and try and get Liam to talk about it.

When his phone rang the next morning not long after six, it took Rick by surprise. 'Hey, I thought you'd be nursing a hang-over until at least lunchtime,' he said by way of greeting to Liam.

'You're right about the hangover,' Liam grumbled, his voice sounding scratchy. 'But the mattress on the spare bed isn't conducive to a lie-in.'

Yikes. 'Things didn't improve between you and Caroline, I take it?'

Liam's chuckle turned into a cough. 'Hang on, let me get a glass of water.'

Rick took advantage of the dead air to pop a couple of slices of bread in the toaster and pour himself a coffee from the freshly brewed pot. The only standing rule in his parents' house was whoever was up first, put on the coffee. No doubt the smell would have his dad stirring before too long, but for now he had the kitchen to himself.

'Right, that's better.' Liam came back on the line sounding much more his normal self.

'So, what happened?' Rick asked between bites of his toast. 'How did you end up in the spare room?'

His brother sighed. 'Before I met Caro I had no idea it was possible to sustain an argument for more than a couple of hours, but we've been having the same one off and on for weeks. Every time I think things have calmed down she has a dig and then we're off again.'

'That can't have made dinner fun, trying to be nice to each other when you're both pissed off.'

Liam laughed, a bitter sound that made Rick wince to hear it. 'Ah, that's where you're wrong, because Caro didn't even make a pretence of it. I mean, I can't stand the couple who were here last night at the best of times, but having them here in the middle of all that turned a bad evening into an absolute nightmare. Lucinda and Caro have been best friends since school, so of course she immediately took Caro's side. And her boyfriend, who by the way is some red-trouser-wearing army plonker called Tarquin Granby-Plungar—'

Rick, who had been taking a sip of his coffee at the time, choked. 'You're shitting me.'

'I shit you not, bro. You thought we had it bad when it comes to names, but I tell you, mixing in the kind of circles Caro does is an eye-opener. Anyway, good old Tarquin clearly thinks he's some kind of banter merchant and he told me I should do what he does and just agree with everything Caro says. Well, you can imagine how well Lucinda took that, and so then they were fighting too.'

'Bloody hell, Liam, I know I shouldn't joke about it, but it sounds like you were in an episode of some hideous old sitcom.'

His brother's laugh was more genuine this time. 'I might as well have been. Really, we should've just knocked it on the head but instead we made the very unwise decision to open more wine. I eventually poured Tarquin into a taxi about half-one this morning. Lucinda was too upset to go home with him and she and Caro ended up in our bedroom with a bottle of Baileys, a box of tissues and the Bendicks mints Lucinda had brought as a gift.'

'Christ, I hate to think about the state of your en suite bathroom this morning. Maybe you were better off in the spare room after all.'

Liam groaned. 'Bloody hell, I didn't even think about that.' He sighed. 'Look, I don't want to make it seem like this is all Caro's fault, because it's really not. She is right, I do make things awkward, but I just get so fed up of having to pretend I care about stuff I find boring.'

'You've not been happy for a while.' Rick made it a statement because there was no room for anything less than total honesty between them.

There was a long period of silence. 'No, you're right, and what's worse is I'm making Caro miserable too. I still care about her but we're not the people we were when we met at university.' He sighed. 'Or maybe we are but we were too blinded by love to see the flaws in our relationship. She's a good person—'

'You just have different priorities,' Rick put in. He raised a hand to rub the ache in his chest. It didn't matter what he thought about Caro; if this really was the end of the line for her and Liam, then it was a sad day.

'Yeah. Yeah, that's it.' Liam made a strangled sound, somewhere between a laugh and a sob. 'Christ, I'm going to have to bite the bullet and talk to her about it, aren't I?'

'I think you should, for both your sakes. But if I can offer one piece of advice?'

'Please.'

'Don't do it today when you're both hungover and upset. Take her out somewhere – not to a restaurant or anything like that. Go somewhere you both like – a park, maybe – so there's enough privacy to be open with each other and space to walk away if things get heated.'

'That's good advice, thanks, and look, whatever happens I'll make sure I'm back for Ma's birthday party, okay? Just let me know the date when Mum's finalised the booking with Harry.'

'It'll be good to see you. It's been too long.'

'Yeah, it has. Hey, how are things there, anyway? How's Anya settling in?'

Rick was immediately on alert at the mention of her name. 'Fine, as far as I know. She was on the beach with Freya yesterday and they seemed to be having a good time.'

'You haven't seen her since she got back?' There was definitely a note of curiosity in the question.

'I've seen her around a couple of times, and I sorted out a job for her helping Uncle Davy at the hotel.'

Liam snorted. 'Way to bury the lead there, bro.'

Rick rolled his eyes even though Liam couldn't see him. 'I've already had a load of nonsense from Ed about this; don't you start.'

'I'm not starting anything! You're the one acting like you barely know who I'm talking about and then the next second you drop the fact you've squared away a job with her – and with Uncle Davy of all people, who is notorious for rejecting anyone's attempts to help. What happened? Did you bump into the devil at a crossroads and sell your soul?'

He couldn't help but laugh. 'Don't be daft. I just found a way to kill two birds with one stone, that's all.'

'Sure, sure, you only helped her out of the goodness of your heart and not because it might make her look kindly upon you.' Liam's tone was gently mocking.

Rick gave an exasperated sigh. 'Give over will you. Why does everyone keep going on about her like she's the love of my life or something? It was just a stupid crush and I'm well over it.'

'Isn't she? Are you?' Liam's voice had grown serious. 'Come on, Rick, this is me you're talking to; you don't have to pretend.'

That stopped him in his tracks. After Liam had opened his heart to him about Caro, didn't Rick owe him at least the same level of honesty? 'It doesn't matter what I may or may not feel about her, I'm sure starting another relationship is the last thing Anya wants or needs.'

'Has she told you that, or are you just assuming you know what's best for her, just like you do with the rest of us?'

Rick shifted in his seat, uncomfortable with the way the conversation was going. 'You make me sound like an arrogant idiot,' he said, unable to keep the hurt from his voice.

'Come on, don't try and deflect, you know that's not what I meant. There's a reason everyone comes to you for help and it's because they know they can rely on you to do your very best for them. I'm just pointing out that it's been eighteen months since

Drew died, and given the mess he left Anya in, do you honestly think she's still mourning him?'

That made Rick sit up and think. 'Well, no, I suppose not, but she's still got Freya to consider...'

'And that would put her off wanting to get involved with you because you're the kind of unreliable guy who would mess around a woman with a kid, not a decent reliable one who would offer his stupidly big heart equally to a little girl as much in need of love and support as her mother?'

Rick laughed, awkwardly. 'When this call is over, I'll have to go and polish my saintly halo. Look, I'll admit I still find her attractive, but we barely know each other.'

'So get to know her! Bloody hell, Rick, it was always a mystery to me why you've been single all these years but now I realise it's because you're basically an idiot when it comes to women.'

'All right, all right, Mr Domestic Bliss.' Rick felt awful as soon as he'd said it, but he'd had enough of Liam's teasing.

'Brutal!' Liam protested.

'Sorry, that was a dick move on my part.'

'Nah, it's all good. Look, I'll make you a deal, okay. By the time I come home for Ma's party I'll have sorted things out here with Caro one way or the other and you'll have talked to Anya and found out how she really feels.'

'Hold on a minute!' Rick protested. 'I never agreed to that.'

'Bwoak, bwoak, bwoak.'

Rick gritted his teeth. Damn Liam for knowing how to push his buttons. Rick could resist most things, but being accused of chickening out of something had always been his downfall. 'Okay, you've got yourself a deal.'

'Great! We can compare notes when I see you in a few weeks. Oh, and while we're at it, Saint-boy, you can tell me how you got Davy to accept some help, because that's little short of a miracle.'

'It was nothing really,' Rick muttered, that familiar queasiness at lying churning his stomach. He had to find time to speak to Davy. He supposed he could pop into the hotel next week on the pretext of seeing how Anya was getting on. That was a perfectly reasonable course of action given he was the one who'd recommended her for the job.

Plus it would be a good excuse to talk to her...

14

'That's it, girl, put a bit of elbow grease into it. Good grief, you need another top off an egg if that's the best you can do.'

Anya raised her head enough to make eye contact with Davy, who was sitting on the closed lid of the toilet like a king on his throne. 'I can do without the running commentary, thanks.' Dropping her head back, she scowled up at the stubborn connection bolt underneath the sink in the bathroom of Room 12. If she could carry a bloody four-year-old and a bag full of shopping, then she could damn well get this bolt loose if it killed her.

'Just offering a bit of encouragement,' Davy offered in an unusually mild voice. She didn't need to be able to see his face to know he was enjoying watching her struggle probably a bit too much.

'Well I can manage fine without it, thanks.'

Once he'd realised how completely useless Anya was at most practical things – well, the ones that had never interested her, at least – Davy had been on a one-man mission to teach her everything he thought she needed to know. This week it was plumbing. The previous week he'd taken her out in the car park and shown her how to jack up a car and change a tyre as well as how to check the oil, refill the washer bottles, and even how a set of jump leads worked. When she'd pointed out she didn't have a car, he waved off her protests, insisting that these were the kind of things she might need to know one day. 'What if you and Freya are stranded somewhere in the future because you can't do something as basic as change a flat?'

Her answer before would've been that she'd call a garage and get someone out to fix it, but when Davy had mentioned how much just the call-out fee was likely to be, she'd blanched and decided that perhaps it was worth learning at least the basics. To her surprise, she'd begun to really enjoy herself. Acerbic comments aside, Davy seemed to be having a lot of fun too. He always had an anecdote to go with every task, some of which made her laugh so hard she couldn't carry on with what he was trying to teach her. And it helped the days to pass. There was a flurry of activity around check-in and check-out times, but there were also a lot of dead hours to fill when someone needed to be around 'just in case'.

She'd even come to enjoy the ritual of the post book as it was a great way to pick Davy's brain. They would settle themselves in his office with a pot of tea and a couple of biscuits in the lull after check-out and go through everything. There wasn't a scenario that came up which he hadn't dealt with before. At first she'd just sat and written down his instructions, but lately he'd begun asking her what she thought they should do. She was surprised how much she'd picked up already. He also always wanted to know what Freya had been up to, and he'd been thrilled when Anya had presented him with a drawing Freya had done for him. It was pinned up on the wall opposite his desk and she often caught him smiling at it.

Ignoring the ache in her arms, Anya went to work on the bolt again. It shifted a fraction then stubbornly refused to move again. Gritting her teeth, she decided to distract herself from the frustration of the moment to talk over something that had been playing on her mind. 'Freya is still insisting on dressing herself.'

Davy chuckled. 'And what was this morning's combo?'

Anya sighed. 'A pink tutu over a pair of fuzzy green leggings I bought her last year to wear as winter pyjamas, and a yellow T-shirt with a sparkly panda on the front. Oh, and a red sou'wester.'

'Ready for all weathers by the sounds of it. Very sensible.'

Anya propped herself on her elbows so she could raise her head and stare at him in disbelief. 'She looks like a scarecrow, Davy! She's got a wardrobe full of lovely clothes and every day she insists on going out looking like I've dressed her in jumble sale rejects. I don't know what's got into her.'

'Have you asked her?'

She narrowed her eyes at him. 'Of course I have, but she just gets upset, so I've had to back off.'

'Poor kid's been through a lot of change.'

She sighed. 'I know. None of which is my fault.'

Davy shot her a sympathetic smile. 'That's not a criticism, pet, far from it. I think you're doing an amazing job coping with everything, especially after all you've been through. Especially having to deal with my grumpy old arse every day,' he said, smile widening into a grin.

'I deserve a medal really when you think about it.'

He laughed. 'That you do. Look, if you want my opinion on it, I reckon it's about Freya trying to feel in control of something. Her whole world has been turned upside down, and for all you've done your best to protect her, she's been through the wringer. There aren't many things she can exert her will over, but what she wears is something that she can.'

Anya considered that for a moment. 'You might be onto something there.'

'Plus, it seems as if what she looks like is important to you, that you want her looking a certain way, presenting a certain image.'

'That makes me sound like I used her as an accessory.'

Davy shook his head. 'No, that's not what I meant, but you've always had a way about yourself ever since you were a kid and it's natural that you want Freya to look nice too. I think all this nonsense with her clothes is her way of testing you. Her daddy's gone, she's lost her home, her friends, everything that was familiar to her, apart from you...'

'You think she's afraid she'll lose me...'

'All kids test boundaries.' Davy shook his head. 'The scrapes and nonsense I've seen two generations of Penrose boys go through as they tried to find their way in the world would turn your hair white.' He pointed to his own shock of white curls for emphasis.

Anya's eyes stung. The urge to drop everything and run as fast as she could to Ma and Pa's and scoop Freya up was almost overwhelming. 'So what can I do to make her feel more secure?'

Davy shrugged. 'Just keep doing what you're doing. Let her wear what she wants and don't let her see that it bothers you. She'll settle down in time once she understands that she's a Penrose now and we look after our own.'

'But we're not, though, are we? Not by blood.'

He made a disgusting noise as though he couldn't believe what she was saying. 'You're one of us in every way that matters, and so is that little girl.'

'Oh Davy, that's a lovely thing to say.' Leaning her weight on one side, Anya fumbled in her pocket for a tissue to blow her nose.

'None of that!' Davy's eyes widened as if horrified at the idea of her crying. 'Stop blathering at me and get that sink sorted, we haven't got all day.'

Smiling to herself, Anya returned to the task at hand. With much muttered swearing she eventually got the bolt about halfway undone when the hotel mobile phone began to ring. 'Do you want to get that?' she asked when Davy made no move to answer it.

'I thought you were the assistant, not me.'

Anya sat up with a huff, only just managing to avoid banging her head on the underside of the sink. She made a threatening gesture towards Davy with the large wrench as she grabbed for the phone with her other hand. 'Good morning. Penrose House Hotel.'

'Hey, it's Rick. Where are you guys? I just popped in to say hello and was surprised to find reception empty.'

Anya rolled her eyes. Everyone was a critic today. 'We're in Room 12 sorting out the sink. We won't be long if you want to wait.' They'd left a sign up asking visitors to call for assistance, the office was secure and no one could get past the reception area without knowing the code to the internal lock.

'No, that's fine.' Rick hung up, leaving her to stare at the phone for a moment. Well, whatever he wanted it couldn't have been important. She put the phone down, put him out of her mind and picked up the wrench once more.

A couple of moments later there was a tap at the door and Rick poked his head around the side. 'Anything I can do to help?'

Anya glanced up at him in surprise. 'How did you get in here?'

Rick shrugged. 'I know the code, of course.'

Of course.

'Now, what needs doing?' As if the bathroom wasn't small enough with her and Davy already in it, Rick decided to join the party, coming to crouch down beside her.

'The sink's backing up, so I'm taking off the pipe to see if I can clear whatever the problem is.'

He ducked his head under the sink, his broad chest all but blocking out the light. 'Do you need a hand?'

Maybe twenty minutes ago when the damn bolt wouldn't move. 'It's fine, thanks.'

'She's got it under control, boy.'

'I'm just trying to help,' Rick protested.

Resisting the urge to whack them both in the head with the wrench, Anya fixed first Rick then Davy with a steely glare. 'Go away.'

Davy chuckled. 'That's us told. Come on, you can make yourself useful and stick the kettle on.'

Fifteen minutes later, Anya was tucking Davy's massive toolbox back under the corner of the reception desk where it lived and trying not think too hard about the revolting hairball she'd fished out of the pipework. Her fingers itched with the need to wash her hands again, even though she'd scrubbed them twice after wrapping the mess in several layers of blue paper towels and disposing of it. The door to the office was closed, which was unusual. When she glanced through a crack in the blinds, Davy had a face like thunder. Rick was leaning against the opposite wall, his hands raised in a pleading gesture. Anya turned away. Whatever was going on between them, they wouldn't thank her for snooping.

She did her best to distract herself. There were half a dozen new emails, all of them sales messages from various suppliers, that she gave a quick scan before consigning to the trash. She'd already printed off the booking details for that day's expected arrivals, but she double-checked them against the diary and reread their details to make sure there weren't any special requests she'd missed.

The office door opened and Rick emerged, looking a little upset.

'Everything all right?'

'Just family stuff. Nothing to worry about.'

It shouldn't hurt to be brushed off like that, but after what Davy had said to her earlier, she couldn't help it. 'Okay. Is that what you came here for, then? To speak to Davy?'

Rick smiled. 'Yes and no. Mostly I was just passing and thought I'd see if you're free for lunch.'

'Oh.' Well, that was unexpected. Though she'd dismissed it at the time, Chloe's teasing comments about Rick having a crush on her came zooming back. A man as handsome as him would surely have his pick of women to choose from, though?

'I just wanted to thank you for making dinner the other night, no big deal.'

'Oh,' she said again, not quite sure whether to feel relieved or disappointed. 'You don't have to do that.'

'Maybe not, but I'd like to. I'm on my way to the café anyway as I've got a meeting in the Hub later.'

'Well I was planning on going there to pick up some sandwiches for me and Davy...'

He smiled. 'Then we can walk there together at least.'

It would seem churlish to refuse and it would be nice to catch up. She'd hardly seen Rick since that first week of her arrival. 'I'll just let Davy know. I'll meet you outside in a minute.'

When she peeked into the office, Davy was staring unseeing

at the drawing Freya had done for him. 'I'm popping to the café to grab some lunch. Any special requests?'

Davy roused himself from his contemplations. 'No, pet. I'm not hungry.'

She frowned. 'You need to eat something...'

He slapped a hand on the desk in front of him. 'Good God, will you stop fussing around me like a bloody mother hen!'

Anya took a step back, shocked at both his tone and his angry gesture. They might niggle at each other, but it was always in jest. Even when she'd made a silly mistake he'd never done more than roll his eyes or call her a twit. 'I'm sorry.'

The flash of temper vanished, blowing over like one of the freak storm squalls that sometimes hit the village, turning the sky from blue to grey and back to blue again in a matter of minutes. 'No, I'm the one who should apologise.' He leaned forward and rubbed the base of his back on the left. 'I've got a bit of stiff hip and it's giving me gyp. I should've known better than to sit on the hard toilet seat earlier.' He smiled. 'I'll have whatever's going. No need to hurry back, I've got everything in hand here.'

Anya didn't believe him for a minute. He might well have a pain in his hip but that wasn't what was upsetting him. It was obvious he and Rick had had words about something. Maybe Rick would give her a clue over lunch, because she didn't like Davy being out of sorts like this. 'Well, as long as you're sure?'

'I am. Oh, hold on.' Davy pulled his wallet out of his pocket and fished out a twenty-pound note. 'Lunch is on me, by way of an apology for biting your head off just now.'

She stared reluctantly at the note for a long moment before deciding there was no point in arguing with him about it. 'Thank you, I won't be long.'

'Take your time. You've got everything ready for this afternoon's arrivals, I take it?'

'Yes.' Anya nodded. 'Everything's laid out on the desk ready, but I'll be back well before then. Mrs Taylor requested oat milk and I've already popped a carton in their fridge.'

Davy smiled up at her. 'I probably don't say it often enough, but you're doing a marvellous job. I don't know what I'd do without you.'

She felt her cheeks warm at the unexpected praise. 'I'm sure you'd get along just fine, but I love working here, Davy. Thanks for giving me a chance.'

A telltale hint of redness showed on his own face as he waved her away. 'Go on with you, girl. I'll see you in a bit.'

15

Rick was grateful at Anya's suggestion he wait for her outside as it gave him time to calm down after his row with Davy. Perhaps row was a bit strong because neither of them had raised their voices, but his great-uncle had been furious with Rick for asking him to consider opening up to everyone else about his condition. When he'd raised the subject of the two of them visiting the doctor so Rick could get a handle on what to expect in the coming weeks and, hopefully – he crossed his fingers – months, Davy had shut him down at once. 'This is my business. No one else's.' Rick had pointed out that Davy had made it his business by telling him, but that had only earned him a nastily snapped comment that if he spent less time being the village busybody it would be to everyone's relief. Something so childish shouldn't have the power to hurt him, but it had stung nonetheless. All Rick had ever wanted to do was help people, and the idea he might have a reputation around the Quay for interfering didn't sit well.

It was a relief when Anya exited the revolving door with a smile. 'Sorry to keep you.'

'Not a problem. I did rather spring it on you at the last minute.' Rick turned towards the road, his hand going out instinctively to shield Anya when a car zoomed past going well over the speed limit. He should have a word with the county council about loaning the village a couple of their temporary speed monitoring signs again, especially now things were going to get busier.

His train of thought was interrupted when Anya pushed his hand away, her expression somewhere between irritated and amused. 'I can cross the road safely you know, Mr No-Not-Now.'

'Mr Who?'

'You must remember the hedgehog road safety campaigns from when we were kids? The little hedgehog asking "Now?" and the big one telling him "No, not now" or them all singing the "Stayin' Alive" song?'

Rick vaguely remembered them now he thought about it. 'Oh, yeah. There was another old song they used as well. What was it...?' His brain was off down a memory rabbit hole of him and his brothers sitting in front of the TV watching CBBC in the days before there were a million and one kids' TV channels and only techy geeks had heard of YouTube.

She rolled her eyes at him. 'Trust you to miss the point.' She strode across the road, leaving him to hurry in her wake.

'So how are you and Freya settling in?' he asked, deciding it was probably best to change the subject before he got in any more trouble. 'You looked like you were having fun on the beach the other day.'

Anya glanced up at him and smiled. 'One of the lovely things about moving here is there's so much more space for Freya to play and explore. We had a nice garden and a park within walking distance, but being close to the sea is another thing altogether.'

'Whenever I get fed up of living in the back of beyond I remind myself how lucky I am and how many people would swap places with me in a heartbeat.'

She looked up at him again. 'Do you really get fed up? You seem so at home here, a real fixture as far as I can tell.'

Rick wasn't sure how he felt about her thinking of him as a fixture, it felt a bit too close to Davy's earlier bit of snide about being a busybody. 'I guess the work I do volunteering on the council must make it seem that way...'

'Well, and being a Penrose, of course. It feels a bit like you run the place, sometimes,' Anya pointed out.

'There's been one or two digs about us being like the mafia over the years,' Rick admitted. 'But you have to remember the first Penrose moved here before there was even a quay, just a handful of tiny stone cottages built into the lee of the cliffs beneath the castle.' Those very same cottages could now be rented by holidaymakers on the lookout for something quirky. Good luck to them, Rick thought, because getting brained by a low beam every five minutes was not his idea of a relaxing holiday.

'I thought your family had always lived in the place Ma and Pa have now,' Anya mused.

He shook his head. 'Oh no, that was the 19th-century modern upgrade. You should ask Uncle Davy about how excited he and Pa were when their parents installed an indoor toilet!'

Anya shuddered. 'It doesn't bear thinking about!'

'The privy was still there when we were kids, you know. We used to think it was a right laugh to go out in the garden for a pee.'

She giggled. 'That's because you were a pack of feral beasts.'

He considered arguing but decided she probably had a

point. 'Speaking of being out in the garden, how's life in the summer house?'

'It's perfect. I thought I'd feel horribly claustrophobic given how small it is, but I love it. It feels like our little space, somewhere hidden away and safe from the world.'

Rick could see why that would be so appealing to her. 'And how's things with Davy?'

She beamed at him. 'Great! He's decided I've been far too sheltered up until now, so he's on a mission to teach me all the things he thinks I should know.'

Suddenly what he'd walked in on that morning made sense. 'Hence the plumbing.'

'Hence the plumbing,' she repeated.

'So me offering to help was a bit like earlier when we were crossing the road.'

'The penny drops!' Her teasing laugh was so pretty it was hard to take offence, but apparently his face had other ideas. 'Oh, don't pout!' she protested. 'I'm only joking. I think it's lovely the way you look out for everyone...' She hesitated, a cheeky grin turning her face impish. 'Most of the time.'

'She giveth with one hand and taketh away with the other,' Rick opined, clutching a hand to his chest.

'Oh, behave yourself.' She gave his arm a little shove with her shoulder.

Rick nudged her back and they continued down the road, their arms brushing now and again as they walked. He tried to ignore his hyperawareness of her, the softness of her skin, the faint scent of her perfume, but it was a hopeless task. 'So you're happy at the hotel, then?' he asked, hoping returning to the topic would serve as a distraction.

'Happy enough.' She sighed. 'I don't mean to sound ungrateful, because I would be in an even bigger hole without at least some money coming in, but it's not what I ever imagined myself doing. Even if it was my dream job, there'd be no point in getting too attached to it, nor to working with Davy.'

That stopped him short. Had his great-uncle confided in her? Surely not, because otherwise why would he have been so angry with Rick earlier? 'How so?'

She gave him a puzzled look. 'I mean, come on, Davy's going to want to sell up and retire at some point, isn't he? Whoever takes over will no doubt want to put their own stamp on the place. Plus there's no guarantee they'd want to keep me on, or any of the other staff for that matter.'

'No, I suppose not.' Davy had told him he had things in hand for the future, and Rick hadn't pressed him on it. It hadn't really occurred to him that he'd sell the hotel, but what else would he do with it? None of the family were in a position to take over from him... unless Anya wanted to, he supposed. It was on the tip of his tongue to suggest that perhaps Davy would hang on to the hotel after he retired and keep Anya on to run it, but that would be disingenuous of him, if not a little cruel, to dangle such a carrot in front of her. 'Do you have any idea what you want to do in the future, or is that just too much to think about right now?' They were almost at the café, so Rick stopped because he genuinely wanted to know what her plans were.

'Chloe wants me to go into business with her,' Anya said, not sounding too sure about it.

Well that was interesting, and if nothing else it was as clear an indication as any that Anya might be looking at sticking around for the longer term. 'Oh really? Doing what?'

'She has this grand idea about us setting up an interior design business together. I'm not sure it'll go anywhere, if I'm honest, but I've said I'll make a few items she can sell in her online shop.'

'Clothes, you mean?' he asked, recalling what she'd said at dinner about making a lot of her own outfits when she was younger.

'Maybe, but I'm more into home furnishings these days.' She pulled a face. 'Well, I used to be, at any rate.'

He pictured the living room at the summer house and how different it had looked from when Chloe had been there, even though the furniture was basically the same. 'You made all that stuff I saw when I came over? The throws and cushions and what have you?' He whistled through his teeth. 'I thought you must've bought it in some high-end place in London.'

Anya ducked her head, but not quite enough to hide her smile. 'Thanks. It was really a hobby more than anything, a way to keep busy. I loved doing it, but it was only ever for me.'

'Well, I think you have great taste, for what it's worth.' It was pathetic, really, how pleased he was when that earned him another shy smile. *Get a grip*. 'And you and Chloe working together sounds like a fantastic idea. Anything that breathes new life into the village is a good thing. We need more local independent traders rather than big chains taking over everything.'

'Chloe thinks there'll be a market for it with all the incomers buying up properties for weekend retreats and holiday rentals.'

Rick thought his cousin had a point. 'I agree with her, plus now you've got your newfound plumbing skills you'll be able to add that to your skill set.' He let his lips curl into a teasing grin that widened further when she rewarded him with another of those joyful peals of laughter. He liked this back and forth with her. He liked *her*.

'It'll take a lot more than knowing how to clean out the U-bend under a sink! But we'd hopefully be able to get Ryan and Matt to give us a hand making a few bigger things.' She covered her mouth with her hand. 'Listen to me getting carried away with myself. I haven't even taken the cover off my sewing machine since I got here.'

'You'll get there,' Rick encouraged, liking the way her eyes shone as she talked about it. 'It's good to have plans, something to strive for.'

'Something to look forward to.'

He nodded. 'Exactly. Look at me. I started out helping Mum in the chandlery on Saturdays to earn a bit of pocket money and now I run my own business.'

'It sounds great in theory, and I want to do everything I can to support Chloe after everything she's done for me; I'm just not sure how much I can practically achieve. Between work and taking care of Freya I'll only have the odd hour here and there once Ryan and Matt sort out a workspace for us. And the fabric I brought with me will only go so far. Once I've used that up, I won't be able to afford to buy anything new, not for a while anyway, because every penny is going towards supporting me and Freya.' She sighed. 'I can't even afford to pay any rent on the summer house and Aunt Helen keeps accidentally' – Anya put the word in air quotes – 'buying too much in the supermarket and filling my freezer. I wish I could tell her to stop...'

She looked so stressed and sad it was all Rick could do not to reach out and pull her into his arms. 'Give yourself a break. It's only been a few weeks, Anya.' He gestured towards the café just ahead of them. 'Come on, let's get some lunch.'

She shook her head. 'I'm not going to stay. I know Davy said I could take my time but he was moaning about his hip aching earlier, so I don't want to leave him on his own for too long.' Tilting her head to one side, she gave him a considering look. 'Did he mention anything about that when you were talking to him earlier?'

Nice try. He thought he and Davy had kept their voices down, but Anya had clearly caught wind that all wasn't right between them. 'Can't say he mentioned it, but a few aches and pains are to be expected at his age.' They reached the door and he held it open to allow her to walk in first.

The smile she gave him didn't quite reach her eyes. 'Of course.'

She brightened up when they walked in and Issy greeted them with a smile. 'Well, two of my favourite people at once, this is a treat. What can I get you?'

Anya perused the glass counter for a moment. 'Can I have a chicken mayo and sweetcorn brown roll for me and cheese and pickle on white for Davy, to take away, please? And pop in a couple of those lovely-looking Bakewell slices as well, as a bit of an afternoon treat.' She fished in her purse and pulled out a twenty-pound note which she offered to Issy.

'You're not staying even for a coffee?' Rick asked, unable to keep the disappointment out of his voice.

She seemed to consider it for a moment. 'I suppose I could. If I rush back too early Davy will only accuse me of fussing again.' She turned back to Issy. 'Add a small latte to that, please.'

'No.' Rick stepped up to the counter. 'The coffee is on me as it was my suggestion.' He sensed Anya bristle beside him. 'Sorry, is that me trying to be too helpful again?'

For a panicked moment he worried he'd killed the mood, until she quirked her lips in a half-smile. 'Normally, I'd say yes, but as this is actually Davy's money I'm spending it'd be a bit cheeky to insist on using it to pay for my drink as well.' She turned back to Issy. 'Make that a large latte, seeing as Rick's paying.'

'Serves me right, I suppose,' Rick said, shaking his head in mock sorrow.

'It does indeed. I'll go and grab us a seat, shall I?'

Rick watched her sashay over to a table by the window that offered a view out onto the beach. When he turned back to Issy she was studying him with a frown. 'What?' He'd meant it to sound casual but failed miserably.

'I was just wondering if you had romantic designs on my friend, Frederick Penrose.'

It was on the tip of his tongue to deny it, but honestly who was he trying to kid? 'And if I did?'

Issy's face broke out into a beaming smile. 'I'd say it's about bloody time. After that pig of a husband, she deserves a decent man like you.'

'That's it?' he asked, having expected a lecture on being mindful of Anya's feelings after everything she'd been through. Not that he needed to be told to tread carefully. When it came to Anya, Rick would always put her needs above his own.

She nodded. 'That's it. Now, what are you having?'

'Um, a chicken salad, please, and a large black coffee.'

'I'll bring them over in a minute.'

Buoyed by Issy's support, Rick was full of confidence as he joined Anya at their table. 'What are you smiling at?' she asked as he sat down.

'Just something Issy said.' He took a deep breath and decided to go for it. 'As you can only stay for a quick coffee now, I was wondering if perhaps you might like to do something else another time.'

Anya huffed an amused laugh. 'You sound like you're asking me out on a date.' When he didn't say anything, her eyes grew round as saucers as his intention sank in.

The anticipation in his stomach turned from a champagne fizz to a lead weight. 'It's a silly idea, forget I said anything.

You've got enough going on, I'm sure, what with looking after Freya and—'

The stream of words cut off as she covered his hand with hers. 'Shh. Just hush a minute and let me think, okay?'

'Okay.' Rick didn't move a muscle. His hand was alive with sensation, the soft heat of her palm resting on the back of it like a promise he didn't quite dare to believe.

'You're right about me having to think about Freya,' she said eventually, making his tender shoots of hope shrivel.

'It's fine,' he said, pulling his hand out from underneath hers. 'I completely understand.'

'Didn't I tell you to hush, just now?' she asked him in something of an exasperated tone. 'Now put your hand back and let me finish.' Trying to keep his face serious, Rick laid his hand back on the table, his pulse thudding as she placed hers back on top of it. 'As I was saying, there's Freya to consider, so I won't be able to go out much in the evenings, but you'd be very welcome to come for dinner again. Or I could get some popcorn and we can sit and watch a film on the TV and pretend we're at the pictures.'

Rick flipped his hand over so they were palm to palm. He closed his fingers around hers, liking the way her smaller hand sheltered within his. 'Sounds perfect.'

'Here are your coffees and your salad,' Issy said, startling not only Anya but Rick, judging by the way he snatched his hand out of hers. Anya didn't take offence as she'd done exactly the same thing. *Good grief, what had come over her just now, holding hands with him in public where anyone could see them*? Clearly Issy had seen more than enough, from the way she was grinning as she placed everything on the table.

'Give me a shout when you want me to make up your sandwiches, okay?' Not content with that cheesy grin, she actually winked at Anya.

'Thanks,' she muttered, looking away before her entire face burst into flames. She immediately locked eyes with a pair of older ladies who didn't even pretend to hide their interested stares. My God, it would be round the village in no time! Panicked adrenaline sent Anya shooting to her feet. The sudden movement made the legs of her chair scrape on the floor, the sound drawing more eyes in their direction. 'Actually, I'd better get back, so if you can make those sandwiches up for me now, please?' She pressed a hand to the sudden tightness in her chest.

Issy frowned. 'You haven't even touched your coffee...'

'*Now*, please?' Anya begged.

Clearly sensing her unease, Issy nodded and hurried back to the counter.

'Is everything okay?' Rick had his hands braced on the table as he stared up at her.

'Oh God, don't you get up too; everyone's already staring at us!' she hissed at him.

Rick's mouth twitched at the corner. 'I doubt that they are, but what does it matter anyway? We haven't done anything wrong; we're just two friends having a cup of coffee together.'

Anya shot him a beseeching look. Why didn't he understand how serious this was? 'I can't be the centre of attention, Rick. I just can't.'

The half-smile that had been teasing his lips immediately fell away. 'Of course. I should've thought, I'm sorry. If you want to forget about—'

'No!' she cut him off, the panicky feeling inside growing worse at the idea she'd put him off already.

She should've said no, should've turned him down gently because, my goodness, if this was her reaction then she was clearly in no fit state to seriously contemplate dating anyone. But he was so kind she just had the sense that everything would be okay if he was near. He was so tall and his chest was so broad her fingers itched to smooth a wrinkle in his shirt just for the chance to see if he was as muscular as he appeared. And how had she not noticed before how soulful his deep brown eyes were?

Something else stirred inside her, a richer, deeper tug underneath the bubbling anxiety, and she felt her breath catch in a different way. *Rick Penrose*. Rick. Penrose. All this time and he'd been right under her nose. Her pulse thudded so hard she raised a hand to her throat, sure he must be able to see it. 'No, just give me some time to get my head around everything, okay?'

He nodded. 'Okay. Can I maybe call you later?'

She smiled, relieved that he was being so understanding. 'Yes, that would be lovely.'

He picked up her cup and handed it to her. 'Don't forget this.'

'Thanks.' She took the coffee to be polite, but there was no way she was going to drink it now. Adding caffeine to the absolute mess of nerves and desire inside her would likely bring on a heart attack. Anya was relieved that Issy had a large paper bag waiting for her with the sandwiches and cakes. She took it without a word and hurried for the door, keeping her gaze locked on the floor.

It was only once she got outside that the tightness in her chest began to ease and she could breathe again. The moment she was out of view of the café's big picture windows she sank down onto the low wall that ran along the edge of the seafront. There were plenty of people out and about on the beach, but it was nowhere near as busy as it had been at the weekend. The sand closest to the high tide line was covered in towels and umbrellas, a few windbreaks here and there (though there was barely a puff of breeze) hammered firmly in to mark out territory. Just a couple of feet further back, there was plenty of space, and the families and couples sitting there were much more spread out. She never understood why some people were determined to be as close to the water as possible, like the ones who crammed into the parking spaces nearest to the door in the supermarket. Give her a bit of room anytime, even if it meant walking a few extra feet.

She watched the comings and goings on the beach for a few minutes, smiling at the shrieks from a couple of little girls who had raced into the sea carrying bright pink inflatables only to turn and scurry out of the shallows as the coldness of the water registered. It would take several weeks of consistent sunshine to warm it by a few degrees, and even then it would be a shock until you got used to it. Anya loved that feeling, the bravery it took to keep striking out into the chilly waves, knowing dabbling about on the edge would only take you longer to become accustomed. She'd have to do the same if she was really going to give things with Rick a chance. All in or not at all. It wouldn't be fair to Freya otherwise. If they fiddled around and took things too slow, she'd get used to him being around and then it would be much harder on all of them if things didn't work out. The tug in her belly earlier told her there might be chemistry, but there was only one way to find out. The thought of being intimate with another man was equal parts scary and exciting. Since Drew's death, it was like that part of her had switched off completely. Though she found herself attracted to Rick, what if she couldn't turn it back on again? The thought of leading him on and then letting him down was almost as bad as the fear of Freya getting too attached.

Her phone buzzed and she set the bag of sandwiches on the wall to retrieve it. It was a WhatsApp message from Issy.

ISSY

What was that all about?? Are you okay??

Before she had a chance to reply, the words *Kat is typing...* appeared on the screen and Anya winced. Issy hadn't just sent the message to her, she'd sent it to their group chat by mistake.

KAT

What's happened?

ANYA

False alarm, everything's fine

If she'd thought that would head things off at the pass, Issy had other ideas. Apparently her first message hadn't been a mistake after all, because her response immediately popped up.

ISSY

Anya and Rick were holding hands just now in the café!!

CHLOE

Whhhaaaaaatt???

Oh God, they'd all seen it.

CHLOE

Details! I demand alllll the details!!

She was tempted to ignore them all, but she knew she'd never get a moment's peace until she said something. Yes there was lots to be nervous about, but if she was going to take a chance, then she doubted there was a better man than Rick to do it with. Taking a deep breath, she sent a reply.

ANYA

Rick and I are going to start dating. NBD.

Issy is typing...
Kat is typing...
Chloe is typing...
Before any of their responses could land, Anya hastily added one more message.

ANYA

Not a word, or I'll block you all!

It was an empty threat, of course, but the three typing bubbles subsided. Shaking her head, Anya tucked her phone away and picked up the bag of sandwiches. She wasn't naïve enough to think that would keep them quiet for long; no doubt the three of them had opened a private chat and were gossiping away behind her back. Fine with her. As long as they weren't bombarding her with questions, she could think things through. Rick would be calling her later to set up their first date and she needed to know exactly what she was going to say to him.

* * *

Though she'd known she'd have to discuss it with her friends eventually, she still couldn't believe it when there was a tap at the door not five minutes after she'd finished putting Freya to bed that evening. She glanced up to find the three of them grinning at her through the glass. Issy was holding a couple of pizza boxes and both Kat and Chloe were clutching bottles of Prosecco. Kat raised her bottle and her muffled voice came through the glass. 'Hurry up, this is getting warm!'

Anya rose and walked to the door but instead of opening it, she turned the lock and yanked the curtain closed, blocking them out. 'Go away!'

'Boo!'

'Spoilsport!'

'Come on, Annie, let us in!'

Sighing, Anya pulled back the curtain and burst out laughing at the three exaggeratedly sad expressions that greeted her. She rolled her eyes and unlocked the door. 'If I let you in, you have to promise to keep the noise down,' she warned them. 'I've just got Freya down for the night.'

'We'll be quiet as mice,' Chloe promised as she all but pushed her way in. At least she paused long enough to peck a kiss on Anya's cheek.

'I got Four Seasons and a Margherita,' Issy said, also stopping to give her a kiss. 'Where's the plates?'

'Top right cupboard,' Anya replied automatically as she grinned at Kat, who at least had the decency to look a little shame-faced about the group ambush. 'I thought better of you, Katrina.'

'It was Chloe's idea,' she admitted, giving Anya a one-armed hug. 'We'll go away if you really want us to.'

'No we won't,' Anya's cousin mock-whispered from the little kitchenette where she'd opened another cupboard and was pulling out wine glasses. Well, to call them glasses was to ignore the fact they were brightly coloured pieces of plastic that looked like they belonged in a picnic set rather than having been designed to grace any dinner table. Given Anya didn't *have* a dinner table and they were eating takeaway pizza, she supposed they were exactly right for the occasion.

They gathered around the coffee table, Issy and Kat on the sofa, Anya in the chair and Chloe happy to sit on the floor. She filled their glasses and handed them out.

'What shall we drink to?' Issy asked as she accepted hers.

'The four of us being together again,' Kat suggested.

Chloe nodded. 'Yes.' She raised her glass and they followed suit. 'To us!'

'To us!' they echoed.

'And,' Chloe added with a sly grin, 'to Annie's soon-to-be-revived sex life.'

Anya gasped. Kat just about swallowed before letting out a choked laugh. Poor Issy turned red, waved her hand in front of her face and eventually had to resort to spitting the mouthful of fizz she couldn't get down back into her glass. 'Oh my God!' she exclaimed, wiping away tears. '*Chloe!*'

Chloe's expression was all wide-eyed innocence. 'What? Don't you think it's something to celebrate? At least one of us is going to be having some fun. It's been such a long time since my nether regions saw any action, my poor lady garden is so overgrown I'm going to need to get Monty Don in to sort it out.'

They all laughed until Anya suddenly remembered Freya and shushed them. 'It's funny actually because I was thinking about it earlier.'

'What? You were thinking about having sex with Rick when the only update we've had so far is that the two of you were holding hands? I feel like we've missed a few steps in this story.' Kat leaned forward, eyes eager, the pizza on her plate forgotten. 'Tell us *everything!*'

Anya shook her head at the overly dramatic tone. 'No, you haven't missed anything, or at least I've kind of rushed ahead in my brain. I know after everything that's happened I should probably take things slowly—'

Chloe grimaced. 'Why the hell should you? You're only twenty-seven, Anya; you deserve to enjoy yourself.'

'There is Freya to consider in all this,' Issy pointed out. 'Anya can't just throw caution to the wind like we can.' She gave a self-deprecating laugh. 'Although chance would be a fine thing!'

Anya nodded. 'Exactly, but I'm almost thinking the opposite, like maybe Rick and I shouldn't hang around too long before we figure out if we're compatible in bed, because I don't want Freya to become too attached and then I find out—'

'What? That he's all sports car on the outside but only a two-stroke engine under the bonnet?' Chloe pulled a face as they all giggled again. 'God, we need to stop talking about this – he is my cousin.'

Kat shot her an amused look. 'Come on now, you were the one who brought it up, and Anya's got a point. It's best to find out these things sooner rather than later.' She turned to Issy. 'Remember that gorgeous surfer I met a couple of summers ago?'

Issy chuckled. 'I remember the disappointed call I got from you the morning after you'd finally persuaded him to shimmy out of his wetsuit.'

'The sea can be quite cold, even in the summer,' Chloe pointed out, though she was grinning from ear to ear.

'Unless he'd been surfing in the Antarctic, I'm afraid there was no hope.' Kat heaved a huge sigh. 'And it wouldn't have been the end of the world if he'd at least been a bit creative.'

Issy snorted. 'What were you expecting from the poor man, a puppet show?'

Kat shrugged. 'Wouldn't have hurt.'

Anya pressed her hand to her side where a stitch was forming because she'd been laughing so much. 'I don't want to start speculating about Rick like that, it's disrespectful. I just meant that if we don't gel in the bedroom then it's kind of a non-starter.' She took a big swig of her Prosecco. 'And the problem might not be with him, anyway.' She looked around at her friends, knowing she could trust them and yet still struggling to find the words to express how she was feeling. 'Drew was... he was the only person I've ever been with. I don't know how to be with anyone else.' She gulped at her fizz again. 'What if I can't?'

'Oh, sweetheart!' Chloe rose up on her knees and leaned over to hug her. 'Is that what you're worried about?'

Anya nodded. 'You probably think I'm being silly.'

Issy set down her glass and reached across the table to take her hand. 'It's not silly at all. It's completely understandable. But if I can offer you a bit of advice, talk to Rick. He's a good guy and he'll want to do the right thing. Give him the information he needs to be able to do that; don't make him second-guess because you're too embarrassed to admit to him what you have to us.'

Kat come over to sit on the arm of Anya's chair and put an arm around her. 'I agree. Whatever else, you can always trust Rick.'

17

Rick had been a little disconcerted to receive a text from Anya asking to postpone their call. He'd been less bothered when he'd been scrolling through his social media later that evening and came across a photo posted by Chloe of her, Anya, Issy and Kat glassy eyed and grinning in a group selfie. He recognised the setting as the summer house and, given the empty pizza boxes and Prosecco bottles on the coffee table, it looked like a fun evening was had by all.

He didn't have much time to dwell on it. The local sailing club held their annual regatta on the first weekend of the school holidays, so the harbour would be a hive of activity over the next couple of weeks as people started getting their boats ready. A steady stream of customers trooped in and out of the chandlery, needing everything from varnish and paint to touch up their woodwork, to replacement ropes and even a couple of new life jackets. His dad was out and about around the harbour, shaking hands, catching up on the gossip and generally running a weather eye over the boats. When he spotted Rick helping one of the customers carry their supplies, Jago came hurrying over to take the box out of his hands.

'Thanks, Dad.'

'My pleasure. Now get back in there and keep that till ringing,' he said, making both Rick and the customer laugh. 'I've got a retirement that needs paying for!'

'Yes, sir!' Rick raised two fingers to his temple and offered a mock salute before heading back inside, where his mum had everything in hand, of course. There was a lull around half-ten, so Rick volunteered to do a coffee run. They had a kettle out the back, but they tended to keep that for emergencies only. Plus it gave Rick a chance to be seen out and about if anyone needed to talk to him. Though his Hub sessions were well frequented, he reckoned at least half of the issues he came across were things raised by people who he bumped into in the street. 'I'm going walkabout,' he said to his mum. 'What do you want me to bring you back?'

Rachel pondered for a moment. 'I quite fancy something cold.'

'What about an iced caramel macchiato?'

She nodded. 'Oh, that sounds lovely. Best get one for your dad while you're at it. The amount of gabbing he's been doing this morning, he'll be parched.'

'He'd call it networking.'

Rachel rolled her eyes. 'I'd call it skiving! At least I know where you get it from.'

'I'm simply serving the needs of the community, Mother,' Rick said, putting on a fake pompous voice.

'Hmm.' Her lips twitched. 'You'll be popping into the hotel, no doubt.'

Rick felt an icy chill ripple down his spine. 'What do you mean?' Had someone got wind of him checking up on Davy?

'Oh, nothing, just something a little bird told me.' She tapped the side of her nose and gave him a knowing smile.

Relief that no one was the wiser about his great-uncle's health issues was tempered rather by the idea he and Anya were already the subject of gossip. 'Well, you and your little bird' – his aunt Helen, no doubt – 'can keep your beaks out of my business.'

Rachel laughed. 'Good luck with that!'

He'd considered it might be wiser to keep away from the hotel, but one look at Issy's rather green-tinged expression behind the café counter made him wonder if Anya was also feeling a little worse for wear. 'Good night was it?' he teased as he reached the front of the small queue.

Issy shot him a glare that could've melted concrete. 'Your cousin has a lot to answer for.'

'Why, what did Chloe do?'

'She went up to the house and fetched a third bottle of Prosecco, that's what she did,' Issy grumbled.

'And forced you to drink it, no doubt.'

'Haha! Right, what do you want anyway?' When he ordered three iced macchiatos and a large latte, she winced. 'Why does everyone want iced drinks today?'

The question bemused him until she switched on the blender to mix everything together. Between the ice rattling around and the whizz of the motor, it made quite a racket. He accepted the tray of drinks and left her to it, smiling to himself as he heard the person who'd been behind him ordering a chocolate frappuccino. It was going to be a long day for poor Issy.

Carrying the four drinks in a cardboard holder, Rick crossed the street and was about to pop into the chemist's to pick up a pack of paracetamol for Anya when he bumped into Morwenna Delaney, the head teacher of the village school.

'Oh, Rick, what good timing!'

'Hello, Morwenna. How's things?'

She nodded. 'Good. Good. Already thinking about what I need to do to get ready for next term. That's actually what I wanted to speak to you about. I've had a couple of people resign from the PTA—'

'Surely you need actual parents on the PTA?' he cut in, trying not to sound too desperate. Morwenna was a lovely woman, but she could be something of a steamroller and he really couldn't afford to get talked into taking anything else on.

She frowned at him for a moment before her eyes widened in amused comprehension. 'Goodness, Rick, there's no need to look quite so panicky. I wasn't suggesting you sign up!'

He blew out a relieved breath. 'You had me worried there for a minute.'

'You do more than enough for our community,' she assured him with a pat on his arm. 'No, I was just wondering if it would be okay to put a poster up in the Hub to see if anyone is interested.'

'Oh, of course, help yourself. If you've got any spares, then we'll put one up in the window at the chandlery as well.'

'Lovely. I haven't got around to making them up yet, but I'll drop a couple off with you when I've printed them off, okay?'

'Whenever you like, and good luck with finding some replacements.'

Morwenna sighed. 'I'm going to need it. The school is barely hanging on as it is. The village might be growing, but the demographic is changing so much that I can foresee a day when I don't have enough pupils to get adequate funds to keep it going.'

Rick frowned. 'I didn't realise things had got that bad.'

She patted his arm again. 'We're not quite on the ragged edge yet, but if we don't find a way to keep our young people around, then it's going to be a problem. Plus so many of your generation are choosing to start your families later, so even those of you who have been able to find jobs and housing aren't keeping my numbers topped up.' She was smiling as she said it.

'Ha! You sound as bad as Mum and Aunt Helen.'

Morwenna laughed. 'Six of you between them and not a sniff of a grandchild; no wonder they're disappointed!'

'Well at least you'll have one new addition to your roster this autumn with Anya's daughter, Freya,' he pointed out.

She shot him a puzzled look. 'Oh, are they planning on staying? I assumed they were only here for the summer. I haven't had any paperwork through to say Anya wants to register Freya for next term.'

'Are you sure?'

Morwenna shrugged. 'Unless it's come through this morning, then absolutely.'

'I'm popping in to see her in a minute. I'll mention it then. I'm sure it's just an oversight.'

'That would be good if you could; the sooner the better so I can finalise my numbers. I'll pencil her in anyway. You don't happen to know the child's surname, do you?'

'Sure, it's Stokes.'

'Lovely, thanks for the heads-up.' Morwenna stepped back from the doorway to make room for him. 'I'll drop those posters off with you in the next day or two.'

When he walked into the hotel reception a few minutes later, Anya looked tired but not as shabby as Issy had been. She glanced up from her screen, the wide, welcoming smile she'd plastered on faltering a little. 'Oh, I wasn't expecting you to visit us again so soon.'

Hmm, not quite the warm welcome he'd anticipated. He held up the tray of coffees even though it was clearly visible. 'I was getting a drink for me and my folks and I saw the state of Issy, so I thought you might be in need of a caffeine boost after last night.'

'She told you about them gatecrashing me? That's why I said not to call.'

He pulled the large latte out of the tray and placed it on the top of the desk. 'Yeah, I figured as much when I saw the photos last night.'

'What photos?'

'Oh, just a couple of group selfies Chloe posted. They popped up on my feed when I was doing my usual pre-bed doomscroll.'

'Ah, okay.' She pulled a face. 'How bad are they?'

'No incriminating evidence, though they might have been taken before the third bottle of Prosecco Issy was just rueing.'

'Ha! Well some of us were sensible and had switched to water by that point. My days of waking up hungover when there's a hyperactive small person to be dealt with are thankfully in the past. Lesson learned, never repeated.'

He grinned. 'I can imagine. Oh, speaking of Freya, I bumped into Morwenna just now and she mentioned that she isn't registered with the school yet.'

He could tell he'd made a mistake as soon as the words had left his mouth from the way her expression shut down. 'Who's Morwenna, and why were you talking to anyone about Freya?'

Rick took an involuntary step back, his free hand raising in automatic apology. 'Hey, I wasn't talking behind your back or anything. Morwenna is the head teacher at the village school and we were chatting about a few things. The topic of school numbers came up, so I pointed out she'd have an addition next term but she said you haven't registered yet. Don't worry if you haven't got around to it; Morwenna said she'd pencil Freya's name in.'

Anya stiffened. 'How does she know what name to put down?'

Rick shook his head, completely baffled. 'She asked me if I knew it, so I told her.'

Reaching up, she rubbed her forehead. 'Look, Rick, I know you were probably only trying to help out, but I really wish you hadn't done that. The reason I haven't registered Freya is because Chloe's helping me with an application to change our surnames and the final documentation hasn't come through yet.'

Oh damn. 'I'm so sorry, I had no idea.' God, he'd really put his foot in it.

She gave him a slightly tired smile. 'Don't worry about it. I'll sort it out with the school when I do the application.'

'Morwenna's dropping off some posters with me in the next couple of days. If you want me to mention—' It took only a raised eyebrow from Anya for Rick to swallow down the offer to help make things right. 'I'll leave you to sort it out.'

'That'd be good, thanks.' The hint of tension around her eyes softened as she reached for the coffee he'd brought. 'And thanks for this, because you guessed right. I could do with a boost. I might not have overindulged, but I haven't had a late night in a while.'

Rick smiled, relieved that he appeared to have been forgiven. 'It looked like you had fun, though.'

She nodded. 'It was so nice to have a bit of adult company, though I'm sorry it meant I had to cancel our chat at the last minute. Speaking of which' – she glanced up at him through her lashes – 'Chloe's volunteered to babysit on Friday night if you wanted to go out and do something.'

'That sounds great. Do you want me to book us a table somewhere? Or we could just go to the Smuggler's Den for a drink?'

She shook her head. 'I'm not sure I'm ready for the local pub. Perhaps we could venture out of the village? I'm happy to drive – Ryan and Helen have put me on their insurance in case I need the car for an emergency, but I'm sure they'd let me borrow it.'

Rick shook his head. 'I can drive.' He hesitated, wondering if this was another one of those situations where he was trying to be too helpful. 'Unless you want to, of course?'

Thankfully, she didn't take offence. 'As long as you don't mind, I'm happy for you to drive.'

'Great. I know a really nice little Italian over in Port Petroc. We can take the scenic route along the coast. What time shall I book for?'

Anya took a sip of her coffee and he could almost see the cogs whirring as she worked out the logistics. 'Eight o'clock? I'll get Chloe to come about half-six so Freya can get used to her being there and then I'll meet you out the front of Ryan and Helen's about seven?'

'Whatever makes things easy for you.'

18

Though Anya had been worried there might be some resistance from Freya about her going out for the evening, when the little girl found out Chloe was coming to look after her, she was too excited to ask many questions. They even had fun choosing something for Anya to wear – thankfully she picked a floaty pale green maxi dress with a pretty floral detail and not the metallic gold catsuit Anya had once worn for a fancy dress party. Like Freya's too-small frog wellies, Anya had no idea how the catsuit had survived the massive clear-out she'd had before their move. One of these days she'd have to see what else had slipped through the net. She still hadn't tackled all the boxes and bags out in the shed, and until she did that Ryan and Matt couldn't get started on converting it into a workspace. A tug of guilt pulled at her. There were so many other things she should be prioritising right now; going out on a date should be way down the list.

Anya eyed her reflection in the bathroom mirror she was using to apply her make-up while Freya splashed around in the bath. *Or perhaps you're just looking for an excuse to back out.* She'd grown increasingly nervous as the day had gone on, and if the butterflies in her stomach didn't settle down soon she wouldn't be able to eat a bite later.

'You look pretty, Mummy,' Freya said.

'Thank you, darling.' Bending over, Anya added a dash of lipstick to Freya's mouth and smiled at her. 'You look pretty, too!'

Freya giggled in delight and they spent the next couple of minutes blowing kisses and giving each other ever-more-extravagant compliments until they were laughing so hard Anya had to wipe off her eyeliner and start again.

By the time Chloe arrived, Freya was in her pyjamas and had transferred her favourite dolls and teddies to the sofa ready for a *Frozen* watch party. 'I hope you don't mind,' Anya whispered as she greeted Chloe with a hug.

'Not at all. It'll be the most fun I've had on a Friday night for a long time.' Chloe held up a carrier bag. 'I've got plenty of supplies to keep us going.'

'I know I'm not going to approve of probably 90 per cent of what's in there, so I'm not even going to ask,' Anya said with a rueful laugh.

'Girls' night secrets,' Chloe said, making a show of hiding the bag behind her back. She cast a critical eye over the shorts and T-shirt Anya had thrown on after her shower earlier. 'You're not wearing that, are you?'

Anya couldn't resist glancing down. 'What's wrong with it?' When Chloe frowned, she grinned. 'My dress is hanging up in the bedroom.' She checked her watch. There was still plenty of time before she had to get changed. 'Do you want a drink?'

Though she'd seen it a hundred times before, Anya still ended up getting caught up watching the film – well, watching Freya watch it, anyway. Snuggled up with her toys, merrily stuffing strawberry bootlaces, sherbet-filled spaceships and all sorts of other sugary delights from the enormous bag of pick 'n' mix Chloe had brought with her, Freya was in her element. Only a nudge from Chloe reminded Anya of the time, and she had to dash into the bedroom, pull on her dress and swap her slippers for a pair of flat, strappy sandals. She picked up the little cream evening bag that had room for a lipstick, a pack of tissues and her debit card. She hoped wherever Rick had chosen wasn't too expensive and tried not to think about all the things the money could be better spent on.

Stop it.

Taking a deep breath, she put her best foot forward and walked into the other room. 'Wow, look at you!' Chloe said, giving her an approving look-over. 'That dress is beautiful. Give us a twirl!'

Feeling giddily self-conscious, Anya turned around a couple of times, letting the floaty skirt of the dress flair. 'I found the material online.'

'You made it?' Chloe's eyes grew wide. 'We must get the workshop sorted and get you back behind that sewing machine because I could sell a dozen of them, tomorrow.'

Anya blushed, absurdly pleased with her cousin's obvious admiration. 'Let's make time this weekend to start clearing things out, then!'

'Deal! Now hurry up or you're going to be late.'

Having given Freya a hug and a kiss, and earned a complaint from her daughter that she was blocking the TV, Anya hurried out of the summer house and through the garden.

Rick was waiting for her on the street, leaning his back against the side of a smart-looking black SUV. The sight of him dressed up was enough to make her catch her breath. In a navy short-sleeved shirt that highlighted the impressive size of his biceps and a pair of tailored cream chinos, he was the dictionary definition of tall, dark and handsome. He straightened up the moment he saw her, the smile curving his lips sending little tingles of anticipation dancing down her spine. 'You look lovely,' he said, reaching out to take her hand. He drew her close enough to lean down and brush a kiss on her cheek. 'Simply gorgeous.'

The rich, amber scent of his aftershave had her eyelids fluttering closed for a second, unable to cope with so many pleasurable sensations at once.

God, you smell good.

Her eyes flew open again, but Rick's warm, friendly smile reassured her that she hadn't humiliated herself by saying it out loud. She needed to say something, though. 'Thank you. You umm, you look nice too, that colour really works for you.'

He brushed a hand over the front of his shirt and she could tell he was pleased at the compliment. 'Are you ready to go?' When she nodded, he used his free hand to open her door, releasing her with the other only after he'd helped her in. He waited until she gathered her dress well clear, then closed her door and circled the bonnet to get in the other side. 'How was Freya? No problems with you going out tonight?' he asked as they fastened their seatbelts and he started the engine.

'She was fine, stuffing herself with sweets and having a lovely time with Chloe.' She wrinkled her nose at him. 'I'm not looking forward to dealing with the after-effects of her sugar rush later, I have to admit.'

Rick shot her a sympathetic grin just as he was pulling away from the kerb. 'I bet. Fingers crossed she'll be fast asleep when you get home.'

'I can only hope!'

There was a lull in conversation as Rick negotiated his way through what bit of traffic there was. The village had grown from the seafront outwards in a higgledy-piggledy maze of narrow streets and dead ends. Even the later parts of the village that had been built in the seventies and eighties struggled to accommodate the combination of parked cars and the popularity of larger, wider vehicles like Rick's SUV.

Once they were out on the coast road, she began to worry less about his paintwork and was able to relax a little more. 'So this place you've booked for tonight, have you been there before?'

Keeping his eyes on the road, Rick nodded. 'Yes, a couple of times. It's not super fancy or anything, but the food is delicious, and if you like seafood they always have a daily special with whatever the chef has bought fresh from the boats that morning.'

She let her head loll back against the seat as she watched the beautiful scenery go by. 'It's been so long since I've been out for a meal that didn't come with fries and a toy, I'm really looking forward to it.'

'I can't remember the last time I went for dinner that wasn't either something to do with the council or a family occasion.' Rick's admission made her feel better, somehow.

She turned her gaze away from the window to watch his profile. 'I thought you'd be much in demand on the Halfmoon Quay dating scene.'

He barked a laugh, his eyes flicking briefly across to meet hers before he looked back at the road. 'The dating scene, such as it is, and I are pretty much strangers these days, I have to admit.'

Curious, she shifted a little in her seat so she could turn more towards him. 'Why's that?'

The nearest shoulder to her raised in a shrug, once again drawing her attention to the tightness of his short sleeve around the thick muscle of his arms. 'I got bored, I guess. Going out on a date when my gut instinct told me it's not going to ultimately lead anywhere began to feel like a waste of time. When I was younger, sure, but a holiday fling with someone who's only going to be around for a week or two at most? That doesn't appeal at all any more.'

'I can understand that.' She recalled her unpleasant encounter with Shelly Dean and what Chloe had said about her being sweet on Rick. 'There was no one from the village you were interested in?'

They reached a junction and, although there was no traffic in sight, Rick stopped the car and looked at her. 'No, the only person I was interested in didn't live in Halfmoon Quay.'

Oh. While she struggled to drag up a half sensible response from her scrambled brain, Rick calmly put the car back into gear and continued driving. 'You never said anything,' she managed to squeak out eventually.

He laughed, not an entirely happy sound. 'I was going to. I'd geared myself up for it, even made sure I was over at Ryan and Helen's on the day I knew you and your mum were due to arrive. I can picture you now, pretty enough to take my breath away in a pink sundress with tiny straps. You'd cut your hair shorter since the last time I saw you, and it had these blonde streaks in it.'

She raised a hand to her fringe in remembrance. 'That was the summer I turned seventeen. Mum finally agreed to let me dye my hair.' It was hard to get the words out because she knew now why he'd never told her how he felt. She wanted to tell him to stop talking, but the lump in her throat was growing bigger and bigger.

'You looked so different, glamorous and so grown up compared to Chloe even though you were the same age.' Rick had to stop at another junction, but this time he didn't turn and look at her as the words kept tumbling from his lips. 'My heart was beating so fast I was sure everyone would be able to hear it, and I was terrified at the thought of speaking to you, and yet deep down I knew this was it, that you'd notice me standing there. That our eyes would meet like in some romcom. And then the other passenger door opened...'

'And Drew got out of the car. Oh, Rick, I had no idea...' She closed her eyes, her heart breaking for the anxious, excited boy she'd heard an echo of in his voice, and perhaps a little bit for herself too. How different things could've been if she hadn't met Drew that day he came in to the department store where she'd had a Saturday job. She and her coworker had even played rock-paper-scissors to see who would get to serve him. Anya had won, or so she'd thought at the time.

A soft hand covered hers and when she opened her eyes, she realised Rick had pulled the car over into one of the viewing point car parks that were scattered along the coastal road. 'Hey, I didn't mean to upset you.'

She turned her hand over so they were palm to palm the way he had when they'd been in the café the other day and threaded their fingers together. 'I had no idea. If I had...'

Reaching out with his free hand, he briefly touched a finger to her lips. 'No. We can't change the past, and if you hadn't met Drew you wouldn't have Freya.'

Anya nodded. 'She's the only thing that kept me hanging on, you know, in the darkest of days. I'm worried already if I should even be here. I can't risk things not working out between us, but I don't know how we can make a go of it without her being involved. It seems crazy to be even thinking so far ahead when we've barely started our first date, but I have to consider Freya in all of this. If she becomes too attached to you and then we split up I don't know what it would do to her.'

Rick squeezed her hand. 'Like I said before, I'm not interested in a casual fling. I've waited more than ten years for the chance to be with you, Anya, I'll do whatever you need me to do to make this work. We can take things as slow as you like and I'll stay away from the summer house if you prefer. Not getting to see each other as often as we might like is a small price to pay if it means protecting Freya. She has to be your priority.'

His gentle reassurance calmed the butterflies in her stomach. 'Thank you. It's not my intention to mess you around or make you feel like I don't want to be seen with you...'

'But you'd rather not be the centre of attention again,' he finished, echoing what she'd said to him in the café.

She shuddered. 'Not if I can help it.'

He reached out with his free hand to cup her cheek. 'May I kiss you?'

She nodded, unable to speak, her heart suddenly hammering so fast. He leaned towards her, stopped suddenly with a laugh as his seat belt jammed, and just like that the tension of the moment melted away. They both fumbled with the release mechanism and leaned in, almost bumping noses in their sudden haste. His lips were soft and there was still a hint of mint from his toothpaste. He slanted his mouth over hers, first left and then right as though seeking the perfect angle, and then his hands were in her hair, and hers rose to press against the smooth cotton of his shirt, the impossible hardness of his chest beneath the material, and she couldn't think, couldn't do anything other than respond to the pressure of his lips as the kiss shifted from a question to something closer to a demand.

'Well,' Anya gasped when they finally broke apart. 'That

puts aside any worries I had about whether or not we had suffi-cient chemistry.'

Rick sank back against his seat with a strangled laugh. 'We might have to wait here a few minutes before we drive on to the restaurant.'

She didn't catch his meaning until he shifted as though trying to adjust his trousers. She made the mistake of glancing down at his lap and quickly turned her hot face towards the window. Oh! Well, that put aside another one of her worries.

She decided to keep that observation to herself.

19

Rick pulled into the large car park near the seafront and stopped the car. 'We've got a bit of time,' he said to Anya. 'We can take a walk along the prom if you like.' She glanced up at him through her lashes and he had to swallow hard before he could speak again. 'I... uh, I could do with a bit of fresh air.'

'That might be a good idea.' A soft pink glow highlighted her cheekbones as her tongue stole out to dampen her lips. It was all he could do not to drag her into his arms and risk them getting arrested for public indecency.

'I'll just go and see if we need a ticket.' He shoved his door open and climbed out before temptation got the better of him and strode over to the large sign above the machine. He'd been here often enough to know that parking was free after 6 p.m., but it was as good an excuse as any to put a little bit of breathing space between them. He counted to thirty in his head, all the while telling himself he needed to get a grip. He was a grown man not an awkward, fumbling teenager and he'd been on plenty of first dates. *Never one that mattered this much though.*

'Do you need some change?' Anya's question made him

jump and he glanced down to see her staring up at him with those shining eyes that made him want to fall into them.

'No. It's fine, I mean it's free.' He tilted his head towards the gap in the fence that led out onto the wide promenade. 'Are you ready?'

'Yes.' She tucked the little clutch bag she'd brought with her under one arm and they began to walk.

It was a lovely evening, the lingering heat of the day countered by a refreshing sea breeze. The beach below them was busier than he'd expected, the people all looking in the same direction. Rick followed their gazes, raising a hand to shield his eyes as he did so. The doors to the lifeboat station were open and a tractor was towing the lifeboat down the slipway. The tide was on its way out and had already left the small pleasure boats that could fit into this narrow section of the bay leaning on their sides like a colourful collection of drunks. As the tractor chugged down the concrete ramp and out across the sand, the crew were busy on deck.

'I hope everything's okay,' Anya said at his side.

'I think it's a training exercise,' Rick reassured her. Unable to resist the urge to touch her, he placed one hand on her shoulder and pointed with the other towards the station. 'There's no siren or flashing light.' He swung his arm back in the direction of the boat. 'And the crew aren't fully dressed up the way they would be for a call-out.' Though they were wearing their bright, waterproof trousers, none of them had jackets or safety helmets on.

Anya visibly relaxed against his hand. 'Oh, that's okay then.' She stepped forward to rest her arm on the rail of the promenade, her smile eager as she watched the spectacle below. Rick moved to lean beside her and she grinned up at him, an excited glint in her eye. 'I've never seen one launch before; do you mind if we watch?'

'Not at all.'

Anya wasn't the only one who groaned in disappointment when all the crew did when they reached the water was turn the boat in a slow circle and hook it back up to the tractor for the return trip up the ramp.

'Come on, let's walk,' Rick suggested. 'We can follow the promenade for a bit and then cut down one of the side streets to the restaurant.'

Still looking a little disgruntled, Anya stepped back from the railing, dropping her bag in the process. Rick bent and retrieved it before she had chance to, keeping hold of it in one hand while he held the other one out to her. With that little glance up through her lashes that filled his head with too many distracting thoughts, she accepted his offer and interlinked their fingers.

They didn't talk much as they strolled along the neatly paved promenade, but it was a pleasant, contented silence and Rick was happy to simply be in the moment. It was surreal getting to experience something he'd wanted for so long, something he'd given up any hope of ever going from dream to reality.

They passed a number of bars with tables and chairs set out for the drinkers to enjoy. Rick thought it would be nice to do that one evening, assuming the rest of the night went as well as it had started and Anya wanted to go on another date with him. Although he knew it was partly down to the size difference, it felt like there were a lot more people out and about here in Port Petroc compared to a typical evening in Halfmoon Quay. The village was bustling during the day, especially during the holiday season, but come evening there simply wasn't enough for people to do. The proliferation of self-catering rentals didn't help as lots of families packed up and tucked themselves away for the evening, but even for those who wanted to venture out, the night-time economy was lacking. They had a couple of restaurants, but they were always booked up, and the handful of pubs didn't offer the same kind of ambience the promenade here had. Perhaps he should survey some of the business owners along the seafront in the Quay, see if any of them had thoughts on what could be done to improve things. If there was enough interest in enhancing the night-time offering for visitors, he could help with things like licensing applications, maybe find some cash down the back of the council sofa to improve the lighting...

'Penny for them?'

Startled, Rick glanced down at Anya, who was studying him with an amused smile. 'Sorry, I was miles away.'

'I could tell! Come on, what were you thinking about?'

Rick hesitated. Should he tell a white lie and talk about how much he was enjoying simply being with her? It was true, of course, but that's not where his train of thought had been when she'd asked. 'Will you be disappointed if I admit it was council business?'

The merry tinkle of her laughter filled the air. 'I would expect nothing less! If it's a problem that's preoccupying you, then I'm happy to act as a sounding board.'

It made a refreshing change for someone to say that, because his family groaned more often than not when he started banging on. 'Not a problem as such, just thinking about ways we might make Halfmoon Quay a more attractive prospect for visitors in the evening.'

Anya glanced around them. 'It is lovely here. I was only thinking how nice it would be to sit at one of these tables and watch the world go by.'

'Exactly!' He gave her fingers a quick squeeze, pleased they were on the same wavelength. 'We could do that next time you have a free evening.'

'I'd like that.' She sighed. 'It might be a while though, because I can't expect everyone to babysit for me – and I'm a bit worried about Freya. She was as good as gold about me coming out tonight, but she's been acting up a little about other stuff. She's not being naughty or anything, but she's got really stubborn about what she will and won't wear. Davy says she's testing me because she thinks it's something that's important to me and deep down she's worried I might leave her too.'

Her pensive expression tugged at Rick's heart. Releasing her hand, he put his arm around her. 'Then we must make sure she feels safe and secure here. Moving won't have been easy on her either, I'm sure.'

Anya rested her head against his chest. 'So much change for her to deal with, but there was simply nothing else I could do.'

'It'll work itself out. And being surrounded by family can only be a good thing for her.'

She turned in his embrace to look up at him. 'That's true. She had so much fun playing on the beach with everyone the other weekend. I know it's asking a lot of you, but she has to come first.'

'It's not asking anything of me that I'm not happy to give. Hey, talking of the beach, the annual regatta's coming up soon. I'll be down there all day as part of the volunteer support team—'

'Well, of course you will be...' She cupped his cheek as she said it, her smile full of tender amusement.

He turned his head to give her fingers a playful nip. 'Don't tease me, we both know I am a hopeless cause.'

Giggling, she stretched up to peck a kiss on his lips. 'I'm sorry, you were saying about the regatta?'

'I just thought you could bring Freya along. There'll be lots of activities for the kids and it would be a good way for her to get to know me a bit better, away from the summer house. The family will all be there, so it won't be like a date or anything.'

'Oh that sounds lovely. Thank you for being so thoughtful.'

Rick winked at her. 'Don't think I won't be trying to sneak you away for a kiss at some point.'

'I should certainly hope so.'

20

When Rick led Anya down a narrow back street and stopped in front of a building with plain white wooden window frames and a small sign above the door that simply said *Deliziosa*, she wondered if he'd brought her to the right place. Nothing about it seemed welcoming and if she'd been walking down the street on her own she'd likely have passed it without a second thought. But the moment he pushed open the door, her mood completely changed as it was like stepping into a different world. A narrow bar lined the right-hand wall, with trailing plants sitting in amongst the bottles. Three pairs of stools were spaced evenly so early arrivals could enjoy a drink. The restaurant seemed huge until Anya realised it was an optical illusion created by a mirror wall above the olive-green leather banquette seating. Each table was covered in a crisp, white tablecloth, with a glass bud vase, candles and sparkling silverware. The napkins were burgundy, the same shade as a good red wine. Like the stools at the bar, the tables were well spaced out, creating an air of quiet intimacy for couples like them wanting to enjoy a romantic date.

A smiling middle-aged woman wearing a simple black dress walked towards them. 'Good evening, my name is Marie and it is my pleasure to welcome you to Deliziosa.'

Rick thanked her and gave his name and Marie ushered them to one of the empty pairs of stools. 'Your table will be ready shortly. Relax and I shall fetch you some menus.'

Rick held the back of the stool while Anya hopped up onto it, then placed her bag on the bar in front of her. She'd quite forgotten he'd been carrying it. 'Thank you.'

'My pleasure.' He sat beside her and she liked the way he didn't try to crowd himself into her space. Drew had always been one for tugging her chair close, sitting with his arm around her or with a hand resting on her knee. She'd thought it romantic at the time, but looking back it felt more possessive, as though she'd been a thing he owned, a pretty bauble he wanted to show off to everyone.

Thankfully the barman approached and distracted her from the uncomfortable memory. 'Good evening, I'm Phil. Great to have you with us this evening. Any allergies we need to be aware of?' When they both shook their heads, he turned to retrieve two small white bowls, one with shiny black and green olives in it, the other a selection of nuts, which he set down in front of them. 'Here's Marie with the menus. I'll leave you to browse, but just let me know when you are ready to order a drink.'

Anya turned and accepted the menu Marie was holding out to her. 'Thank you.'

'You are very welcome. Your table is ready when you are, but please, there is no hurry at all, so take your time.' She handed the second menu to Rick before gliding off to clear plates from a nearby table.

'Are you happy to sit here for a minute?' Rick asked her as he unfolded his menu.

'If you are.' Unable to resist the plump olives, Anya popped one in her mouth only realising after a couple of chews that there was a touch of garlic in the oil dressing coating them.

Rick must've seen something on her face. 'What's wrong?'

She swallowed and shook her head. 'Nothing. They're delicious, just a bit garlicky.'

'Ah.' With a grin he reached out and popped a couple in his mouth. 'In case you let me kiss you again on the way home.'

Ducking her head to hide her blush, Anya buried her nose in her menu. 'Play your cards right and we'll see,' she murmured, enjoying the rich chuckle that elicited from him in response. Maybe she hadn't forgotten all the rules of flirting after all. Feeling pleased with herself, she studied the menu. It wasn't a huge selection, no more than a half-dozen choices each for starter, main and dessert, but everything sounded so tempting she had no idea how she'd ever settle on one thing. While she mulled over her options, she turned the page and looked at the drinks list. There was a nice selection of wines by the glass, which was good to see, and she might have one with their meal, but she didn't want to overdo it. 'I think I'll start with a glass of sparkling water.' She reached for her bag and pulled out her debit card. 'What would you like?'

She saw the hesitation in Rick's eyes, could tell he was fighting the instinct to tell her he'd pay, and was relieved when he simply said, 'I'd like a bottle of alcohol-free beer, please.' She had no doubt he would offer to pay for their food, and honestly it would be a blessing if he did because her budget would struggle to stretch to it, but she didn't want to take his generosity for granted.

Phil must've been keeping an eye out, because he appeared

in front of her and took their drinks order with a smile. While he went to fetch them, Anya turned her attention back to the menu. 'I don't know what to choose,' she confessed to Rick.

'How hungry are you?'

'Quite, but I also know if I order a starter I'll probably regret it, especially with these nibbles as well.'

'We could stick with what we've got and just order a main each, then; maybe share a dessert if we get that far?'

'That sounds like a plan. Now, if only I could decide between the chicken in mushroom and brandy sauce or the fillet steak.'

Rick raised an eyebrow 'No pasta?'

Anya glanced down at the fantastic array of dishes. 'They all sound tempting but when you live with a small child then at least 50 per cent of your meals are pasta based.'

He placed a hand over that section of her menu. 'Definitely no pasta, then! I'm torn between the lamb chops and the pork belly.'

'Pork belly,' Phil said, setting down their drinks in front of them. 'If you're looking for a recommendation, that is.'

Rick closed his menu. 'Sold.' He glanced back at Anya. 'Any closer to making a choice?'

She loved chicken, but again it was almost a daily staple at home. 'The fillet steak.'

'A fine choice,' Phil said. 'Medium?'

'Yes please.'

'Great. I'll let Marie know. Are you happy here, or shall I bring your drinks over to your table.'

Anya gestured to Rick that she didn't mind and he smiled at Phil. 'I think we'll go to our table now. Can we bring these with us?' He pointed at the bowls of snacks.

'Of course. I'll bring them with your drinks. We've put you

over there in a quiet spot.' Phil nodded towards an empty table in the far left corner beneath the mirrored wall.

Rick stood and offered Anya his hand as she climbed down from her stool, releasing it afterwards so he could fetch her bag from the bar. Again she was struck by the thoughtful way he looked out for her. It wasn't for show, it just seemed to be something innate within him. What her mother would consider old-fashioned good manners.

They were just settling into their seats when Phil appeared carrying a tray. As well as their drinks and snacks he set down a plate with a cheese-topped garlic bread, its four quarters still steaming from the oven. 'Compliments of the chef.'

'Thank you,' Rick said with a smile, and he waited until Phil had walked away before he raised the plate and offered it to her. 'Do you want some?'

Several reasons to refuse popped into her head – it was swimming in garlic and there was enough melted cheese coating the top and filling the centre to block several arteries. It would be messy and greasy and there would be no way to eat it politely. Plus she always ended up with a little food belly when she ate bread. She met Rick's eyes. Would any of that bother him?

You can always trust Rick.

'I'm having an existential crisis about the bread,' she admitted with a wry grin.

Scrunching up his brow, Rick set the plate down again. 'In what way?'

She raised a hand to the sudden heat rising on her cheek, wondering why she'd said anything. 'Because I'm worried about stinking of garlic, about not being able to eat it nicely...' She trailed off before deciding that if she was going to be honest with him then she might as well put it all out there. 'And about getting bloated.'

Reaching out, he ripped one of the quarters off the round loaf and held it out to her. 'For as long as I have the privilege of spending time with you, I will always want you to eat the bread, Anya.'

The little knot of tension in her stomach unfurled. Accepting the greasy, cheesy chunk from him she ripped the corner off and stuffed it into her mouth. She chewed with relish, her cheek pouching out like a hamster's. Eyes shining with approval, Rick tore off his own piece and joined in. God it was good. Not just the bread, though it was soft and warm, the cheese rich and creamy, the bite of the garlic adding the perfect complement. It was the fact she felt like she could be completely herself and Rick wouldn't judge her. She'd barely swallowed the first piece before she pulled off the next, and the next. Her fingers were covered in buttery grease, and she had no doubt her chin would be shiny with it too. When she reached for the plate to help herself to her second quarter there was nothing but approval in Rick's gaze. It made her want to lean across the table and kiss him, greasy garlicky mouth and all.

21

They walked back to the car via the promenade again. The chairs and tables were mostly empty, the drinkers having gone inside now the sun had set. The smell of fish and chips wafted on the breeze and Anya pressed her free hand to her middle. 'I ate so much tonight that I can't believe I'm even tempted, but I haven't had fish and chips for years.'

'I'll treat you another time,' Rick offered as they moved towards the centre of the prom to avoid a couple resting against the railings as they shovelled hot chips into their mouths with tiny wooden forks. Seagulls squabbled at their feet and the man tossed another chip towards them, sending the birds into a frenzy. With a gentle tug, Rick guided Anya in a wider arc around the people eating, and just as well he did because the next moment one of them shouted in alarm as a greedy gull flapped into the air to snatch a chip out of his fingers.

Anya reared back into Rick, a look of horror on her face. 'I think I'll pass on the fish and chips,' she murmured.

'There's a reason we always eat ours at home,' Rick told her with a grin. 'When I treat you, I can bring supper round to the summer house.'

He expected her to smile, but when she looked up at him there was a furrow etched between her brows. 'Maybe not there.'

He could've kicked himself for being so stupid. Hadn't he promised her he would keep his distance if that was what she needed? 'Sorry, I wasn't thinking.'

Anya's hand pressed closer against his chest. 'I don't want you to think that I am ashamed of you, or that I want to keep you a secret.'

'It's fine, Anya. I get it.' He wrinkled his brow as he racked his brain. 'You're always welcome at mine. Although that doesn't help with the Freya situation and I doubt the idea of hanging out at my parents' place holds much appeal either.' Past Rick had thought he was being smart by not moving out and putting most of his money into his business rather than a mortgage. Past Rick was a dickhead.

Anya pulled a face. 'I don't really fancy bumping into your dad on the landing.'

He cupped her face and kissed her. 'No, I can see why that wouldn't appeal. Don't worry, I'll figure something out, and in the meantime there's always the back seat of my car!'

He'd meant it as a joke, but there was a hint of mischief in Anya's eyes as her hand slid down his chest and around to his back. 'How far do the seats go back?'

Rick shifted his feet so they were either side of hers and their bodies were touching from chest to hip. 'They fold completely flat and the rear windows have a pretty dark tint on them.' Laughing, he placed his arm around her. 'I can't believe we're talking about having sex in my car.'

'Do you have any better suggestions?'

He racked his brain again. He could book a hotel room, but they could spend ages trying to find somewhere and Anya wouldn't want to stay away from Freya for too long. With them both working full time and her childcare commitments, evenings like this might be few and far between. But still, this was their first date and he didn't want her to think he was only after one thing. 'There's no rush, we can take our time, make sure you're ready.'

She pressed her body into his. 'I don't know if I'll ever be ready, I don't even know if I can be with anyone else, but I want to try. I could spend months hovering on the edge of this, dipping a toe in now and then, but the only way I'll know is if I dive right in.'

Though her words were bold and brave, he could hear the tremor in her voice. He wanted to drag her against him, lose himself in the promised heat in her eyes, the soft tempting curves of her body, but he had to be sure this was the right thing. 'And what if you find out the water's too deep?'

She raised a hand to caress his cheek. 'Then I trust you to pull me back into the shallows.'

Rick turned his head to press a kiss to the tips of her fingers. 'You can always trust me.' He would do right by her if it killed him, and if the tightness of his trousers was anything to go by, it might just. But tonight wasn't about him, it was about them, it was about Anya and respecting her need to do this. 'I know somewhere we can go.'

They didn't speak much for the rest of their walk back. Inside, Rick was at war with himself. Anya deserved the best that he could give her – a soft bed, champagne, romance – but her fingers played up and down over the back of his hand, teasing and tempting with how good they would feel on other parts of his body. By the time they reached the car it was hard to think straight. He unlocked it, but didn't immediately open the passenger door. 'Anya...'

She reached up and pressed a finger to his lips. 'There are a hundred reasons not to do this, I know, but those all belong to the woman who is scared to care about someone again, who is worried about her child, who doesn't have any idea how she's going to turn her life around. I don't want to be her, not right now. I want to be the woman I see when you look at me. Beautiful, confident, desired and desiring.'

Unable to stop himself, Rick reached out and cupped her neck, the hot silk of her hair gliding over his fingers like a caress. 'You *are* beautiful, Anya.' As he drew her towards him, he bent his head to press a kiss to the pulse point on her neck. 'The most beautiful woman in the world.' He breathed the words against her skin, felt her shiver against him, and his doubts about whether it was too soon were no match for the need thundering in his blood. 'You are all I've wanted, all I've dreamed about. It was always you. Only you.' He traced his lips up her throat, capturing her mouth when she turned her head to meet his. Her hands raised to clutch at his shoulders as they kissed, his own pulling her closer still. The contrast of the hard metal of the car at his back and the soft curves of her body fitting against the front of him was intoxicating.

Laughter burst in the distance, shocking them both apart. Rick scanned the car park, but there was no one in sight. He looked down at Anya, her hair rumpled from his fingers, her lower lip plump from the pressure of his mouth, and it was all he could do to yank open the door instead of grabbing hold of her again. 'Get in.'

While Anya settled herself, Rick opened his window and fiddled with the radio until he could find something soothing and mellow. He turned the sound down low, enough to fill the silence without being overwhelming. When he glanced over, Anya had her head back against the seat, her eyes closed. He looked down at where her hands rested in her lap, saw the way she was gripping them together, and he knew what he had to do. *Take her home.* Not saying a word, Rick put the car into gear and began to drive.

The roads were quiet and it didn't take long before they were back in Halfmoon Quay. It was only as he turned into the top of the road where his aunt and uncle lived that Anya stirred beside him. 'I thought...'

Rick pulled into an empty space half in the glow of a street lamp and stopped. He turned off the engine and released his seat belt so he could turn to face her properly. 'I meant everything I said to you earlier, and you don't know how hard it was for me to bring you straight back here.'

In the amber glow of the light he could see the confusion on her face, the hurt and disappointment. 'Then why?'

'Because I promised that you could trust me. Because I know you have doubts about this, and I never ever want to make you regret anything when it comes to us.'

She reached a beseeching hand towards him and he took it. 'But I want to be with you.'

He nodded. 'I know, and I want to be with you too. So much I could punch myself in the face right now.' Her pretty laugh did much to break the tension between them. 'But not in a snatched moment because that's what our circumstances dictate right now.' He didn't mention the things she'd said about being scared, being worried for Freya and confused about her life, but they weighed heavy on him. 'My body might feel like that of a stupid, horny teenager right now, but my head says no. My heart says not yet.'

She heaved a sigh that sounded like it had been dragged up

from her toes. 'You are the most lovely, most infuriatingly thoughtful man I know.'

He raised her hand to his lips and kissed it. 'Can I take you for lunch one day next week? We can park up at one of the lookout points.'

'Will lunch involve some kisses at least?'

'Lots and lots, I promise.' Leaning forward, he traced her jaw with his thumb, relishing the way she automatically arched towards him. As their lips touched, a sense of certainty settled deep within his core. When the time was right, when her doubts and worries had faded and he'd proved to her she truly could trust him, then he knew they'd be magnificent together. For now, he'd settle for this.

And lots and lots of cold showers.

22

Her aunt and uncle's house was in darkness apart from a muted glow behind the curtains of one of the upstairs bedrooms. Anya quietly eased the side gate open and closed as she let herself into the garden. Her stealthy route to the summer house was somewhat ruined when she triggered the security light and the entire rear of the house and garden were lit up. She hurried down the path to find Chloe already waiting with the summer house door open. 'Hello, did you have a nice time?'

'Yes, it was lovely, thank you. Any problems here?'

Chloe shook her head as she stepped aside to let her in. 'Nope. Freya went to bed about an hour and a half ago and I haven't heard a peep from her. I looked in not long ago and she was crashed out.'

'Thank you again for looking after her.'

Her cousin beamed. 'It was my pleasure. Really, I had an absolute blast. Any time you want me to sit for you, just say the word.'

'Thanks, well, we'll see how it goes.'

Chloe narrowed her eyes. 'That doesn't sound very promising. I thought you said you'd had a lovely time with Rick.'

'I did, it's just...' Anya shrugged. 'I don't know.'

'Okay, let me put the kettle on, because this sounds like it might take a while.'

Anya would've preferred a bit of time to process the evening on her own, but Chloe had done her a favour and there was no polite way to get out of it. A few minutes later they were settled side by side on the sofa, each holding a steaming mug of tea. Chloe faced her, one arm resting on the back of the seat cushions, her cheek propped on her fist. 'So what happened?'

Anya blew the steam on her mug, trying to find the words to describe the confusion inside her. 'Rick didn't want to sleep with me.'

'Oh my God!' Chloe blurted.

'Shh! Don't wake Freya.'

'Oh my God,' Chloe repeated in a stage whisper. 'You guys certainly didn't waste any time. I know you said when we were chatting the other night that you wanted to make sure the two of you were compatible, but I didn't think you'd try and jump his bones on your first date!'

'We didn't even get as far as that.' With a sigh, Anya slumped back and closed her eyes. 'It's my fault. We were having such a nice evening and it was just so good to feel something again, to have someone look at me with desire in their eyes.' To have Rick look at her that way.

'And Rick rejected your advances?' Chloe's brows drew down. 'I find that hard to believe.'

Anya rolled her head to the side to meet Chloe's eyes. 'Even though I wanted us to take things further I, uh, I was really nervous and I think perhaps he sensed that.'

'Ah, that makes more sense.' Chloe sipped her tea. 'So where did you guys leave things?'

'He wants to take me for lunch next week.'

'That sounds nice?'

'Oh it is! Don't get me wrong, Rick was incredibly kind and understanding and he said he's happy to wait until I'm ready.'

Chloe nudged Anya with her knee. 'But...'

'I don't know. Is there a but, or am I just making more of this than there needs to be? It's been so long since I felt anything like this, I don't know if I can trust myself to know when the time's right.'

With a laugh, Chloe pushed to her feet and then drained her mug. 'I think you just need to go with the flow, Anya, enjoy the moment and not fret too much about the future. If it's meant to be, it's meant to be.'

Anya frowned up at her. 'Is that it? That's the best pearl of wisdom you can manage?'

Laughing, Chloe set her empty mug on the coffee table. 'What do you want from me? Did you miss the bit where I've been single since before they built the pyramids?' Bending down, she gave Anya a hug. 'All jokes aside. If you can't trust yourself right now, trust Rick.'

Anya hugged her back. 'Maybe you're better at this advice thing than you realise.'

* * *

She'd been a bit nervous about meeting Rick for lunch the following Monday, but he never made any reference to their conversation, and any doubts she'd had about him being put off by her blowing hot and cold were dispelled when he'd produced a gorgeous hamper of food from the boot of his car. She had no idea when he'd found the time to put it together, but knowing he'd gone to the effort gave her the confidence to follow Chloe's advice and just enjoy the moment.

That was the last time they'd managed to see each other before the regatta the following weekend, but they'd messaged or spoken most evenings, even if it was just a quick call to wish each other goodnight.

As she and the rest of the family made their way towards the beach on Saturday morning, Anya found herself taking a firm grip on Freya's hand. There were cars everywhere and the path along the sea wall was crowded. Anya was grateful to Matt for scooping Freya up and onto his shoulders, out of harm's way, when she was almost knocked over by someone trying to push past. 'Is it always like this?'

Chloe tutted and rolled her eyes as she was shoulder barged by someone else. 'It's one of the most popular events of the year. Hopefully things will be better when we get down on the beach.'

They reached the top of the steps and Anya wasn't the only one who stopped to survey the crowded sand with dismay. 'Or maybe not.'

'Come on,' Ryan said as he started down. 'Jago messaged me earlier and said they'd staked a claim near where Rick normally has his gear set out.'

Anya wasn't sure they'd ever find them in the chaos below but she fell into line between Matt and Chloe and did her best to walk in her uncle's footsteps as much as possible. Somehow they made it through the noisy crowds to find Jago, Rachel, Harry and Ed guarding the corners of the space they'd claimed near the lifeguard's hut and lookout point.

'You made it!' Rachel jumped to her feet and reached up to lift Freya down from Matt's shoulders. 'Hello, poppet! Don't you look nice?'

Anya bit her lip and thanked God Rick's mum was a kind soul, because Freya had chosen a pair of thick bottle-green dungarees with a Peppa Pig patch on one knee where Anya had covered up a hole caused when Freya had fallen over in the park. Underneath them she was wearing a red and white polka dot swimsuit and she had a pair of black trainers with rhine-stones covering the toes. A pink bucket hat completed the ensemble. She got their towels laid out and then, as casually as she could manage, she asked Ed, 'Is Rick not with you guys?'

The moment she'd asked him she regretted it because a huge grin spread across his face as he turned and pointed.

'Lover boy's over there with the rest of the do-gooders.' His smile vanished as Chloe gave him a sharp jab in the side and leaned over to hiss something in his ear. Eyes wide, Ed turned to look at Anya and mouthed, 'Sorry!'

Anya narrowed her eyes at him but didn't say anything; after all, it was her own fault for asking. Thankfully Freya was busy chatting to Rachel and Jago about something and hadn't heard what he'd said. Deciding it would be a good idea to change the subject completely, she said, 'I haven't been to a regatta weekend before, how does it work?'

Aunt Helen wrinkled her brow. 'Have you really not been to one?' She paused as though thinking about it. 'I suppose you and Lisa always visited a bit later in the school holidays. There's all the boat races, of course.' She leaned closer to Anya and dropped her voice to a conspiratorial whisper. 'Between you and me, I find them impossible to follow and I just clap when everyone else does.'

Anya grinned. 'Thanks for the tip.'

Helen winked. 'Anyway, as well as all that, there's lots of events for the kids – sandcastle building, hoop tosses, foot and swimming races for various age groups. You should sign Freya up for something.'

Anya glanced around at the crowds. 'I'm not sure about that, it's very busy.'

Helen pointed to a small section of the sea very close to the shore that was clearly roped and marked with bright red buoys. 'That area is for the little ones to play in. It's always well super-vised, so she'll be safe there if you want to take her paddling.'

Raising a hand to shade her eyes, Anya surveyed the area. It was a little less busy than the rest of the shallows and there were lots of parents with children, from toddlers to a few years older than Freya. 'That's a good idea; she needs kids her own age to play with. Freya?' she called out. 'Do you want to go swimming?'

Though she was covered from head to toe in sunscreen, Anya still made Freya pop a T-shirt on over her swimsuit to protect her shoulders and back. 'Hold tight to my hand, darling, until we get to the water, okay?'

'Yes, Mummy.'

They trooped down to the children's zone, Chloe, Helen and Rachel with them carrying various toys and a set of armbands for Freya. Anya winced as the cold water lapped at her toes.

'Oh that's, umm, refreshing!' Rachel gasped as she waded out until she was knee-deep in the water.

Knowing it was better to just get on with it, Anya and the others followed her into the shallows. 'Hold Freya for a sec will you, Chloe?' Anya requested.

'Sure.' Chloe came and braced a hand on Freya's shoulder.

'Arms up. Let's get these on and then you can go and play.' With a bit of wriggling and silent swearing, Anya got the armbands on her daughter. The moment Freya was released she launched herself into the water, sending up a huge splash, which soaked the front of Anya's floral cover-up she'd pulled on over her swimsuit, making her shriek.

Freya's giggles were a dead giveaway that she'd done it on purpose, and Anya scooped up a handful of water and splashed her right back.

'Not fair, Mummy!' she protested, her attempts to plant her hands on her hips somewhat hampered by the water wings.

'Lesson learned, huh?' Bending down, Anya picked Freya up and spun her around in a circle just to hear her laugh again.

Having set her down, the five of them began to play catch with the ball they'd brought with them. After a few minutes, Anya noticed a little girl watching from nearby. 'If it's okay with your mum, you can come and play,' she offered, making sure she addressed the comment equally to the blonde woman standing next to the girl.

The woman smiled. 'That sounds like fun, don't you think?'

They moved outwards to expand the circle and accept the pair into the game. The ball flew past Rachel's shoulder and was grabbed by a little boy nearby. Before they knew it, the circle had expanded to over a couple of dozen people and multiple balls were being tossed around. Freya was in her element, and she and the little blonde girl who'd first joined in were holding hands as they chased around trying to catch one of the balls.

'Having fun?' a deep, familiar voice asked at Anya's shoulder.

She turned to find Rick grinning down at her, his eyes hidden behind a pair of sunglasses. He was wearing a sleeveless baggy vest over a pair of knee-length shorts, the muscular curve of his arms emphasised by the way they were folded across his broad chest. God, he was enough to make a woman weak at the knees. 'Do you want to play?'

It was only when the curve of his mouth turned wicked that Anya realised there was a much less innocent interpretation to her question. 'I'm heading over to my storage shed to fetch some life jackets for the group of teens I'm supervising; you could give me a hand if you like?'

She glanced over to where Freya was playing. 'I can't leave her.'

Rick's fingers touched the inside of her arm, a featherlight caress gone almost before she felt it. 'Five minutes. Mum's here and Helen and Chloe.'

Her heart pounded. It had been almost a week since they'd seen each other and every inch of her skin felt alive at the prospect of a few stolen moments together. 'Chloe? Can you keep an eye on Freya, please?'

Chloe glanced over and Anya could tell the moment she clocked Rick's presence by the way her eyes widened. 'Sure.'

'I'm going to help Rick fetch some life jackets for his youth group.'

'*Sure.*' Chloe waved her hand. 'Take your time, we'll be fine.'

She wondered about letting Freya know, but she was happy and it would take longer to explain than to get to where the life jackets were. Plus there was the risk Freya would get upset at her going or want to come with them. *Five minutes.* With one final quick check that her daughter was fine, Anya turned to Rick. 'Let's go.'

The inside of the shed was dark and cool and quiet compared to the bright, hot noise of the beach. She barely had time to adjust to the difference before she was in Rick's arms and she forgot about everything else beyond the sweet, heady warmth of his embrace. 'I missed you,' Rick murmured when they finally broke for air.

His lips teased across her cheek, and she sank her fingers into his thick hair as she leaned into him. 'I missed you too.' She wanted time to stand still, to forget about everything beyond the door of the shed and focus only on him. Turning her head, she stole another kiss, and another. *Enough.* Anya cursed her conscience but still shifted her hands to Rick's shoulders and applied the faintest of pressure.

The moment he felt her pushing him away, Rick made space between them. 'We should get back.'

Regret and understanding shone in his eyes. And something darker, something so very tempting. Laughing, Anya raised a hand and blocked the upper part of his face. 'Don't look at me like that; you'll make me forget myself.'

Rick grabbed her hand and pressed a kiss against her palm. 'I like it when you forget yourself.'

Snatching her hand away, Anya ducked underneath his arm. 'Rick Penrose, you are a very bad man!' His deep, rich, wicked laugh followed her across the shed to where the shelves were filled with stacks of neatly organised equipment. 'Are these the life jackets we need?'

'That's the ones,' he said, coming over to lift a stack down and hand it to her before loading himself up with another pile.

They stepped outside and a wall of heat and light made Anya's eyes water behind the lenses of her sunglasses. She rested her back against the wall of the shed while Rick set down his jackets and locked up. 'Okay?' he asked once he was ready to go.

He was turning her world upside down and she wasn't sure if she'd ever be simply okay ever again. 'I'll speak to Chloe and see if she'll sit for us again.'

Rick glanced around to make sure no one was watching then bent his head to press one last hot, swift kiss to her mouth. 'That sounds like a very good idea.'

They were almost back at the paddling zone when Rick swore low and harsh beneath his breath. 'What the hell are they playing at?' Before Anya knew what was happening, the life jackets he'd been carrying thudded at her feet and Rick was running full pelt into the water, his arms waving above his head as he shouted, 'Hey! Hey! Get back beyond the flags!'

She tracked his movements and spotted what he must've already noticed: a couple of lads whizzing around the bay on a jet ski. They were zooming in circles, their speed churning up the water. A wave they'd created hit Rick, almost covering his chest, and her brain finally processed the danger as the first high-pitched scream sounded and then she was running for the water too.

Chaos. It was chaos as the unexpected waves ripped through the paddling zone, catching everyone by surprise. Several children disappeared beneath the water, the force knocking them off their feet. Anya's entire focus narrowed down to Freya's pink bucket hat as she ploughed through water that felt thicker and heavier than liquid concrete. A woman carrying a little girl cut in front of her, blocking Anya's view, and another wave hit, causing more shouts of fear and anger. She scrambled around the woman and Freya was further away, the rush of water carrying her out of reach of Rachel. Thank God she had her water wings on because they were the only thing keeping her afloat.

'Mummy!'

'I'm here!' Anya pressed on and had almost reached Freya when Rick got there first, scooping the little girl up into the safety of his arms.

'I've got you, I've got you,' Anya heard him say as she waded over, her breath coming in panicked gasps.

'Is she okay?'

'She's fine. She's fine, just a little frightened.' Rick's big hand was rubbing circles over Freya's back, her face buried in his neck, her arms clinging to him like a limpet.

The adrenaline began to fade, leaving Anya exhausted as the others waded over. 'Who was that idiot?' Helen demanded, a furious scowl twisting her face.

Rick shook his head. 'A couple of stupid kids who don't know any better. The lifeguards chased them off.'

Anya was about to say they'd better make sure they chased them all the way out of the village when she heard someone crying and turned to find a little boy standing on his own about twenty feet away. His face was red and Anya looked around to see who he was with. Realising he was alone, and knowing Freya was safe in Rick's arms, she waded over to him and bent at the waist. 'Hello? Where's your mummy?'

The little boy sniffed and knuckled his cheeks. 'Dunno.'

'Shall we see if we can find her?' Anya held out her hand and he grabbed for her like he would a lifeline. Her heart went out to him and she leaned down and scooped him up onto her hip. 'There we go, it's okay, we'll find her.' There was something vaguely familiar about him but she couldn't place him. 'What's your name, darling?'

More sniffles. 'Leo.'

Anya gave him a reassuring smile. 'Hi Leo, I'm Anya. Come on, let's find your mummy.'

She was about to ask him what his mother looked like when a piercing scream came from the beach. 'Leo? Where's Leo?'

Anya turned and her stomach gave a little lurch as she spotted a distraught-looking Shelly Dean scanning the water as she tried to hold onto two squirming babies. Bracing herself for another confrontation, Anya secured her hold on Leo and hurried towards the beach as quickly as the water would allow. 'Shelly! Shelly!' she called out. 'I've got him.'

Shelly's head snapped towards them. 'Leo!'

'He's fine, he's fine.'

They met on the edge of the sand. 'He wanted to play and I thought it would be okay because there were loads of adults in the group.'

'It's okay, it's not your fault.' Even as she tried to reassure Shelly, guilt gnawed at Anya's belly. She'd thought Freya would be okay too, had put her own selfish needs first.

She glanced behind to see Rick and the others approaching, Freya still clinging to him like a little monkey. 'Chloe, give us a hand,' she called. Her cousin splashed up. 'Grab one of the babies, will you?' Anya nodded towards Shelly.

They did a bit of juggling and soon both she and Chloe had an armful of smiling, plump, oblivious baby each while Shelly clung onto Leo, who had burst into tears the moment he was safe in her arms.

'Thank you, thank you,' Shelly repeated over and over.

'It's fine, he's fine.' Any hurt she'd felt at the way the other woman had spoken to her when they'd met previously vanished in the face of her obvious distress.

Her aunt Helen placed a hand on Shelly's back. 'Come on, let's all go and sit down.'

They settled on their towels and Rick immediately set Freya down in Anya's lap. 'I'm going to speak to the lifeguards, find out if they caught up with those idiots.' His hand settled on her shoulder. 'You okay?'

'Yes, thanks to you.'

His fingers flexed against her skin for a second before he removed them. 'I'll be right back.'

Freya snuggled close, curling up like a kitten, and Anya wrapped a spare towel around her and rocked gently. 'I couldn't find you, Mummy.'

Hot guilt lanced through her once again. 'I'm sorry, darling. I'm here now.'

23

Just over a week after the debacle at the regatta, Rick parked his SUV in the car park around the back of the hotel and let himself in the rear entrance using the key code. Anya had been understandably reluctant to spend time with him since the near miss with Freya, and he couldn't blame her. Given how guilty he felt about persuading her to sneak away for a few minutes, he could only imagine how bad Anya must've been feeling. Not that she'd spoken to him about it. When he'd tried to raise the matter, she'd clammed up. At least she'd carried on speaking to him though, and he eventually persuaded her to go out with him for lunch.

He had a picnic lunch in a cool box in the boot and they were going to drive to one of the viewing points just outside the village. He hadn't even thought about mentioning her offer to get Chloe to babysit again. It would take time for her to feel okay about leaving Freya for anything other than work, and Rick was prepared to wait as long as she needed.

He wandered along the back corridor of the hotel, noting

how tired some of the paintwork was starting to look. Everything was spotlessly clean, but there was a slightly depressing air about the space. Might be worth mentioning it to Anya or Davy because it wouldn't take much to brighten it up – a couple of framed prints on the wall to draw the eye up and away from the scuffed and faded skirting boards.

All thoughts about flaking paintwork shot out the window when he walked into Davy's office to find him pale and clammy. Anya had one arm around his waist as though trying to hold him up, her face almost as white as his great-uncle's. 'I'm fine,' Davy was saying, though there was no heat in the words. He sounded exhausted.

'What happened?' Rick demanded as he rushed over to take Davy's weight.

'I don't know,' Anya replied. 'I just gave him the cushion I made for his chair and when he stood up to put it behind him he keeled over.'

'I did not keel over, girl!' Davy growled, sounding a bit more like himself. 'I just stood up too quickly, that's all. Let me sit down and stop fussing, the pair of you.'

Anya scowled at him. 'Next time I'll let you fall on your stupid face, you stubborn old fool!' She might have sounded furious, but Rick could tell she was really scared for Davy.

Rick helped his great-uncle into his chair then stepped back so he could look at both of them. 'What do you mean next time? Has this happened before?'

'It's nothing, bit of a blood sugar drop,' Davy protested, though Rick didn't miss the way he wouldn't meet Rick's eyes. *Yes, you should feel bloody guilty.*

'He had a wobble last week when he was climbing down a stepladder after changing a lightbulb in reception,' Anya stated in a flat tone. 'Though that time it was down to him being a bit light-headed because he hadn't had any lunch.'

'Two funny spells in a week? Sounds like we need to take you to the doctor and find out what's going on,' Rick said to Davy.

'No! I'm fine. It's probably just a virus or something.'

'A virus.' Rick tapped his index finger as though counting off. 'A drop in your blood sugar.' He tapped his middle finger. 'Light-headed from skipping a meal.' He tapped his ring finger. 'I think we definitely need to find out which one it is, don't you?' The foul glare from Davy might've scared off another person, but Rick was absolutely at the end of his tether, and sick with worry to boot because he knew it was none of those things. He turned to Anya. 'Can you do me a favour and fetch Davy a glass of water while I try and talk some sense into him?'

She snorted. 'Good luck with that.' But she did at least leave the room.

As soon as she was gone, Rick rounded on Davy, who already had his mouth open as though about to voice another protest. 'No!' Rick snapped. 'Not another bloody word from you. We are going to the surgery right now or I swear to God I am going to phone Mum and let her deal with you, because I can't go on like this.'

'You wouldn't dare!'

Rick didn't bother to answer, just pulled out his phone and began to scroll through his contacts for his mum's number.

'Okay, okay,' Davy agreed. 'But not a word to anyone else.'

Rick put his phone away just as Anya returned with a glass of water and a plate of biscuits. 'In case it really is just your blood sugar,' she said as she put them down in front of Davy.

'I'm going to give him a lift up to the surgery,' Rick told her. 'We'll have to give lunch a miss, I'm afraid.'

Her look of relief told Rick he wasn't the only one who'd been worried about Davy, and guilt was a tight knot in his gut. Well, once he'd been in with Davy to speak to Doc Ferguson – and there was no way he was sitting outside and giving Davy the chance to bullshit him afterwards – he would at least know just how bad things were. And then he and his great-uncle were going to have another chat, because Rick had told Anya she could trust him and being caught between that and his loyalty to Davy was tearing him apart.

* * *

Doc Ferguson gave a double-take when Rick walked into his office on his uncle's heels. 'Rick, good to see you.' He turned to Davy. 'And it's good to see you too. I'm pleased you've agreed to be open with your family about your condition, because you're going to need their support.'

Davy slumped into the plastic chair closest to the doctor's desk, his mouth set in the same belligerent line it had been in since Rick insisted on coming in with him. Rick swallowed a sigh as he took the second chair and smiled at Doc Ferguson. He'd got through the door, which was a miracle in itself. 'Thanks so much for giving up your lunch break to see us.'

Doc nodded like it was nothing then turned back to Davy. 'I hear you've been having a couple of dizzy spells. Can you tell me in detail what happened?'

Davy shrugged, looking more like a sulky teen than a man definitely old enough to know better. 'It's like I've been telling the boy here: I stood up a bit too quick, that's all.'

'And you had a wobble on a stepladder last week,' Rick reminded him, keeping his tone light. 'And yes, we will be having a conversation later about you going up one in the first place.'

Doc huffed. 'Good luck with that. I've been doing some shifts with the air ambulance team and I swear half our call-outs are to gentlemen in their, *shall we say,* twilight years, who have fallen off things. I had one the other week who decided to try and prune a tree in his garden with a ladder and a rented chainsaw.'

Rick shuddered. 'I don't think I want to know.'

Doc grinned. 'Luckily the chainsaw went one way and he went the other, but it could've been fatal.'

'I was only changing a damn lightbulb, not scaling the north face of the bloody Eiger,' Davy grumbled. 'Now can we get on with this farce, because I've got a hotel to run.'

Rick sat back and let Doc do his thing. He ran through the basics, taking Davy's blood pressure, checking his eyes and inside his ears in case there was any sign of an infection or inflammation that might be causing balance issues. He kept up a constant stream of chatter with questions interspersed about how he'd been eating and sleeping. With the physical examination done, Doc began tapping away on his computer, noting down every grudgingly given titbit of information he managed to winkle out of Davy.

'My hip's been giving me a bit of trouble,' his great-uncle eventually admitted. 'But that's to be expected, isn't it, at my age?'

Doc stopped typing and sat back in his chair, no sign of his earlier good humour. 'It could be, but we won't know until we have a proper look.'

Davy shook his head. 'What do you mean a proper look? I don't want someone slicing me open!'

Doc smiled. 'No slicing, just a scan for now. I know you have

strong feelings about treatment, Davy, and while I don't neces-
sarily agree with your approach I cannot force you to accept my
recommendations. I do think it would be wise to at least get a
scan so we know what we are dealing with here.'

'All right then, but only a scan.'

Rick gave a little sigh of a relief. 'I can take you to the
hospital when your appointment comes through.'

Doc Ferguson nodded. 'And in the meantime I can write a
prescription for some pain relief that should help you sleep a
little better, Davy. How does that sound?'

'Yeah, thanks. That's probably what's causing the dizzy
spells: me being tired.' Rick and Doc exchanged a silent glance.

Rick waited until they were back in the car before he turned
to his great-uncle. 'This can't go on you know, keeping everyone
else in the dark.'

Davy scowled at him. 'Don't start that again. I don't need
another lecture, just take me back to the hotel.'

Rick shook his head. 'No, Davy, I'm serious. I know you want
to enjoy what time you have left, but given your condition, situations like this are inevitable. You can't keep acting like nothing's going to happen.'

'I know exactly what's going to happen, boy, you don't need
to remind me!'

'Then why won't you tell the rest of the family? They love
you as much as I do and they deserve the chance to come to
terms with what's happening too. You can't keep shutting them
out and pretending it's for their own good. They'll be upset
when they find out, there's no avoiding that, but if you leave it
too long they'll be devastated you didn't let them support you
when you need it the most.'

'I don't need their support, I don't need anything other than
to be left alone. Why can't you understand that?'

Rick rubbed at the tension headache building between his eyes. 'And why can't you understand that you are tearing me apart? I promised Anya I'd always be honest with her. Don't you think she deserves that after everything Drew put her through? By forcing me to keep your illness a secret, you're making me lie to her, Davy. She knows there's something wrong, it was obvious earlier how worried she is about you.'

'Well, if I tell her I don't need her at the hotel any more she won't have to be worried about me, will she?' Davy snapped.

Horror flooded through Rick. 'You wouldn't do that. You know how much she's relying on that job to make ends meet.'

'Blackmail's not so nice when you're on the other end of it, is it?'

Rick struggled to process what he was hearing. 'So that's where we're at? If I tell anyone in the family about you being ill, you'll sack Anya?'

Davy didn't reply, just turned his head to stare out the passenger window.

Disappointed, Rick started the engine and drove them back to the hotel in silence. He knew Davy was lashing out because he was scared and in pain, but Rick couldn't let things go on like this. He didn't really believe Davy would get rid of Anya, but if he did then Rick had plenty of savings in the bank. Living at home might not be ideal, but he'd been squirrelling away every spare penny that hadn't gone into building his business and there was enough there to see her through until she could find something else.

He pulled up outside the front of the hotel and his great-uncle got out and slammed the door. Rick let him take a couple of paces up the path before he lowered his window and called out, 'You've got until after Ma's party to work out how you're going to break the news to everyone.'

Davy turned to glare at him. 'Or what?'

'Or I'll tell them myself. Let me know when you hear about your scan.' Without waiting for a reply, Rick pressed the button to close his window and drove off. He couldn't face seeing Anya, not with everything bubbling so close to the surface. One look from her and he'd give the game away. All he could do was hold his nerve and hope Davy saw sense sooner rather than later.

24

Anya was curled up on the sofa trying to finish off the apron she was making for Ma's birthday. It wasn't the most glamorous gift, but she'd never seen Ma in her kitchen without one and Anya had found an old cotton skirt she'd picked up in a charity shop once for fifty pence when she'd been sorting through the bags in the shed. It had a cream background and was covered in beautiful butterflies in every colour of the rainbow. She'd found a pattern online and it hadn't taken more than a couple of hours to cut out the pieces and stitch them together on her sewing machine. The skirt had been hemmed with white lace and Anya was using that to add a little bit of detail to the front pocket of the apron.

Her phone vibrated next to her and Anya reached for it, expecting it to be Rick calling to say goodnight. They hadn't had a chance to rearrange a meeting since their aborted lunch date the previous week but they'd spoken every evening after Freya had gone to bed. They'd even watched a movie 'together' on Saturday night, using a watch party function on a streaming app. Anya had cancelled all her memberships months before, but Chloe seemed to have a subscription to everything going and had left them all logged in on the TV in the summer house. It hadn't been quite as good as being able to snuggle up together, but being able to chat and share jokes with Rick had been better than sitting on her own. Freya was showing no ill effects from the events at the regatta and Anya was doing her best not to be to clingy with her. They'd even been back down to the beach for a paddle, because she hadn't wanted Freya to develop a fear of the water. They'd not gone in deeper than Freya's knees but it had been enough to reassure them both. Shelly had called into the hotel to thank her and they'd ended up arranging a playdate as Leo would be starting at the village school in September as well. Anya wasn't sure if they'd ever be close, but she couldn't afford to be at odds with someone she was likely to bump into frequently at the school gates.

Instead of Rick it was her mum and she was trying to video call rather than just send a text, which had been their usual method of communication since they'd fallen out.

'Hi Mum, what a lovely surprise!'

She recognised the abstract blue and green print on the wall behind her mother. It was the one hanging in the dining area of the open-plan ground floor of the two-storey villa her mum shared with her husband, Bill, in the mountains above Las Palmas in Gran Canaria.

'Hello, love, how are you?'

A little surprised, but very relieved that the cold war appeared to be over, Anya crossed her legs and settled down to chat. 'I'm good thanks. How about you? You're looking well. How's Bill?' She was so excited they were talking again that the questions tumbled out one after another.

Lisa laughed. 'We're fine, aren't we Bill?'

'What's that?' Anya heard Bill say in the background.

'It's Anya, she was asking how you are.'

Bill popped into the background, clutching a spatula. 'Hello! All good, all good, I'm just making us a spot of supper. Fajitas,' he added with a wink. 'Your favourite.'

Of course Bill would remember a little thing like that. He was one of the good guys. She'd always kept him at arm's length and yet he'd never held it against her. She'd yearned so long for a father figure and still she hadn't let herself trust him to fill the empty space in her heart. 'I miss your cooking, Bill!'

'Bring Freya for a holiday and it'll be my pleasure to cook for you both every day.' The way he beamed at her rare compliment was bittersweet. He really did deserve better from her.

Her mum nodded. 'Yes, do come. We'll pay for the flights – and no arguments, young lady.'

Anya shook her head. 'As if I would bother arguing when I know I'm not going to win. Honestly, it would be lovely to see you both,' She made a point of including Bill in her smile as she said it. 'We might have to wait until a bit later in the year, though. Freya is starting school, so it would have to be October half-term, or maybe Christmas.'

'Well I can't wait until Christmas, so October it is. And how on earth is Freya old enough to be going to school? It feels like only yesterday you were bringing her home from the hospital.'

Anya shook her head. 'That was a long time ago, Mum.' They both fell silent and Anya knew she wasn't the only one experiencing a pang of regret. How delighted they'd all been when Freya was born. How happy.

'Let us know the dates and I'll look for flights,' Bill said, bringing Anya back to the present. 'I'd better go before I burn my chicken!' He blew a kiss and disappeared from view.

'Bill never changes, does he?' Anya said, meaning it as a compliment. 'I don't think I've ever seen him in a bad mood.'

'No, he's like that morning, noon and night,' her mother said in a voice full of affection. 'Sometimes I wonder how I got so lucky. Speaking of which, are we booking two flights, or three?'

Anya gasped. 'Who told you?'

Lisa rolled her eyes. 'Helen, of course, though I must say it's a poor do when I have to hear from my sister that you're going out with Rick Penrose of all people!'

Anya frowned. 'What do you mean "of all people"?'

Her mother waved a hand. 'Oh, just a turn of phrase, no need to get your back up. I mean he was sweet on you back in the day, but don't you feel it's all a bit sudden?'

Sweet on her? Was she the only one who'd had no idea? 'We're not rushing into anything, Mum, and we are being careful around Freya for the time being, but he's been very kind and I really like spending time with him.'

Lisa's gaze softened. 'Well, you certainly deserve a bit of kindness after everything you've been through.' She smiled. 'So we'll hold off on booking a ticket for him just now?'

Anya laughed. 'For now.' She stared at her mum through the screen, wishing she could reach out and give her hug. 'Thanks for calling, Mum. I'm sorry things have been difficult between us these past months.'

'I'm sorry too, though I do wish you'd have let us help you. You have no idea how hard it's been having to sit by and watch you hit rock bottom. I've been there myself and I never wanted that for you.'

Anya pressed a finger to the corner of her eye where she could feel a tear burning. 'I know, but I couldn't risk seeing you back there again either, and honestly, trying to salvage anything would've swallowed every penny you and Bill have.'

Lisa blew her nose. 'But you've lost everything. Your beautiful home that you worked so hard on.'

Anya sighed. 'It wasn't a home though, not really, because the whole thing was built on a false foundation. It was a fantasy, Mum, a Disney castle where I got to play princess for a while.'

Her mum sighed. 'I was as guilty as anyone for ignoring the red flags, but I so wanted a happy ending for you. It's been awful seeing you brought so low.'

'It's not so bad. I have Freya and she's thriving. I have a job which is giving me enough to put food on the table, and I have plans for the future.' She told her mum about her and Chloe going into business together.

'That sounds wonderful, I'm so proud of you.' Lisa's smile faltered. 'I wish I was there to help you. If Helen hadn't stepped in, I don't know what you would've done. I feel so far away.'

Anya wagged a finger at the screen. 'None of that, now, Mum. It'll be October before you know it.'

Lisa took a deep breath. 'Yes, you're right, but a mother's guilt is something that never goes away. In fact I think it gets worse as you get older because the stakes are so much higher.'

Anya pulled a face. 'Gee, well that's something to look forward to.'

Her mother laughed, exactly as she'd intended. 'My pleasure.' Her face grew serious as she extended her fingers towards the screen as though she could reach out and touch Anya. 'The guilt might grow, darling, but so does the love.'

Anya reached out, pressing her fingers to her own screen. 'I love you, Mum.'

'I love you too. Speak soon.'

* * *

On Saturday morning Anya was up early. Ryan and Helen were hosting a barbeque that evening and the plan was to finally empty the shed so Ryan and Matt could install the shelving and workbenches she and Chloe needed while they helped Helen with preparations for dinner. While Freya finished her breakfast, Anya moved her daughter's play table and chair outside underneath the shade of a tree. When she came back inside Freya had put her bowl and spoon on the counter next to the sink.

'That's a good girl, thank you. Now, do you want to come and choose which crafts you want to do?'

'Can I do some painting?'

'You can do whatever you like. Where's your smock?'

By the time the others walked out the back door, Freya was set up at her table. Picking up a deck chair, Helen set it next to Freya's table. 'I'll keep an eye on her.'

'Are you sure?'

'Of course. If we all try and empty the shed we'll just get in each other's way.' She turned to Freya. 'What are you going to paint for me?'

'A butterfly!'

'Oh, my favourite. Now then, what colours are you going to use?'

Grateful once again for her aunt's never-ending well of enthusiasm, Anya left them to it. Ryan handed her a pair of work gloves. 'There's probably all sorts of loose nails and splinters so better safe than sorry.'

'Thank you.'

For the next half an hour Anya, Chloe, Matt and Ryan systematically emptied the shed and ferried the contents upstairs to the box room in the main house. Once the shed was emptied, Matt and Ryan headed back to the shed while Anya and Chloe surveyed the piles of boxes and bags. 'I didn't realise I had accumulated so much stuff,' Anya said with a sigh.

Chloe put her arm around her shoulder and gave her an encouraging squeeze. 'I'm glad, because it means we've got plenty of stock. Come on, it won't take us long to get it sorted.'

'Guess who called in to see me at the hotel the other day,' Anya said a bit later as she was sorting through a bag of offcuts.

Chloe glanced up from the box of yarn she was sorting into colour combinations. 'Who?'

'Shelly.'

All eyes, Chloe set the yarn aside. 'No! Really? What did she want?'

'To say thank you for rescuing Leo.'

'Well, I should think so too.' Her cousin snorted.

'And she apologised for being horrible to me; we had quite a good chat actually. Did you know her husband was working away?'

'I can't say I did, but then again we don't really mix in the same circles.' Chloe seemed to consider that for a minute. 'Actually, I'm not sure who she hangs out with these days.'

'I got the impression she's pretty lonely and managing three small kids is clearly getting her down.' Anya folded the square of fabric she was holding and sat back on her heels. 'I felt sorry for her, actually, and I've arranged a playdate for Freya and Leo next weekend.'

'That's kind of you, especially after she was so rude.'

Anya shrugged. 'I figured I need all the friends I can get, and Leo and Freya are going to be classmates for the next few years.'

'Good point. Hey, if she's really struggling, why don't we speak to Mum about inviting her and the kids over?'

'What, today?'

'Why not? The fridge is packed full, so it's not like we're going to be short of food – and that's before we add whatever Rachel and Jago bring with them.'

Anya finished folding the contents of the bag and reached for the next one. 'Let's see what your mum says.'

25

By the time Rick had finished up and put all his gear away he was ready to go home and fall face down on his bed for a few hours. He should be grateful business was thriving, but it was too much for him to handle on his own on busy weekends. He'd have to do something about hiring some help, but not tonight. Tonight he was going to relax and have fun with the people he loved. Knowing he was going to be seeing Anya, even if it was with the rest of the family around, was enough to give him a lift and by the time he was showered and changed he'd shaken off his tiredness. It wasn't far to Ryan and Helen's so they decided to walk. Somehow his mum had found time over the past couple of evenings to prepare desserts so they were laden down with a cheesecake, a treacle tart and a huge trifle.

They followed the path down the side of the house to find everyone sitting around the large, rectangular patio table. 'Here they are!' Helen called out by way of greeting as she stood. 'We were just wondering where you'd got to.'

His mum leaned forward to kiss Helen's cheek. 'Sorry, we

got here as soon as we could.' She raised the box with the cheesecake. 'Shall we put these inside?'

'Yes, come on through and grab a drink while you're at it.'

Rick's parents followed Helen while he scanned the garden with a frown. 'Where's Anya?'

Chloe got up with a laugh. 'Don't panic, lover boy, she and Shelly are giving the kids a bath and putting the twins down for a nap.'

That stopped him in his tracks. 'What's Shelly doing here?'

Chloe took the trifle he was holding and carried it towards the back door. 'She's having a hard time with Jason being away so we invited her to join us,' she said to him over her shoulder before disappearing inside.

Rick caught up with her in the kitchen where Helen and his mum were trying in vain to make room in the fridge for the desserts they'd brought. 'Is he still away? I thought it was just for a couple of weeks.'

Chloe raised an eyebrow at him. 'Of course you'd know what's going on.'

He lifted a hand to rub the back of his neck. 'I just remember Jason coming into the Hub a while back when he was looking for work.'

'It's good that you know what's going on with everyone,' Chloe reassured him as she handed him a bottle of beer then leaned back against the kitchen counter next to him. 'I feel a bit bad that I never thought to check in with her myself. Now I wonder what else is going on with other people that we used to hang out with. Even if we're not good friends, we should at least try to be good neighbours.'

Not liking how downcast she looked, Rick nudged her foot with his. 'I bet it was your idea to invite Shelly today.'

Surprised, Chloe met his gaze. 'How did you know?'

'We're not so different, you and me.'

She laughed and clapped a hand to her chest. 'Don't say that!'

They left their mothers to do battle with the fridge and went back outside. Rick handed a second beer to his father, who had taken up post behind the huge gas barbeque next to Ryan. Rick beat a retreat and went to join Chloe as she sat down with Matt at the table. 'No Ed?'

Matt shook his head. 'Nope. He had a better offer.' His cousin air-quoted the last two words.

Rick grinned. 'Have you worked out her name yet?'

The three of them were still laughing and speculating about who Ed's love interest might be when Anya and Shelly emerged from the summer house with Freya and Leo. The children immediately broke off to go and sit at a little table under a tree while Anya and Shelly joined the rest of them on the patio. Shelly set a baby monitor on the table in front of them. 'Hopefully they'll sleep for a couple of hours.' She looked as much in need of sleep as anyone.

Chloe reached for a bottle wine in an ice bucket. 'Anyone want a glass?'

Shelly half-laughed, half-sighed. 'I'd love one but I'd better not.'

'We've got some sparkling water and loads of ice – how about a spritzer?' Chloe offered.

'That sounds good,' Anya said, scooping her hair off her neck and tying it up with a scrunchie she'd been wearing on her wrist. 'I swear it's getting hotter by the minute.'

It was pretty close. They could normally rely on a breeze off the sea to freshen the air, but there hadn't been a breath of it all day. Rick raised the bottle of beer to his cheek, enjoying the shock chill of the cold glass. 'It's only supposed to get warmer over the next few days.'

She smiled at him. 'Good for business.'

'Depends what your business involves,' Matt said with a grunt. 'Dad and I have a loft conversion project starting on Monday.'

They all shot him looks of sympathy. Working on the beach might be hard but Rick couldn't imagine trying to function in the trapped heat of a roof space. 'It's great that you're busy, but that doesn't sound like anyone's idea of a good time.'

'You've got that right.' Matt clinked the neck of his beer bottle against Rick's. 'Shouldn't complain, though, because we've never had so much work. We're almost at the point where we might have to start turning jobs down.'

Chloe returned with a large bottle of sparkling water, Helen and Rachel behind her carrying several tall glasses and a tray of ice cubes. While they made spritzers, Rick turned his attention to Shelly. 'How long is Jason away for?'

She scrubbed a hand through her thick curls. 'Don't ask.' Rick winced but before he could apologise, she did. 'Sorry, I didn't mean to jump down your throat.'

'It's fine, it can't be easy on your own with the kids.'

Shelly glanced over her shoulder to check the children were still occupied with their crafts. 'Jason wants us to join him.'

Anya reached out to her. 'You never said anything.'

Shelly wrinkled her nose. 'Because I've been trying not to think about it. I don't want to move away from the Quay, it's all I've ever known. I want the kids to grow up here not in a city, but it's not fair on Jason either, never getting to see them while he has to go where the work is.'

It was a growing problem for their generation, for the village as a whole. If they didn't find a way to keep the young families around, the place would slowly die. Rick was reminded about the conversation he'd had with Morwenna about dwindling pupil numbers. He wished he had the answers.

'Creating our own business is all about trying to preserve our future here in the village,' Chloe said, raising her glass towards Anya. 'And now the workshop is ready, we should celebrate our new start.'

Anya raised her glass. 'To us. It's going to take us a long time to build it into anything significant though.'

'Mighty oaks from little acorns grow,' Rachel said, also raising her glass. 'At least the two of you are giving it a go.'

'Exactly!' Chloe said, then turned to Shelly. 'Hey, you used to be pretty good at art when we were at school. Do you still paint?'

'The only painting I do these days is finger painting with the kids,' Shelly said with a laugh. 'I can't even find the energy to repaint the kitchen walls.' Her smile faded. 'Not that I'll have to worry about that if we move.'

Rick's heart went out to her. There must be something he could do. He'd have to do some scouting around, see if he could dig anything up.

'Well at least have a think about it,' Chloe urged Shelly. 'And if inspiration strikes, we might be able to sell prints of anything you paint on our website. It wouldn't make you a lot, but it'd be a start.'

'And it would be nice to do something for yourself,' Anya added. 'I know it's hard to find time. I struggle and I only have Freya to look after, but it's important to make time for a little bit of creative self-care if you can.'

'You're assuming even if I could find the time that my paintings would be any good.'

'You won't know until you try.' Anya patted her leg. 'Maybe

we can pool resources like we did earlier with the children one
evening and then we could work on a few ideas.'

Rick shoved aside the thought that this would give him even
less time alone with Anya, not liking the selfish hunger that
came with it. Anya was her own person and she could choose to
spend time with whoever she wanted. He liked that she was
making friends, that she was seeking to help someone else even
when her own circumstances were far from secure. It would
take ages for her and Chloe to get anywhere with just a website;
what they needed were other outlets. When the answer hit him,
he was amazed he hadn't thought of it before. Excited, he
turned to Chloe. 'You should speak to Kerry Wilson at the
Curiosity Cave!'

Chloe frowned. 'Why would I do that?'

He leaned forward, eager to share his idea. 'Because she
sells the sort of stuff you're talking about putting on your
website. If you sold through her as well, you'd get more
business.'

'And less money. We'd have to pay her commission, plus the
fee she charges for simply displaying things in her shop.'

Deflated, Rick sank back in his seat. 'You've already thought
of it.'

'No, but I've done my research. I'm not an idiot, Rick, I've
checked out the competition already.' Chloe took a large swig of
her drink, clearly annoyed.

'I didn't mean to suggest that you were, I was just trying to
help.'

Chloe set her glass down on the table a little harder than
necessary. 'Have you ever tried not helping?'

Rick felt like he'd been slapped. 'I'm sorry.'

Freya and Leo ran up to show off their colouring in, giving
Rick a welcome excuse to slip away from the table. He couldn't

just duck out of the evening, but he needed a bit of space, so he wandered across the grass, trying to figure out what he'd done wrong. His meandering led him over to the pair of sheds.

'Do you want to see the workshop?'

Startled, he turned to see Anya watching him with a sympathetic expression on her face. 'I don't think Chloe will want me poking around in there, somehow.'

'Come on, Rick, don't be like that.' Brushing past him, Anya pushed opened the door to the shed and beckoned him inside.

The smell of freshly cut wood filled the air and he spotted a small pile of shavings that had been swept into the corner. A long bench lined one side of the shed, two short-backed stools tucked under it. Anya's sewing machine sat in front of one stool, with several boxes of pencils, pens and tools in front of the other. The wall opposite was covered floor to ceiling with shelves. Clear plastic boxes lined several of the shelves, neatly printed labels describing their contents. 'Wow, it looks really great. I can't believe how much you've got done today.'

Anya's soft hand slipped into his. 'Hey, I'm sure Chloe didn't mean to upset you.'

He looked down at her. 'I don't understand what I did that was so bad, it was only a suggestion.'

She sighed and squeezed his hand. 'You didn't wait to be asked, and you didn't make it a sound like a suggestion. You told Chloe she *should* talk to Kerry.'

'It was just a turn of phrase. I wanted to help, you must see that.'

Releasing his hand, Anya folded her arms over her chest and leaned against the shelves behind her. 'But this is our business, mine and Chloe's, and it's important to us. We might make some mistakes – in fact, I'm sure we will – but that's on us, not you. You don't have to take everything on your shoulders, Rick.

You need to let us take responsibility, to make our own decisions about it.' Unfolding her arms, she closed the distance between them and placed her hands on his chest. When she spoke again, her voice was softer, coaxing. 'I'm not saying I won't need your help – I'm sure I will – but can you maybe try and wait until I ask?'

Rick closed his hands over hers. 'I'll try. I really didn't mean to upset anyone.'

She went up on her tiptoes and pressed a sweet, soft kiss to his mouth. 'I know, and I know Chloe didn't mean to snap at you either. It's been a long day and everyone's tired.'

He released her hands so he could put his arms around her and draw her close against him. 'This is nice.'

Her hands shifted to his back, tracing small circles at the base of his spine that threatened to short circuit his brain. 'It is. I'm definitely going to ask Chloe about babysitting again.'

'That would be good.' The subject made his thoughts drift to Shelly. 'Sounds like Shelly could do with a babysitter too.'

Anya leaned back enough so she could look up at him. 'She needs to see her husband.'

Rick nodded. 'I wish there was something I could do to h—' He cut himself off with a rueful laugh. 'I really do need to work on that.'

Anya kissed him. 'Don't ever feel bad for having a good heart, Rick, and I really wish there was something we could do. I don't even know what Jason does for a living.'

'He's a builder. I know he did a bricklaying course at the local college, but I don't know if he does other stuff...' He trailed off as the cogs in his brain began to turn.

'You've thought of something.'

Rick raised an eyebrow as he glanced down at her. 'Aren't you a bit fed up of my ideas?'

Anya gave him a little shake. 'Don't keep me in suspense. Spill it!'

'It might be nothing, but Matt was talking about how much work he and Ryan have on. There's so many refurbishment projects around, with people snapping up places as holiday homes, that he was saying they're almost turning work away. I don't know if Jason has the right skill set, though.'

'But it would be worth asking the question.' Anya leaned up to kiss him again. 'It's a good idea.'

He tightened his arms around her and pulled her in for another kiss. 'I thought you wanted me to mind my own business.'

She laughed. 'I didn't say that. I'm going to need all the support you can give me, but I also need to stand on my own two feet for a change.'

He leaned forward and pressed his forehead to hers. 'I'll do my best, I promise.'

26

'Morning, Anya! Lovely day for it,' Jim said as he swung through the revolving door. Now the hot weather had really kicked in he'd shed his fleece and had teamed his ever-present shorts with a short-sleeved uniform shirt that already looked a little worse for wear. Even with a fan beneath the desk blasting cool air onto her, the back of her own shirt was sticking to Anya's back. She couldn't imagine how much hotter he must be lugging that massive sack around in the full heat of the sun. Not that he seemed bothered about it. Come rain or shine, Jim was bright and cheery. Perhaps she should ask him what he had for breakfast, because a slice of toast and a cup of tea wasn't putting any kind of pep in her step.

'Morning. What have you got for me today?'

'Oh, the usual: bills, bills and more bills!' Face wreathed in that ever-cheerful grin, he dropped half a dozen envelopes bound up in a rubber band on top of the reception desk, then rummaged in his bag. 'And there's a parcel for you to sign for, as well.'

Anya made an incomprehensible squiggle on the screen of

the electronic scanner he held out to her. If anyone had ever managed to produce anything close to their actual signature on one of those damn things it would be a miracle.

Or witchcraft.

She frowned at the label on the box for a second then spotted the supplier's name in the corner. 'Fab! That's the new drain trap I ordered for Room 12. I wasn't expecting it so soon but I can fit it this afternoon before the new guests check in tomorrow.'

Jim grinned. 'You're a plumber now too, are you? Is there no end to your talents?'

'Ha! More like there's no start to them. Poor Davy had no idea how useless I was when he took me on, but he's teaching me all sorts of things I should probably already know.'

The postman frowned. 'You shouldn't put yourself down like that, lovie. I think the way you're trying to turn your life around is remarkable. A lot of people would've stayed beaten by what you've been through, but here you are dusting yourself off and starting again. There's a lot to be said for that.'

Anya didn't know whether to be embarrassed or pleased, so she opted for pleased. It was silly to think she could pretend everyone didn't know her circumstances and Jim would be horrified if he thought he'd said anything to upset her. 'Thanks, Jim. It feels like a long road sometimes but I'm getting there.'

'That's all that counts.' He looked past her, frowning when he saw the office was empty. 'Where's his lordship?'

'He's making us a drink. He'll be back any minute if you want to hang on.'

'My, how the tables have turned! One of these days I'll walk in and find you sat in that office with your feet up, you mark my words!'

'I doubt it somehow, but I appreciate the vote of confidence.'

Jim tapped the top of the desk. 'Well, let's see where you are this time next year. Right, places to go, people to see!'

'Bye, Jim!'

Anya set the box to one side and lifted down the little stack of post. She took off the rubber band and popped it in the empty butter tub sitting on the desk. When the tub was full, she would stick them all in a spare envelope and give them back to Jim. She had no idea if he used them again, but it felt better than throwing them away. She had just finished slitting open the envelopes when Davy came back with the tea things balanced on a tray. 'Do you want tea here?' He spotted the post. 'Jim's been, has he?'

She nodded. 'Yup. Not much today. Take the pot through to the office and I'll join you in a minute. It won't take long to jot what's here down in the book.'

'All right, pet. Come through when you're ready.'

Anya grinned at him. 'Oh, and the tap arrived, so guess what we're doing this afternoon.' She patted the top of the box.

'And there was me thinking I'd be able to sit back and relax on my lovely new cushion,' Davy grumbled, but he was smiling as he did so.

'No rest for the wicked, isn't that what they say?'

Davy rolled his eyes as he stomped off into his office with the tray. 'I wish someone had told me at the time when all these supposed wicked things were happening, because they passed me by!'

Laughing, Anya started separating the post from the envelopes, opening each letter and scanning the contents. Gas bill. Invoice from the cleaning company they used. A sale flyer from the company she'd ordered the tap from. Well, it hadn't taken them long to put their details on a mailing list. Anya slid out the last letter and unfolded it. The first thing she spotted was the familiar blue NHS logo in the top right-hand corner and the name and address of the county hospital underneath it. Why were the hospital writing to Davy, she wondered, before realising it wasn't her business. Davy didn't get a lot of personal mail, so it never occurred to her to check for it before she started opening the post. She quickly folded the letter closed but not before the word *oncology* caught her eye. Oh God, oncology meant only one thing. Without really thinking about what she was doing, Anya smoothed out the letter and read it. It was details of an appointment for a CT scan with an accompanying printout about what to expect and what preparations needed to be taken in advance. The final paragraph advised the results would be reviewed by the oncology department, who would write to his GP within one to two weeks.

Anya's stomach heaved and she pressed a hand to her mouth and swallowed hard. Still clutching the letter, she walked into Davy's office. He looked up with a smile. 'That was quick.'

She placed the letter on his desk. 'I opened this by mistake. I didn't realise what it was.'

Davy glanced down and his smile vanished. Without a word, he yanked open the top drawer of his desk, shoved the letter inside and slammed it shut again. 'It's nothing.'

'Davy...'

'I said it's nothing. Now, have you finished sorting the rest of the post? Your tea's getting cold.'

Anya sank down in the spare chair. He couldn't possibly expect her to pretend she hadn't seen what she'd just seen and act like nothing had happened. 'Why didn't you tell me you were ill?'

He scowled at her. 'Because it's none of your bloody business, that's why. Christ alive, if it's not Rick snooping around, it's you.' His brows lowered until they almost hid his eyes. 'He put you up to this, didn't he? I might have known he'd set you spying on me!'

She rocked back. 'What are you talking about?' None of this made sense. Surely Rick wouldn't have kept her in the dark over something like this. What about the rest of the family? The questions whirled around in her head and she didn't like any of the answers her brain was coming up with. 'What's Rick got to do with this?'

Davy snorted. 'Don't try and play the innocent with me, girl. I didn't come down in the last bloody shower. He's been black-mailing me ever since he found out I have cancer – how else do you think you got a damn job here? It's not because you're an administrative wizard, is it? Didn't know your arse from your elbow when you walked through the door, and as for helping me? I've done nothing but hold your hand since the day you started.'

Anya winced, the words hurting as much as if he'd reached out and physically struck her. 'I've tried my best, Davy. I'm sorry if you feel it's not been good enough. If you didn't want me here, you should've said something.' Rick should've said something. Chloe should've said something. 'Who else knows about this?'

Davy shook his head. 'No one, and that's the way I want it, do you understand? I've already got that boy meddling in my business, I don't want the rest of them on my back as well.'

Anya shook her head, unable to take it all in. 'Rick's the only one who knows? Why didn't he say anything?'

'You'll have to ask him yourself, won't you, because I'm done talking about this.' Davy waved an angry hand towards the door. 'Go on, get out. I'd rather the damn cancer got me than the pair of you nagging me to bloody death.'

As if moving on autopilot, Anya rose and walked out. She paused at the reception desk only long enough to grab her handbag from the cabinet drawer. Her little stash of tea bags, tissues and other bits and pieces she ignored. In a daze she pushed her way out of the front door, raising a hand to shield her eyes from the glaring rays of the sun. She tried to open her bag to fetch her sunglasses but her fingers couldn't grasp hold of the zip and when she looked down everything was blurry. A hot, fat tear splashed on the back of her hand, followed by another and another. Anya wrenched open her bag, fumbled for her sunglasses and shoved them on, grateful they had over-sized lenses that covered half her face.

Sniffing back the tears, she hurried down the street, desperate to go home and get away from Davy and all the cruel things he'd said to her. She made it half a dozen steps before remembering it was one of her aunt Helen's days off, so she would be in the summer house with Freya. Not home, not until she'd calmed down a bit, because she couldn't let Freya see her upset. The café then? Issy had plenty of space out the back where Anya could hide until she could pull herself together. And help her understand what was happening. Reaching beneath her sunglasses, Anya quickly dashed away her tears then crossed the road and began following the sea wall towards the café.

No one else knows.

She stopped in her tracks. If what Davy had told her was true, then the only other person who knew about his illness was Rick. If she told Issy – and how could she ask her advice without explaining everything – then she'd have to tell Chloe, and Helen and Ryan. And Ma and Pa. Oh God, did Pa not know? Had Davy honestly kept such a terrible thing from his own brother? How could Anya be the one to break the news to him? She couldn't, it wasn't her place, and deep down she didn't want to be the one who did it. Didn't want to be involved at all. She wished she could turn back the clock, take a couple of minutes to properly check the post before she opened it, realise the letter was addressed to Davy personally and hand it to him.

Only she was involved, because Rick had involved her. He'd put her right inside the heart of it and not even had the decency to warn her. She scanned the crowded beach, her gaze skipping over the mass of sunbathers, the colourful windbreaks and towels until her eyes locked on the bright green beach flag flapping in the breeze. Anger bubbled inside her and Anya changed course again, jogging towards the steps that led down onto the beach. Her progress was hampered by the number of people spread out everywhere and the sand getting inside her sandals. She bent and yanked them off, hooking the straps over one finger. The sand was hot beneath her toes, but better than that horrible gritty feeling.

She spotted Rick in the crowd. It wasn't hard given his height, plus the bright green hat and T-shirt he was wearing with his business branding on it. She was a few feet from him when he spotted her, his face lighting up.

'This is a nice surprise!'

Don't you dare smile at me. Before she realised what she was doing, one of her sandals was hurtling across the short distance between them. He stared at her open-mouthed as it bounced off his chest and dropped to the ground.

'Anya! What the hell?'

She raised her other sandal and Rick lifted his arms as he ducked his body to ward off a second blow. 'How could you?' she demanded. 'How could you do that to me?' The final words were almost lost in the choked sob escaping her throat.

'Anya? Oh my God, what's wrong?' His momentary shock overcome, Rick closed the distance between them and pulled her into his arms. At least he tried to, but she fended him off, still brandishing her sandal like a weapon.

'How could you do it to me?' she railed. 'You promised me, Rick. You promised that I could trust you and now I've found out you've been lying from the start. Oh God, you're just like him! I thought you were different, that you and I could have something special together. I'm such an idiot.'

His arms tightened around her again and though she wanted to shove him away, her knees wouldn't hold her up. She twisted her hand into the front of his T-shirt and pressed her face into his solid chest as she sobbed. 'Davy's got cancer, and you never told me. He's dying, isn't he?'

'Shit.' Rick buried a hand in the back of her hair and held her close. 'I'm sorry, Anya. I'm so sorry. You don't know how much it's been killing me not to say anything to you, but I gave him my word.'

The flash of anger was enough to stop her tears and she pulled herself free of his arms. 'Oh well if you gave him your word, I suppose that's all right then!' she snapped. 'What about your word to me, Rick? Or doesn't that count?'

'Of course it counts, but what was I supposed to do? Davy told me it's too late to do anything but he knows the family will push him into trying anyway and he just wants to be left alone to enjoy what time he's got left. I didn't know what to do.' He held out a hand to her. 'Anya, please. Can we go somewhere and talk about this? I'm so sorry I kept it from you, but Davy's told you now, so at least it's out in the open and he's obviously coming round to the idea of facing up to things.' He sounded so relieved, like a huge weight had been lifted off his shoulders. A huge weight he'd hung around her neck instead, without any warning.

She shook her head. 'Davy didn't tell me. I opened a letter

from the hospital by mistake.' The shock of it hit all over again. *Davy was dying.* Rick had just said it was too late to do anything. The pain was like a knife shredding her insides. 'How could you do that to me?'

He held out a hand to her, his face a mask of grief and pain. 'I'm sorry I lied to you.'

He didn't get it. 'It's not the lie, though God knows that's bad enough. It's the fact you put me in that situation in the first place. You let me get attached to him and all the while you knew that he's going to die. You let me get close to him, to care about him and now he's going to leave me and I can't go through all that again. I can't.' She turned away, the tears falling too hard to continue speaking. It didn't matter, she had nothing else she wanted to say to him.

'Anya, wait. *Please.*' He placed a hand on her upper arm to stop her but she shook him off.

'No, let me go. You've broken my heart, Rick Penrose, and I'm never going to forgive you.'

27

Rick stared after Anya in disbelief. Not at what she'd said to him but the fact he'd put her in such a terrible position. The long-term implications of her and Davy working together had never occurred to him. He'd been too focused on finding a quick solution to both issues. He'd told himself he was doing right by both of them, but had he really considered anything beyond what would make life easier for him? Anya was right about him inserting himself into everything. It hadn't been his responsibility to find her a job, so why had he done it? *Because you wanted her to be grateful to you.* No, not grateful, but he'd wanted to do something that would make her notice him, make her think kindly of him and perhaps give him a chance for their friendship to develop into something more. He'd thought he was being so clever, and look where it had got him. She would probably never want to speak to him again and, honestly, he couldn't blame her.

And what about Davy? Rick had promised to respect his wishes and keep his secret and yet from the moment he'd found out he'd been doing everything he could to circumvent that promise because he hadn't liked the burden of it. Blackmail, that's what his uncle had called it and he was right. *Shit.* Rick needed to talk to him and apologise. He needed to speak to Anya too and try and persuade her to help him keep Davy's secret. It wasn't fair to ask, not after he'd put so much on her shoulders already, but what else could he do?

He took half a dozen steps before reality stopped him in his tracks. His gaze scanned across the water, past the swimmers to the windsurfers and paddle boarders further out to sea. He couldn't just run off and try and fix this awful mess he'd made because he had customers out there. Responsibilities. Trudging back to his post, Rick picked up the clipboard he used to keep track of his rentals and ran through the list. There was a group of four paddle boarders who were due back within the hour. He raised his head and searched the bay again until he spotted the familiar bright yellow life jackets he issued. They had followed his advice and stuck to the water sports zone on the right-hand side nearest the quay wall. He glanced back down to his list... That left the couple who'd rented a double kayak and the photographer who'd hired a jet ski so he could access some of the more remote bays along the coast. He was a regular customer of Rick's, so he didn't have any worries about him being back on time. He surveyed the neat rows of unused equipment in front of him. Even if his current rentals returned soon, he still had to drag all this stuff up to his lockup and secure it.

Frustrated at his inability to do anything, Rick pulled out his phone and sent both Davy and Anya messages, apologising and asking if they could talk later. To Anya's message he added a request not to talk about Davy being ill to anyone because it was his responsibility to sort it out and he'd already put her in a terrible position.

He heard nothing back from either of them.

It was Anya who was his most immediate concern given the state she'd been in when she'd walked away. Who would she go to? Issy, maybe? No, the café would be busy. Chloe would still be at work and he didn't have Kat's number, though she'd probably be working too. What would he say to them, anyway? He could warn them that Anya was upset and that it was his bloody fault, but they would want to know why and he couldn't tell them without betraying his promise to Davy. Rick tucked away his phone and stared once more out at the sea. For the first time in his life it felt like there was nothing he could do to help two of the people who meant the most to him. And he hated it.

All the customers had come back at their expected times and Rick was busy tidying up when his brother, Ed, came traipsing towards him, hands in his pockets. He was hard to miss, not just because the crowds on the beach had thinned out as people packed up and headed back home to start thinking about their dinner plans. Unlike everyone else, dressed in casual attire, Ed was still wearing the smart dark trousers and white collared shirt that were standard office wear for most men. He had at least taken his shoes off and was carrying them under one arm. Rick hoped he wasn't going to take after Anya and start flinging them at his head. A strappy sandal was one thing, but a black Oxford dress shoe would hurt like hell.

As his brother got close, Rick recognised the hangdog expression all too well and he swallowed down a sigh. 'What have you done now?'

Ed scowled. 'Why do you always assume it's my fault?'

'Because it usually is.' Rick checked his watch. 'You've finished early, not that I'm complaining because you can give me a hand with these.' He nodded at the paddle boards he'd been stacking onto his wide-wheeled trolley.

'I'm not exactly dressed for it,' Ed said, gesturing down at his clothes.

'And I've got neither the time nor the patience to listen to you whine about whatever's put that look on your face, so you either work and chat or you can piss off and leave me in peace.'

Ed gaped at him. 'Okay, forget my problems for a minute. What the hell's the matter with you?'

Rick shook his head as he turned away and bent to lift another board onto the trolley. 'Nothing, I'm just busy.'

Dropping his shoes onto the sand, Ed leaned over at the waist to roll his suit trouser legs up to his knees, then grabbed the next board. 'Since when are you too busy to help someone? You are literally the St Bernard of Halfmoon Quay trotting around rescuing everyone.' Ed grinned, clearly impressed at the comparison. 'If only you had a little keg of brandy strapped around your neck, you'd be perfect.'

Not feeling remotely amused, Rick planted his hands on his hips and glared at him. 'What if I'm sick and tired of helping everyone? What if I've decided it's time to mind my own damn business and look after number one for a change?'

Ed mirrored his body language. 'Then I'd assume there was an alien invasion while I was at work and you've been body-snatched.'

Rick huffed out a breath. 'Stop trying to make me laugh, you annoying brat, and get to work.'

With Ed's help the boards were soon stacked and they trundled across the sand to his lockup, where they quickly unloaded them onto the racks Ryan and Matt had installed. They were on their way back when Ed stepped in front of Rick and he had to stop or risk mowing him down with the trolley. 'What?'

Ed tilted his head to one side. 'You're really not curious about why I left work early?'

Rolling his eyes, Rick dodged around him and dragged the trolley back towards where the jet skis still needed to be loaded. 'I can't say it's top of my priority list to listen to your latest attempt at self-sabotage, no.' He lifted the front of the first jet ski with a grunt, glad he'd only put a few out that morning.

'That's a bit harsh,' Ed complained as he bent to lift up the other end. Rick stared at him over the top of the jet ski for a long moment before his little brother sighed. 'But probably fair.'

Rick set down the vehicle on the trolley and grasped at his chest as if shocked. 'What's this? Ed Penrose discovers self-awareness at the ripe old age of twenty-five? 'Tis truly the end of days.'

'Oh do piss off,' Ed said, managing to hold onto a wounded expression for all of two seconds before he burst out laughing. 'God, you are in a brutal mood today. Whatever's happened to you, I don't like it. I want the old Rick back; he's nice to me even when I have been a complete idiot.'

That stopped Rick in his tracks. It wasn't fair to take his bad mood out on Ed, regardless of the way he seemed to lurch from one scrape to another. 'What did you do?' he asked, making sure to keep his voice soft.

His brother looked away, one foot scuffing through the sand. 'I got involved with someone at work that I shouldn't have.'

Oh bloody hell. 'Who?'

Ed's cheeks began to flame as he risked a peek up at Rick through his lashes. 'Umm, the head of area sales?'

Rick closed his eyes for a second. So not even a regular coworker. 'Go on.'

'We umm, kind of had a thing at the staff Christmas party—'

'This has been going on since Christmas?' Rick interjected.

Ed shook his head. 'No, not really. I mean, I thought it was a one-off dirty snog in the photocopying room, nothing serious. But she split up with her husband a couple of months ago, and well, one thing led to another.'

Rick shook his head as he turned to pick up the next ski. 'I've changed my mind, I don't want to know.'

Ignoring him, Ed picked up the other end of the ski and carried on yapping. 'It was all going so great and there was a temporary job on the sales team which she arranged for me to move into.'

Rick sighed. 'Of course she did.'

'Hey,' Ed protested. 'It was a good deal. Not only did I get the chance to spend more time with her, but the money was way better too.'

With both skis loaded, Rick began the trek across the sand again. He didn't need to ask what happened next. 'She changed her mind and went back to her husband and your temporary job vanished, right?'

Ed stopped short. 'How did you know?'

Because it was glaringly obvious to everyone, apart from you apparently, how things would play out. 'So now what?'

Ed fixed him with the beseeching stare he'd been using to twist their entire family around his little finger since he'd been old enough to speak. 'Didn't you say something about needing extra help for the rest of the summer?'

Not knowing whether to laugh or cry, Rick instead dug a hand in his pocket and pulled out the keys for his lockup. He tossed them to Ed, who just managed to catch them before they hit him. 'Fill your boots.' Without another word, Rick turned and walked away.

'Hey! Where are you going?' Ed called after him. 'I can't manage this stuff on my own.'

'If you want a job then you'll figure out a way,' Rick called back, not turning round.

28

Rick was running by the time he reached the top of the steps, barely pausing at the kerb to let a car pass before he sprinted across the road towards the hotel. He needed to talk to Anya, but not until he'd found out exactly what had happened between her and Davy. The reception area was empty and so was the office by the looks of things. Davy must be making a cup of tea, because if he was off doing something around the building he always made sure to lock up the office. Rick dodged past the desk, intent on heading down the corridor to the kitchenette, when he spotted a foot sticking out from behind Davy's desk and then he heard a soft moan.

'Davy?' He ran into the office to find his uncle flat on his back on the floor, white faced and sweating. He had his hands pressed to his stomach as he moaned again. 'Bloody hell, what's wrong?'

'Just help me up,' Davy muttered through gritted teeth as Rick crouched down beside him.

'But if you've fallen over, I'd better not move you until the ambulance arrives,' Rick protested as he pulled out his phone.

'I didn't fall and I don't need an ambulance, I've just got a bit of a stomach ache. Now help me up, please.'

Shocked by the desperate pleading in his great-uncle's voice, Rick put an arm around his shoulders and began to lift Davy. The old man cried out and Rick immediately lowered him back down. 'Enough of this, I'm calling for help.'

He got through on 999 and, after what seemed like a million questions, the call handler told him an ambulance would be with them as soon as they could. 'Any idea how long?' Rick asked, shoving a worried hand through his hair as he stared down at Davy. 'He's got cancer and I'm not sure how bad it is but he's got an appointment for a scan soon.'

'We're very busy at the moment, sir, I'm sorry. Can you give me details on his condition and I can add them to the notes for the paramedics?'

Rick swallowed. 'I... I don't really know, I'm afraid.' He glared down at his uncle, wanting to yell at him that this was why it was wrong of him to shut everyone out. They needed to know stuff like this. But it was only his fear making him want to rage, a fear he saw reflected in his great-uncle's eyes. 'Can you at least give me an idea of how long we might be waiting?' he asked the call handler.

'As I said, we are very busy and all our teams are out on priority calls.'

Rick wanted to snap that this was a bloody priority, but again he held his tongue. Davy was clearly in severe pain, but he was breathing okay and he was lucid. There would be people out there in a much worse state. 'An hour?' he asked. The call handler didn't reply. Bloody hell. 'Two?'

'At least,' she said. 'I am very sorry but we will get there as soon as we can.'

Rick looked down at Davy. He couldn't leave him just lying

there on the floor and his car was parked back at home. 'Okay, that's too long, so I'm going to take him to the hospital myself. Thanks for your help but can you cancel the request?'

'Are you sure you can move him safely?'

'Yes. I've got plenty of people to help, don't worry. Thanks for your time.' He rang off and immediately dialled his father's number. 'Dad, I'm at the hotel and Davy needs to go to the hospital but I can't leave him to get my car.'

'What's happened?'

'It's not for me to say, Dad, but please, I really need your help.'

Jago huffed out a breath. 'Fine. Let me call Ryan. I know he and Matt were working locally today, so he's your best bet. You and I are going to have a talk later, lad.' The phone went dead.

Rick knew there would be a reckoning with his father, but he couldn't worry about that now. He plucked the cushion Anya had made off Davy's chair and gently lifted his great-uncle's head enough to pop the cushion behind it. 'Help's on the way,' he assured him, reaching down to brush the sweaty strands of hair away from his forehead. Davy didn't even try to argue, just clenched his teeth and nodded again, his hands pressed underneath his belly.

The phone rang and it was Matt. 'We're a couple of minutes away. Front or back door?'

Rick frowned and considered their options. 'Front. I'll open the fire door at the side and I think if you can help me get him to his feet we can walk him out.'

'No probs.'

The silver pickup with *Penrose and Son* emblazoned down the side pulled up outside just as Rick had unlocked and secured the fire door open on its heavy magnet. Rick only had time to meet Ryan's worried gaze from the driver's window before Matt ran around the front of the truck to join him. 'Where is he? What happened?'

'He's in the office,' Rick said, leading the way. 'I don't know what's wrong, something to do with his stomach because that's what he keeps holding. I tried for an ambulance but they said at least a couple of hours.'

'Stuff that,' Matt said, shaking his head before he put on a bright smile. 'Blimey, Uncle D, what's all this, then?'

'What does it look like, you stupid boy?' Davy managed to grumble.

Matt laughed, not taking the least bit of offence. 'If you're still complaining, it can't be that bad. Come on then, old man, let's get you up.'

With his cousin's help, it was almost no effort to get Davy up. He was skin and bone, Rick discovered as he slung an arm around his great-uncle's waist, and between him and Matt they carried him towards the door. Ryan was out and on the pavement, the wide back door of the pickup open, and they quickly settled Davy on his back across the seats. Rick ran back inside the hotel, grabbed his uncle's mobile and keys off the desk and locked the office door. He pulled out his own phone and sent Anya a message.

> I know you hate me but Davy's ill and we're taking him to the hospital. Can you watch the hotel?

His phone rang a couple of seconds later. 'I'm on my way.'

Rick sighed in relief that at least she was reading his messages. 'I've locked the office, do you need the keys?'

'No, I have a spare set.'

'What about the phone?'

'I'm only around the corner, so I'll be there in a couple of minutes, just stick it in the top drawer of the desk.'

'Done.' Rick ran towards the exit, kicking the fire door free of the maglock as he passed so it would close behind him. 'Thank you.'

'I'm doing this for him, not for you.' She was silent for a moment. 'I haven't said anything to anyone yet, but you must know this deception can't go on.'

'I know,' Rick said, propping his phone under his chin as he climbed into the back and lifted Davy's head up so it could rest on his lap. His eyes met his uncle's through the rear-view mirror and he knew it wasn't only his dad who would have something to say to him about the situation. 'I'll sort it out, somehow.'

Anya was silent for a moment. 'Call me later when you know what's going on.'

By the time they got to the hospital, the tops of Rick's legs were wet through from the sweat pouring off Davy, and his great-uncle was struggling to speak. What he did manage to say wasn't making much sense and all Rick could do was hold onto him and murmur that everything would be all right. Between the three of them they managed to carry Davy into the reception area, where something like a dozen people were already waiting in the neat row of plastic chairs lined up in front of the desk.

The receptionist took one look at them and she must've pressed some kind of secret bat signal on her desk because moments later two men and a woman all dressed in pale green hospital scrubs came running through the large double doors. The woman immediately turned back the way they'd come while the two men hurried over to them. The younger of the two turned to Ryan and addressed him.

'Hello, I'm Dr Hillman. What's the problem?' He had black-framed glasses and fine blond hair that was swept back from his forehead in an untidy tangle as if he'd run his hands through it many times. He couldn't have been much older than Rick, but he exuded an air of quiet calm and authority.

'This is my uncle Davy – sorry, David Penrose. Best speak to Rick as he's the one who found him.' Ryan gestured in Rick's direction.

Davy groaned and the older man in scrubs came to help Rick and Matt who were still holding Davy up. 'Hello there, Davy, I'm Jamie. All right then, we'll get you sorted out in no time. Look, here's Nicky with the trolley now.' The female nurse who had disappeared had returned in short order with a porter who was pushing a trolley. Jamie glanced up at Rick and Matt. 'You okay to lift him?'

'Absolutely,' Rick said.

'Whatever you need,' Matt said at the same time, and between them they got Davy up onto the trolley.

'Room three is free,' Nicky said to Jamie, who nodded and they immediately began pushing the trolley back towards the double doors.

Rick, Ryan and Matt made to follow them, but the doctor raised a hand to hold them back. 'I can't have all of you in there, sorry.' He looked at Rick. 'You found him?'

Rick nodded. 'He was lying on his back in his office, pale, sweating and holding his stomach. He said he hadn't fallen when I asked him.'

The doctor nodded. 'And do you know how old he is?'

Rick shrugged. 'Not sure. Eighty-something. We had Pa's eightieth last year and Davy is a couple of years older than him.'

'Don't worry, someone will be out in a minute to take down some proper details. I need to get in there and do the examination. Is there any pertinent information we should know about – any pre-existing conditions?'

Rick swallowed hard. 'He... he has cancer.'

'He what?' Ryan exclaimed.

Ignoring him, Rick kept his eyes on the doctor. 'I don't know the details but I think it's pretty far along from the little bit he's told me. He's supposed to be having a scan. A letter arrived today but I don't have the details.'

The doctor nodded. 'That'll do for now. Take a seat and I'll come and talk to you again as soon as I can.' He placed a hand on Rick's arm. 'Try not to worry, he's in good hands.' And with that he pushed through the double doors and left Rick to face the music.

Taking a deep breath, Rick reluctantly focused on his uncle and cousin. Both were frowning, but Ryan looked furious whereas Matt just seemed a bit confused. 'I can explain—'

'Outside. Now.' Ryan turned on his heel and marched towards the front door.

Matt winced. 'I have no idea what's going on, but you are in the shit, mate. I've never seen him so mad.'

Rick sighed. Both his uncle and father shared the same relaxed, sunny outlook on life, and Rick could count on the fingers of one hand the number of times he'd seen either really lose their temper. Keeping Ryan waiting wasn't going to make things any easier, so Rick followed after him, Matt on his heels. His uncle was standing on the pavement about thirty feet from the entrance, hands on his hips, his mouth pulled into a tight line.

'I'm sorry,' Rick said as soon as he was close enough.

Ryan shook his head. 'I don't want to hear it. Just tell me what the hell is going on.'

Rick opened his mouth, then closed it again as he spotted a

familiar red estate car pulling into the car park. It was more abandoned than parked in the nearest available space, and seconds later Rick's parents emerged.

Matt placed an arm around his shoulder. 'You know that shit you're in? It just got about ten times deeper.'

29

By the time Steve, the night manager, arrived Anya hadn't heard anything from Rick. 'Poor old boy,' Steve said as they swapped seats behind the desk. 'I hope he'll be all right.'

Anya nodded. 'Me too.'

'And you've no idea what's wrong? What did the paramedics say when they arrived?'

'I think Rick took him to hospital. I don't really know because I wasn't here at the time.' She sighed. There wasn't much point in pretending everything was okay because Steve would find out sooner or later. 'My job here wasn't working out, so Davy and I decided to part ways this morning. I only came back because there was no one else to fill in.'

Steve rocked back, eyes wide. 'I thought you and Davy were getting on like a house on fire. What happened?'

She shrugged. 'It's fine.' It wasn't anything close to fine, but she wasn't going to get into it. Steve was a nice guy, but she wasn't about to bare her heart and soul to him. 'It was only ever a temporary measure, something to get me back on my feet until I got settled in.'

'Oh, sure. No, no, I get it. Well, for what it's worth I think it's a shame because Davy's never been happier than since you started working here.'

Which Anya supposed only went to show that Davy could be as deceptive and false as his great-nephew. 'Well, I need to get back to Freya, so I'll leave you to it.' She shouldered her bag and took a few steps towards the door.

'Hey, Anya?' She turned to look back. 'If you hear anything about Davy, will you drop me a text?'

She nodded. 'Of course.'

'Thanks.' Steve's brows drew down. 'If they keep him in, who's going to look after this place?'

'That's something the family will have to sort out.' She'd agreed to come back because it was clear Rick had been in a state earlier, but she hadn't forgiven Davy for what he'd said to her. She hoped he was going to be okay, but he wasn't her problem. Perhaps her mum had been right all along and she should've taken Freya and gone to stay with them. After all, there was nothing keeping either of them here. It had been kind of her aunt and uncle to invite them to stay, but they would surely be relieved to let everything go back to normal. She felt a twinge of guilt about leaving Chloe in the lurch, before brushing it away. Her cousin had likely only included her in her business plans because she felt sorry for her. Chloe would be just fine on her own, and no doubt glad to get her home back once they moved out.

She let herself into the summer house about fifteen minutes later to find Chloe and Freya sitting together on the sofa, *Frozen* once again playing on the TV.

'Not this again!' Anya said, dredging up a smile from somewhere. Whatever her problems, Freya didn't need to get drawn into them.

'Mummy!' Freya jumped up and ran over for a hug. 'Chloe wants to stay for tea. I told her we're having nuggets!'

'It was an offer too good to refuse,' Chloe said, holding out her arms to catch Freya and pull her back up on the sofa. She turned to meet Anya's eyes as she set her bag down on the kitchen counter across from them. 'Mum had something to do, so I said I'd hold the fort.' The brightness of her tone was a stark contrast to the worry etched on her face. Obviously word about Davy had started to spread around the family.

'Thanks. I got held up at work, but I'm glad you've agreed to stay for tea. The nuggets are optional, though.'

Chloe pressed her hands to her chest as though shocked Anya would even suggest such a thing. 'No way, I'm only here for the nuggets.'

Anya laughed as she opened the little freezer above the fridge and pulled out two bags. 'Right then, potato faces or chips?'

With Chloe's help, Anya managed to make everything seem normal for Freya. After dinner, Anya found a pack of cards and they played snap and go fish until it was time for Freya's bath. The excitement of the extra company soon wore her out and she was yawning her little head off as Anya dried her and got her into her pyjamas. She didn't even want Anya to read her a story, happy to lie down with her audiobook and her coloured light painting patterns across the room.

Anya pulled the bedroom door to and found Chloe with a dishcloth in her hand, drying the last of their dinner things. 'Oh you didn't have to do that.'

Chloe set aside the towel and gave her hug. 'It was the least I could do. Have you heard anything yet?' She sniffed back a sudden tear. 'I suppose it's a miracle he made it to the age he has without anything serious until now, but when Mum told me earlier about Davy having cancer—' She stopped herself, eyes widening in horror. 'Oh, I shouldn't have broken it to you like that! I wasn't thinking!'

Anya hugged her again. 'I found out this morning. Let me see if I've had a message from Rick.' She went to double-check her phone, but there wasn't so much as a text. 'Nothing.'

Chloe swallowed, but did her best to smile. 'No news is good news, isn't that what they say?'

Anya hugged her again. 'Let's hope so. Do you want a coffee?'

Chloe nodded. 'Let me message Mum and see if she's spoken to Dad since he called her earlier.'

They'd just sat down when there was a quiet tap on the door and Helen let herself in. 'Your dad just called, so I thought it'd be easier to come and update you both rather than trying to explain it all in a text.'

Anya jumped up. 'Come and sit down. The kettle's just boiled; do you want a drink?'

Helen shook her head as she took a seat in the armchair. 'I am awash with tea as it is.'

Anya sat back down. 'How bad is it?'

Her aunt gave her an appraising look. 'You knew?'

'About the cancer? Only since this morning. I opened a letter about Davy needing to go in for a scan by mistake. We had a bit of a row about it.' She rubbed a hand over her face as a wave of tiredness washed over her. 'And then Rick and I had a much bigger row about it.'

'Poor Rick,' Helen said, shaking her head. 'He's in everyone's bad books.'

'So he bloody well should be!' Anya clamped her mouth shut for a moment. 'Sorry, never mind about that now. What did Uncle Ryan tell you?'

Helen raised an eyebrow at the outburst but didn't address it, saying instead, 'Well the good news is that the immediate problem is a nasty urinary tract infection. Davy's hooked up on an IV and getting strong antibiotics and some painkillers and he's a lot more comfortable. They're going to keep him in overnight as a precaution. They've also arranged for him to have a scan in the morning so they can get a better idea about his cancer.' It was her turn to rub a hand over her face. 'Turns out he's not been to have one yet. Poor Rick is beside himself because Davy gave him the impression that it was all far too late to do anything, when it turns out he hasn't even had a full diagnosis since his initial blood test came back.'

Anya rocked back in her seat. 'What are you talking about? I assumed he was beyond help. When we were arguing earlier he said he'd rather let the cancer get him than have me nagging him to death.' *And he'd let Rick believe the same thing.*

Helen's eyes widened. 'I thought Rick must've been confused, but if Davy's let you think the worst as well? I simply don't understand what he's been playing at.' She muttered the last more to herself than Anya. 'We can sort all that out once we have the full picture. In the meantime, it looks like you'll be on your own at the hotel for a few days. Do you think you'll be able to manage?'

Anya held her hands up. 'The hotel's nothing to do with me any more. Davy made it clear to me this morning what he really thinks of me, so you'll have to find someone else to cover until he's back on his feet. I was thinking I might take Freya over to stay with mum for a few days.'

'Anya!' Chloe exclaimed. 'You can't leave Davy in the lurch. I'm sure whatever he said, he didn't mean it. And what about Rick?'

'What about him? He lied to me, Chloe! Worse than that he

put me in a situation where I'd have to spend every day with a man he thought was dying. I trusted him, I trusted Davy, and it was so nice to have someone teach me all the things I missed out on growing up. You have no idea what it's like, because your dad's always been here. And you had all the rest of the family looking out for you too. I had no one, only Mum, and she was working all the time.'

Chloe leaned in to hug her. 'I know it was hard for you, but look on the bright side: things with Davy might not be as bad as you feared.'

Anya leaned away until Chloe released her. 'Coming to Half-moon Quay was supposed to be different. It was supposed to be my chance to start again, to escape the fantasy world I'd built around myself and Drew and get to grips to with real life. But if this is real life then it can get stuffed, I'm not interested!'

Aunt Helen leaned forward and placed a comforting hand on Anya's knee. 'Come on, darling, I know you've been through an awful time, and you've had a bit of a nasty shock today, but things aren't that bad.'

'Aren't that bad? I wasted ten years of my life on a compulsive liar only to find I've got myself mixed up with another one! Well it serves me right for getting involved with anyone. Rick and I are done and that's all there is to it. I have Freya and she's all I need.'

'Back the truck up there for a second!' Chloe exclaimed. 'I'll admit that Rick's messed up big time, but there's simply no comparison between him and Drew.'

'He promised I could trust him and now I find out he's been lying to me.'

Chloe rolled her eyes. 'And I promised my arse I'd stop eating chocolate, but here I am still filling out a pair of size sixteen jeans!'

'You said before that you wanted to stop living in a fantasy,' her aunt interjected in a gentle voice. 'But it sounds to me as if that's exactly what you're still looking for. You have every right to be upset with Rick for keeping the truth about Davy from you, we're all a bit angry with him about that, but can't you at least try and see things from his point of view?'

'You mean the point of view where he needed someone to keep an eye on Davy and get into my good books at the same time?' Anya scoffed.

'Oh, I think that's a bit harsh,' Chloe protested.

Anya glared at her. Whose friend was she supposed to be anyway? 'He blackmailed Davy into giving me that job, and before you make excuses for him, Davy told me so himself. Said he wouldn't have given me a job if Rick hadn't forced him to and that I was more hindrance than help.' She rubbed her chest as though she could soothe away the ache of remembering his ugly words.

'That doesn't sound like Rick. Doesn't sound like Davy either for that matter.'

Anya sighed. 'Well maybe it's just me that men are awful to. I must give off some kind of pheromone that brings out the worst in them.'

Helen shook her head. 'What would you have had Rick do?'

Why was this so difficult for them to understand? 'I would've had him tell me the truth so I could make up my own mind about whether I wanted to work with Davy. I never would've let him get so close to me if I'd known he was so ill.'

'That's you wanting the fantasy life again, though. You can't insulate yourself from pain. It's simply not possible. And running away to your mum's isn't going to make things any better either.'

'I'm not running away! I'm just choosing to take my life in a different direction. You were all very kind to take me in, but coming here was a mistake, I see that now. All I've done is disrupt everything. You'll have your hands full dealing with Davy over the coming months anyway.' Yes, going to see her mum and Bill was exactly what she needed to do. Feeling something close to relief, she turned to Chloe with a smile. 'And you'll get your lovely little home back.'

Chloe just stared at her. 'What about our plans? What about the business?'

Anya quirked her lips; it was sweet of Chloe to try and pretend that her leaving wouldn't be the easiest thing for all of them. 'Oh, come on, we both know you were just being kind when you included me. You'll make a great success of things on your own.'

'But I want *us* to make a great success of things, Annie.'

Anya patted her cousin's knee. 'You'll be fine without me.'

'And what about you?' Helen asked, quietly. 'Will you be fine? Is that what you want for the rest of your life, because it sounds like a very lonely existence to me. What about Freya?'

Anya tilted her head as she gave her aunt a quizzical look. 'What about Freya? She's my priority in all this. Thank goodness I kept Rick at arm's length when it came to her, because she won't have to suffer losing another man in her life.'

Helen bowed her head for a moment. 'It's like history repeating itself.'

'What are you talking about?'

'You sound just like your mother after your father left. She swore off men for years, said she didn't need anyone else because she had you. It might've been fine for her because she didn't have to risk getting hurt again, but what about you? What about what you said to Chloe earlier about having no one around when you were growing up to show you how to do things. What about all those times you came home from school and had to let yourself in because Lisa was at work?'

Anya swallowed around the lump in her throat. 'This will be different.'

Helen shook her head. 'Pain is the price we pay for love. You keep talking about wanting to live in the real world, but thinking you can have a life without any more pain is the *real* fantasy here.'

Anya scoffed. 'That's easy for you to say because you and Ryan have always been happy together.'

Helen sat back in her chair and let out a hoot of laughter. 'My God, is that what you think? I love Ryan more than anything but if you knew even half the mistakes he's made over the years, you wouldn't believe it. And that's before we got onto all the times I messed up. There's no such thing as perfection when it comes to marriage or a relationship, and yes, sadly, there are some experiences that are truly terrible. I wouldn't wish what Drew put you through on my worst enemy, but you cannot waste the rest of your life being too afraid to try again.'

'But I did try again,' Anya protested, scrubbing an angry hand across her eyes as hot tears began to prickle.

'And you got hurt. But the only reason you got hurt is because you care about Rick, and you care about Davy too. Drew was only able to cause you so much pain because of how much you loved him.'

'But he didn't deserve my love!'

Helen leaned forward and took her hands. 'No, he didn't, but you didn't know that at the time. You had a lovely life, and you made a beautiful child together. And then you lost it all, and that has to hurt more than anything else ever has in your life.'

'I never really had it, though, did I?'

Helen squeezed her hands gently. 'But you didn't know that,' she repeated. 'You've never let yourself grieve properly because you think you don't deserve to mourn Drew, but that's denying the truth of what you experienced at the time. If you don't let yourself come to terms with that, you'll never be ready to move forward. You have to stop punishing yourself, Anya. It's time to forgive yourself.'

Anya let that sink in for a bit. 'Even if what you say is true and I do all of that, I'm still not sure I can ever forgive Rick for lying to me.'

Helen leaned back again, steepling her fingers under her chin. 'Whether you can forgive him or not will be up to you. I'm not going to tell you that you shouldn't be mad at him, because God knows I'm furious with him for keeping all this to himself, especially when he's somehow only got half the story. But I know why he did it. Or at least I can hazard a good guess. Rick has always been a good boy, you see,' she said, a fond smile spreading over her face. 'He's always been the one of those four who did the right thing. He never misbehaved, never forgot to do his homework. Never ran out into the street to chase a football.'

Anya recalled the way he'd put an arm out in front of her when she'd gone to cross the road. 'He's very cautious.'

Helen nodded. 'Liam was the golden boy with the big brain and the scholarship. Harry was the wild one who ran off the rails and Ed was the baby of the family, especially after his accident. Rick, on the other hand, he just tried not to be a bother to anyone. When his mum needed help running the chandlery, he was the one who stepped in. When the parish council almost had to fold because of a lack of members, he was the first to volunteer. When he realised there was a resource gap for the village, he founded the Hub.'

'You make him sound like a saint.'

Helen scoffed. 'Oh he's hardly that, he's just someone who's always tried to help wherever he's seen a need for it.' She shook her head. 'The sad thing is, I don't think anyone has ever stopped to ask him what *he* needs.'

Anya's phone beeped and she reached for it. It was a message from Rick.

> Davy ok, will explain tomorrow. Ed's doing Hire Hut so I will cover at the hotel until D back on his feet.

It was hard not to laugh, because of course Rick would be the one to sort things out. *He wouldn't have to if he hadn't made a mess in the first place.*

> Thanks

She began typing a follow-up query about whether he was okay but she deleted the words before she sent them. While Helen had given her a new insight into why Rick might behave as he did, she couldn't gloss over things. Setting the phone aside, she looked at Helen and Chloe. 'I won't make any rash decisions about going to Mum's, but I'm going to have to have a long hard think about whether staying in Halfmoon Quay is the right thing for Freya and me in the long run.'

30

Anya is typing... The words teased him for a few seconds, then stopped, started again, and then nothing. Rick stared at his screen, willing her to carry on the conversation, but after five minutes of silence he sighed and tucked away his phone. The loss of light from the screen plunged the back seat of his parents' car into darkness, which at least had the benefit of Rick no longer being able to sense his father's laser-like glare via the rear-view mirror every time he looked up. Rick shifted in his seat and stared out the passenger window, though there was nothing to see beyond the glass. The Stygian dark of the unlit country road made the atmosphere in the car even more stifling, locking Rick inside a box of his own shame and regret.

What else could I have done?

His mind kept circling back to the same question, not as a plea of self-justification but to batter himself constantly with answers that seemed so obvious with the benefit of hindsight. He could've taken his mum or dad into his confidence about Davy, talked it over with them and found a way to help his great-uncle without turning the whole thing into a circus. He could've let Anya find her own way. There were plenty of part-time jobs around the village this time of year that didn't need much in the way of experience. He hadn't needed to create one for her.

You've broken my heart, Rick Penrose. The remembered words cut as deeply as when she'd said them. How could he have been so stupid? So careless and inconsiderate of the trauma she'd suffered since Drew's death. His gut shrivelled every time he thought about it.

After what felt like an eternity, they pulled up on the block-paved drive in front of the house. The external security light illuminated the car as the three of them got out. There wasn't any danger from trespassers or would-be car thieves in the village, rather it had been fitted by Jago after he and Rachel had been woken once too often by the late-night key fumblings of one or other of their errant sons. It wasn't the only change they'd had to make to the house to accommodate their growing brood. Rick could still remember the summer they'd installed the practical, if not so aesthetically pleasing, paving slabs beneath his feet. His parents had sacrificed the small front garden to meet the parking needs of several teenage boys all desperate to own their own car. It had been hard work laying the slabs, but a lot of fun.

Jago stalked past Rick without a word. He unlocked the front door and disappeared upstairs. His mum laid a hand on Rick's arm. 'He just needs a bit of time to calm down.'

Rick nodded. 'I don't blame him for being angry with me.'

She reached up to cup his cheek, almost having to go up on tiptoe to do so. 'He's not angry with you, not really. He's angry with himself because he feels responsible for not noticing there was anything wrong with Davy.'

'But that doesn't make any sense!'

His mum smiled. 'No more sense than you feeling like you had to shoulder the burden of his illness alone.' Rick cringed a little, making her shake her head in gentle bemusement. 'Two peas in a pod, that's you and your dad.'

He didn't bother to deny it, because he knew it was true. Jago had always been Rick's role model growing up. 'He shouldn't blame himself, because Uncle Davy did his damnedest to hide things from all of us. I wouldn't have noticed if Maud hadn't sought me out in the café and asked me to call in on him.' He frowned. 'Has anyone thought to let Maud know? Maybe I should text Issy...'

'Stop it.' His mother shook his arm gently. 'Tomorrow will be soon enough to think about things like that.' She tilted her head towards the stairs. 'Why don't you go up and try and relax? You've had a horrible day.' Her mouth quirked in a little smile. 'By the sounds of it, you've got some company waiting for you up there.'

Above the dull buzz of the shower running in his parents' en suite, he caught the strains of a TV, followed by familiar deep laughter. 'What are the twins doing here?'

'Why don't you go up and find out?'

Not the least bit in the mood for company, Rick dragged himself reluctantly up the stairs. He paused for a moment outside the door to his sitting room, which had been left ajar, and took a deep breath.

'I can see you lurking out there,' Harry called.

Rick plastered a smile on his face as he pushed the door wide. 'I was trying to wake myself up from the nightmare of you two invading my space.'

'Haha!' Ed pointed at an ice bucket of bottled beers sitting in the centre of the coffee table. 'Sit down and have a drink. You look like crap.'

Harry shuffled over on the sofa to make room for Rick to sit next to him while Ed grabbed one of the beers, twisted off the cap and passed it to him.

'Thanks.' Rick took a long gulp, the cold bitterness a balm as it slid down his parched throat. The coffee in the machine at the hospital had been undrinkable and the vending machine next to it full of unappetising junk food and the sort of glow-in-the-dark coloured energy drinks that gave Rick the shakes just looking at them. 'To what do I owe the pleasure of your company?'

Harry reached down to unzip a padded bag by his feet, producing a tinfoil-covered plate and a knife and fork, all of which he set down on the coffee table in front of Rick. 'I thought you might be hungry.'

The scent of rich, meaty gravy hit Rick's nostrils and his empty stomach immediately growled in appreciation. Setting down the beer, he tore off the foil. 'What's this?'

'Beef bourguignon with Hasselback potatoes and wilted greens.'

Rick nodded, unable to talk around the forkful he'd already shoved into his mouth. He closed his eyes for a second to savour the exquisite flavours but he was too hungry to take his time and was soon scraping the last bit of gravy-soaked potato up. When he set the plate down, Harry grinned at him.

'Better?'

Leaning back, Rick placed a hand on his full belly and sighed. 'Much. Thanks, mate, you aren't half bad at that cooking lark.'

Harry barked out a laugh. 'Right, well, now we've fed and watered you, it's time for what we really came here for.'

The lazy relaxation that had been creeping over Rick vanished in an instant. 'What's that?'

'To take the piss out of you, of course!' Ed replied, his face-splitting grin matching his twin's. If it hadn't been for the white scar bisecting Ed's right eyebrow, they really would be impossible to tell apart.

'Rick... Rick... Rick,' Harry was saying as he shook his head. 'How the mighty have fallen.' He looked over at Ed. 'It's a sorry day, bro, to see such a giant of integrity brought so low.'

Ed pulled a sad face. 'A very sorry day indeed.'

Rick couldn't help himself as he started to laugh. 'If that's what you came for then you know where the door is.'

'Come on,' Harry said. 'You have to admit it's kind of funny.'

Ed grinned back at him. 'It's glorious! I like Rick being in the shit even more than I like seeing you screw up.'

Harry shot him the middle finger. 'So what did Dad say?'

All humour fell away as Rick's gut clenched and his delicious dinner no longer sat so easily. 'Nothing.'

'Nothing?' Ed echoed.

Rick shook his head. 'Not a word.'

The twins exchanged glances.

'Ooh, he's big mad,' said Ed.

Harry nodded. 'The only thing worse than getting one of Dad's disappointed-but-understanding chats is the big freeze.' He patted Rick on the leg. 'You're really in the poop, aren't you?'

'Neck deep, I reckon,' Ed said, not at all helpfully.

'Up to his chin at least, maybe even touching bottom lip.' Harry raised a hand to indicate the level and the pair exchanged a grin.

'Did you honestly only come here to torment me, because believe you me, I'm more than capable of doing that without any assistance from you two chuckle hounds.'

'Nah, mate.' Harry sat back, throwing one arm across the

back of the sofa. 'Matt messaged and told us what happened and we wanted to make sure you're okay.'

'I'm the last person you should be worried about. If I hadn't kept quiet about Davy he might already be having treatment. What if...' Rick had to pause so he didn't choke up. 'What if it's too late?'

Ed's expression was completely sober as he leaned forward. 'A couple of months can't have made that much difference and besides, from what Matt told us it sounds like there's only one person to blame in all this and that's Uncle Davy.'

'He always was a stubborn old goat,' Harry grumbled. 'And Ed's right. If Uncle D decided to stick his head in the sand about his condition then that's on him.'

Somewhere in the back of his mind, Rick knew they were right but that still didn't excuse what he'd done. 'I forced him to give that job to Anya, told him I'd tell everyone he was ill unless he took her on.'

Harry looked at him for a long moment then shrugged. 'I don't see the problem. The hotel's been getting a bit much for Uncle D for a while. Anyone with eyes could see it and you know both Dad and Uncle Ryan have tried to persuade him to slow down well before now.'

Ed nodded. 'Exactly. And Anya clearly needed a job asap given the hole that wanker left her in. I, too, am failing to see any problem here.'

Rick sighed. 'I put a bereaved woman who's lost her husband in the worst possible circumstances in close proximity to someone I thought was also going to die soon.'

'Oh.'

'Shit.'

'Yeah.' Sinking back against his cushion, Rick took a morose sip of his beer. 'She hates me, and she's got every right to.'

'I doubt she hates you,' said Ed, ever the optimist.

'Oh, no, I'm pretty sure she hates you,' Harry said, never one to pull his punches. 'But there is one bit of good news in all this: Uncle D might not be dying – well, not quite yet, at any rate.'

'I suppose there is that. But I don't know what I'm going to do about Anya.'

'I don't think there's anything you can do,' Ed said. 'Not right now.'

'But there must be something.' Rick raised a hand to rub his temple where a headache had started to pulse. 'I can't think straight, I'm too tired. But I'll work something out.' He had to. Anya was too important to him to let one mistake ruin everything. Even if that mistake seemed pretty insurmountable right now.

'You never change, do you?' Harry snorted. 'Mr I-Can-Fix-Everything. I hate to break it to you, but I reckon the only chance you have of getting this right is by not doing anything.'

'What are you talking about?'

'Some things are simply beyond your control. Whether Anya can come to terms with what's happened is up to her, not you. Whether she then decides to forgive you...' Harry shrugged. 'Also up to her.'

'What about losing her job at the hotel? She's got Freya to think of, and like Ed said, Drew left her right in the hole. I've got some savings—'

Harry held up his hands, his expression one of pure disbelief. 'You've got to stop, Rick, seriously. You're going to have to let her get on with it. Anya's mistakes are hers to own, and hers to rectify. You can't swoop in like Prince bloody Charming and slay all her dragons in the hope she'll swoon at your feet in eternal gratitude.'

'I think it was the prince in *Sleeping Beauty* that had to kill the dragon, not the one in *Snow White*,' Ed pointed out.

Harry raised his bottle and pointed it at Ed. 'Not helpful, bro.' He turned that pointing bottle towards Rick. 'If you really care about Anya, you're going to have to do something you've never done in your life, and that's let her learn to stand on her own two feet. She doesn't need an over-protective big brother, she needs a partner, someone who will stand by her not in front of her.'

Rick scrubbed a hand through his hair as the painful truth finally sank in. 'There's really nothing I can do, is there?'

'Afraid not.' Harry's eyes were full of sympathy as he patted Rick on the leg. He raised his beer, stopped with it hovering near his mouth as a sly grin appeared. 'At least Ed's still a hope-less case, so you can channel all that big brother energy into sorting him out.'

Ed laugh-groaned. 'Hey, come on, I'm not that bad.' They both stared at him for a long time until he lowered his head and sighed. 'Okay, yes, I am that bad, but that's all behind me now. I'm turning over a new leaf.'

Rick would believe that when he saw it.

31

Anya woke the next morning tired, but determined to seize control of her life. What Helen had said the night before was true. Running off to stay with her mum wouldn't solve anything; in fact, it would only put Anya further behind. Freya deserved the security Anya had never had, surrounded by friends as well as family. The summer would be over in a few short weeks and school would be starting. While she was cleaning up after making breakfast, she put a quick video call in to Chloe. 'Hey, I know it's early but I wanted to catch you before you go to work.'

'Hey. No probs, what's up?'

Anya glanced towards where Freya was sitting in front of the TV. Anya had stopped feeling guilty about using the telly as a part-time babysitter; sometimes she just needed five minutes' peace to get on and do something, and *Numberblocks* was at least educational as well as fun. Freya was absorbed in whatever was on the screen, the square of toast in her hand forgotten. Still Anya turned her back and lowered her voice. 'That paperwork thing you were sorting out for me, can you chase it up?'

'The name change? Yes, of course.'

'Great. I really need it asap so I can get Freya registered for school.'

Chloe went quiet as the implication of what Anya was saying sank in. 'Oh, fab, I mean, yes of course I'll chase it up. Do you want me to print off the copy of the registration form and the automated receipt email I got back? You could always take them in to Morwenna and see if you can kick-start things at her end while you are waiting for the official certification to come through.'

Anya considered it for a moment. 'That might be a good idea, thanks. And if you've got time this weekend perhaps we can have a look at a few designs I've found online. I was thinking tote bags might be a quick and easy thing I can knock out, and with school coming up, maybe pencil cases, laptop covers and what have you. They'd be a great way to use up some of the odds and ends of material I have.'

'Sounds perfect! I'll get onto Dad and ask him to finish off those last bits in the workshop and we can get everything out of the spare room too.' She paused. 'You sound a lot better than last night.'

'I feel a lot better. Look, I've got a few things to sort out, so can we catch up later?'

'Sure. I need to jump in the shower anyway. I'll pop in when I get home and drop those copies off with you.'

'That would be lovely. You can stay for dinner again if you like. It's fish fingers, mash and peas.'

'Sounds too good to refuse!' Chloe winked. 'See you later, Annie.'

Anya looked over at Freya. Her toast was all gone and she wasn't sure what she was watching now, but she was giggling and Anya decided that was at least as important as learning to count. She flicked through her contacts and made a second call. 'Hi, Ma. I'm sorry to call so early.'

'Hello, dearest! Don't worry about the time, we've been up since just after five. We don't sleep late and what with this business with Davy...' A gusty sigh filled Anya's ear.

'You must be worried sick about him, but Aunt Helen seemed to think it wasn't all bad when she was here last night.'

'No, that's true. Jago's arranged for some cover at the quay, so he's going to take Ron up to the hospital to see him. Hopefully they'll find a doctor to tell them the truth about what's going on while they're there.'

Of course they'd be visiting Davy; Anya should've thought about that before she rang. 'So you won't want Freya today, then? That's what I was calling to check.'

'Oh no, drop her off as normal. I'm not going up to the hospital, because I'd only brain Davy with a bedpan if I'm within striking distance of that stubborn old fool.'

Anya laughed as she pictured it. 'I think they're made of cardboard these days.'

'Well I'd stab him with a scalpel then!' Ma chuckled.

'So bloodthirsty, Ma!' Anya exclaimed. 'I never would've thought it of you.'

'I never thought of myself as having a violent streak either, but these Penrose men, sometimes they drive you to think the worst.'

'I know what you mean.' She didn't want to take a scalpel to Rick, but she wouldn't mind giving him a jab with a sharp pencil, maybe a kick in the shin while she was at it, stupid bloody man. 'Are you sure about having Freya for the day? I can make other arrangements if you need me to.'

'Absolutely sure. You drop her off as soon as you are ready. It's my baking day anyway, so we will have lots to keep us busy, and it'll be good to have her company rather than sitting here and fretting.'

'As long as you're sure?'

'I'm positive. See you soon, dearest.'

Right, that was one thing sorted. On to the next.

'I didn't expect to be seeing you again so soon,' Steve said when she walked into the hotel reception about half an hour later. 'I thought you didn't work here any more.'

'Seems I'm a glutton for punishment, doesn't it?' she said, rounding the desk to drop her bag on the floor. 'Right then, anything I need to know about?'

The handover with Steve didn't take long and Anya was logged in and scanning through the couple of emails he'd flagged for her while he went and fetched his lunchbox from the fridge in the kitchen. Not a *lunch*box, she supposed, when he was eating his sandwiches at ten o'clock at night.

'Here you go,' Steve said, setting a mug of hot water down beside her. 'I didn't add milk because I know you like that herbal stuff.'

'That's kind of you, thanks.' Anya bent over and pulled a tea bag out of her stash in the bottom drawer.

'What you got?'

'Raspberry and lemon.' She held up the little sachet to show him.

Steve mock-shuddered. 'Good grief, give me a cup of good old builder's tea any day.' He tapped the edge of the desk. 'I'll be off, then, if you're sure you'll be okay?'

'I'll be fine, thanks. Do you want me to text you later if I get any update on Davy?'

'That would be great, thank you. I meant to thank you for the message you sent last night too. It was a real weight off my mind.' He sighed. 'I've grown fond of the old boy, even with all his quirky ways.'

Anya smiled. 'Me too.'

There was a heavy thud-thud-thud and Rick came dashing through the revolving door. 'Sorry I'm late, Steve! I had a bit of nightmare this morn...' Rick trailed off as he spotted Anya ensconced in her usual spot behind the desk. 'What are you doing here?'

'What does it look like?'

Steve shot a quick glance between them. 'Oh, trouble in paradise. That's my cue to leave.'

'No trouble,' Rick called after him as Steve headed for the door.

'No paradise, I think you meant to say,' Anya said, but not until Steve was safely inside the revolving compartment.

Rick stared at her for a long moment, his eyes full of regret. 'Yes, that too.'

Breaking his gaze, Anya shuffled the papers on the desk in front of her. 'Well, as you can see I've got everything in hand here, so you can concentrate on running your own business.' She'd almost said minding your own business, but even though she was still upset with him, it wasn't in her nature to be deliberately mean. Though she might still fancy a punt at one of his shins if he was foolish enough to get too close.

'What about when Davy gets back?'

Anya glanced up. 'That's for me and him to sort out.'

Rick closed his eyes for a second. 'Of course. Well, I'll leave you to it. If you need anything...'

'I'll be fine.'

He smiled then. 'I know you will. It might not seem like it from the way I've acted, Anya, but I never doubted you, not for one minute. You're one of the strongest people I've ever met and I wish nothing but good things for you.'

Damn him for being nice to her. 'Take care, Rick.'

32

The day passed without incident and Anya received an update from Ma and Pa when she went to collect Freya.

'They're letting him home tomorrow. The antibiotics are doing their thing and he's much more comfortable,' Pa told her as she sat down for the obligatory cup of tea with them. 'I tried to persuade him to come back here, but, well, you can imagine how that went down.'

'I sure can.' Conscious of small ears, she framed her next question casually. 'And the other matter?'

Pa gave her a very relieved smile. 'Manageable, by the sounds of things.'

Anya blinked hard to ward off a sudden rush of tears. 'That's good. I'll have a chat with housekeeping in the morning and we'll make sure his suite is spick and span, and between us Steve and I will keep an eye on him.'

'That would be a weight off my mind.'

Though she'd half expected it to be Rick who brought Davy home the following morning, it was instead one of the twins –

Harry, Anya figured as he came closer and she could see there was no scar.

'Delivery for you.'

'Thanks, I guess. Hello, Davy.'

Davy gave her a sheepish glance from under his brows. 'Hello, pet.'

She folded her arms. 'Is that it?'

He shrugged. 'I reckon so.'

'Good. I'll leave Harry to get you settled and I'll come up in a bit to make you a pot of tea.'

'I'll be fine in the office,' Davy protested. 'I don't need any mollycoddling.'

'Behave yourself, Uncle D. The doc only let you come home because you promised to be on bed-rest for the next couple of days.'

Davy scowled at Harry. 'No one likes a grass, boy.'

Harry seemed entirely unfazed. 'You don't scare me, Uncle D, but Mum bloody well does and if she finds out I let you get away with any nonsense she'll have my guts.' He pointed towards the door that led to the stairs. 'Come on, let's get you sorted. Kitchen prep started half an hour ago, so I need to get to the restaurant.'

Anya let Davy get himself settled in before she placed the 'back in five minutes' sign on the front desk and made sure she had the hotel phone in her pocket. She climbed the stairs to the first floor and made her way down the corridor to the corner suite of rooms where Davy lived. When she knocked he told her it was unlocked, and she found him in his chair by the window with its rather uninspiring view out over the car park.

He turned to regard her. 'It's a lot tidier in here than I left it. That your doing?'

She nodded as she crossed to the little kitchenette in the

corner. 'I got housekeeping to change the bed and push the hoover around. It's always nice to have clean sheets, I think, especially when you've not been feeling your best.'

'It is, thank you.' He was silent for a moment as she made herself busy filling the kettle and sorting out cups and the teapot. 'Leave that for a minute will you, and come and sit down.'

There was only one chair, so Anya perched on the edge of the bed facing him. 'I don't want to fight with you, Davy. If you want to replace me, that's your prerogative, but you'll need someone to help you here.'

Davy held up a hand to forestall her. There was a livid bruise on the back of it, probably from where he'd had to have an IV line. 'I owe you an apology. I could tell you that I wasn't myself the other day, that it was the pain talking, but that would be a coward's excuse. I lashed out at you because I was scared to death, and I'm afraid I took that out on you.'

She sighed. 'I know you didn't want me here, Davy, that Rick forced you to take me on.'

'Forced me?' Davy wheezed out a laugh, then winced and pressed a hand to his side. 'I was struggling well before I banged my head, I just didn't want to admit it. It was easier on my ego to pretend otherwise, but when Rick insisted I took someone on, it was a huge relief.'

'You really hurt my feelings.' It was important for her to say it. To stand up for herself and make him understand they couldn't just brush everything under the carpet.

'I know, pet. And I am more sorry than I can say. I know I don't deserve it, but please try and find it in your heart to forgive a silly old fool with more pride than sense.' He sat forward on the edge of his chair, clasping his hands together between his knees. 'Having you here has been a blessing. More than a blessing: a joy. I hadn't realised how lonely I was, how much I'd closed myself off from everyone, until I had you around and about the place.'

Anya rubbed her cheek where she could feel a blush of pleasure beginning to glow. 'It's been special for me too.'

Davy's eyes lit up. 'So you'll stay?'

Anya glanced away, not liking the weight of that hope on her shoulders. 'I don't know yet. It depends on what you choose to do next. If you don't want to undergo treatment then I will respect your decision, but I don't know if I can bring myself to sit by and watch you fade away, Davy. You won't have any problem replacing me, and I'll bridge that gap until you do.' She hesitated. It would be easier to walk away now, to protect herself as much as possible. But her aunt was right, life couldn't be lived in a bubble. 'If you decide to fight, however, I'll fight with you, every step of the way.'

Davy shook his head. 'You've already done more than enough, I wouldn't have you go through that.'

Though her heart ached, Anya managed a wobbly smile. 'You don't get to make that decision for me. For all your grumping and growling, I've grown rather fond of you.' She rose, needing to get out of there before she started bawling her head off. 'Right, I'd better get back downstairs. Let me sort out your tea.'

Davy was silent until she set a clean cup, a small jug of milk and a pot of tea on the table beside his chair. 'Thank you.'

'My pleasure.'

He held out his hand to her and she took it without hesitation. His skin was warm, almost papery beneath her fingers. She held it gently, conscious of the bruise. 'I'm going to see the doctor as soon as he gets my results through and I've already promised to take either Jago or Ryan with me.' He huffed in amusement. 'It'll be both of them, if I know anything about my family.'

Anya smiled. 'Bloody Penrose men, you're all as stubborn as each other.'

'Aye, aren't we just. Anyway, I can't make any promises until I know the full picture, but I'll follow the doctor's advice.' He gave a little chuckle. 'I thought I'd made my peace, that I was ready to accept I'd had my allotted time and shuffle off quietly. Then you showed up and I've watched you dig yourself out of rock bottom and it makes me ashamed that I didn't show the same kind of courage. Not just about the cancer, but years ago.'

Anya knelt beside his chair. 'What happened?'

Davy's smile was soft and sad. 'Oh, nothing earth shattering. Just that I thought I'd met the person I was supposed to spend the rest of my life with, but she had other ideas. I kind of gave up after that. Withdrew into my shell and even when there might have been another chance at happiness, I didn't take the risk.' He reached out and stroked her hair. 'Don't close yourself off to love. I know you've suffered more than anyone at your age should ever have to, but if a foolish old man is allowed to offer one piece of wisdom, it's to always keep your heart open to possibilities.'

Anya lowered her head. 'It hurts too much.'

Davy's gnarled fingers stroked her hair once more. 'You only think it does, but when you reach my age and look back on all the chances you've missed, it'll hurt so much more.'

She lifted her watery eyes to meet his. 'He lied to me.'

'I know, but only because he was trying to do the right thing by me. I should never have put Rick in that position and I'll regret it for whatever days are left to me that I'm the one who caused problems for the two of you.'

She sighed. 'It wasn't just you. I rushed into a relationship with Rick before I was ready. I mean I thought I was, but it's become clear to me over the past couple of days that it all got a bit too much too soon.' She quirked her lips in a wry smile. 'You Penrose men are too damn easy to love and it was so nice to have someone to lean on. But Rick deserves someone who can give support, not just take it, and that can't be me until I learn how to stand on my own.'

'There's nothing to say you can't try again. Take your time.' He gave her a bittersweet grin. 'You've got plenty of that at least.'

'You're as bad as your great-nephew, always wanting to fix things,' she admonished, though she smiled as she wagged her finger at him. 'If I'm sticking around here, you need to promise to keep your nose out of my private life.'

Davy grinned, a hint of his old sparkle in his eyes. 'I've got better things to do than worry about what you're up to. I've got plans of my own, including for this place.'

Whatever she'd expected him to say, it wasn't this. 'I thought the hotel meant everything to you.'

Davy sighed. 'So did I. Turns out you're never too old to learn what's really important in life.' He squeezed her fingers. 'Don't worry, I'll see you right.'

She shuffled closer to lean her head against his shoulder. 'Don't worry about me, I'll be fine.'

'I know you will.' Davy turned his head and brushed a kiss against her temple. 'And I intend to stick around if I can and watch you go from strength to strength.'

Anya sat back on her heels. 'I'm going to hold you to that. So, are you going to tell me what your plans are for the hotel?'

Davy tapped the side of his nose. 'It's all in hand. You'll see.'

33

The heat of the past few weeks had broken with a spectacular downpour which entirely suited Rick's own gloomy mood as he wove his way through Port Petroc towards the railway station and parked up in the twenty-minute pickup zone. According to the train company's app, the rush hour service from London was running only five minutes late – a miracle in itself. A handful of taxis filled the rank opposite and several other cars formed a queue behind Rick's SUV. The train pulled in and Rick turned on the engine, activating the wipers so he could peer through the heavy rain as people emerged from the front of the station. They peeled off in different directions, some towards the taxis, others putting up umbrellas or lifting the collars on their summer jackets as they headed out on foot. A group of four men dashed across the road and into the pub, which made Rick smile before he turned his attention back to the station entrance.

Where is he?

The rush of people had slowed to a trickle, the last few stragglers making their way out, and then a familiar figure stepped into view, struggling with two large suitcases, one of which appeared determined to steer off in the opposite direction to where Liam wanted it to go. Clicking off his seat belt, Rick jumped out and ran over to help, wincing as a large raindrop managed to sneak inside his shirt collar, splatting down his neck. 'Blimey, I thought you'd missed the train for a minute!' he exclaimed as he grabbed the handle of the rogue case.

'Bloody lift's out of action,' Liam grumbled. 'So I had to wrestle these up the stairs and over the footbridge.'

They hurried towards the car, Rick pressing the button so the automatic mechanism on the boot opened it by the time they got there. 'You sure you've brought enough with you?' he asked as he heaved the first case into the rear compartment. 'You look like you're planning to stay for a month, not just a couple of nights.'

'Yeah, about that...' Liam lifted the other case and wrestled it in beside the first.

Rick shut the boot and stared at him in surprise. 'What's happened?' Another raindrop splashed off the end of his nose. 'No, tell me in the car.'

They jumped inside and Rick turned the air up full blast to fight the mist forming on the inside of the window from the sudden rise in humidity caused by their wet clothing.

'Caroline and I broke up,' Liam said, not looking at Rick as he put on his seat belt.

'I'm sorry to hear that, I knew things weren't great when we spoke the other week, but still, it's a shock.'

'What does it say about us that we were both more relieved than sad to admit it was finally over?' Liam propped his chin on his hand and stared at the side window. 'At least I didn't have to feel bad about moving out. Lucinda and that awful Tarquin bloke split up as well, so she's moved into the spare room and is paying half the rent.'

Liam fell silent and Rick concentrated on the light traffic through Port Petroc and out onto the main road back to Half-moon Quay. Even if the weather hadn't been terrible, he was keen to avoid the scenic route. Not that it stopped him from thinking about Anya. She seemed to fill his every waking thought, even more so than for the brief time they'd been together. 'If it's any consolation, things didn't work out between me and Anya either.'

Liam shifted in his seat and Rick could feel his eyes on him. 'No! Oh, mate, I'm so sorry, what happened?'

Rick spent the rest of the journey going over it all. 'Harry reckons there's nothing I can do to fix things, that I'm just going to have to wait and see if Anya can forgive me at some point.'

Liam gave a soft chuckle. 'Good luck with that.'

'Oh come on, the twins have already given me enough grief. Why didn't anyone bother to tell me you all found me so over-bearing?'

'Not overbearing, but maybe a little over-caring. There are a lot worse things to be than the kind of person who wants everyone around them to be happy, Rick.'

'But maybe I need to try a bit less hard to fix everything.'

'Exactly. You know what the most surprising thing about all this is? That Harry's the one dishing out sensible advice.'

Rick laughed. 'He's changed a lot since he's been working with Russ at the restaurant.'

'Sounds like it. How's Ed getting on?'

'Still hopeless! He's working for me at the moment thanks to an affair at work that turned sour.'

Liam groaned. 'What was he thinking?'

'I don't think there was a lot of thinking going on, certainly not with his brain, anyway.'

'What about his course?'

Rick pulled the car up onto the drive. 'Thankfully, that's the one thing we don't have to worry about when it comes to Ed; he's still as dedicated to his studies as ever.'

'That's good.' Liam stared up through the car window at their parents' house, his expression unreadable. 'Here we are, then.'

Rick turned off the engine and looked at his brother. 'How long are you planning on being home for?'

Liam shrugged. 'Your guess is as good as mine. I've taken a leave of absence from work. I had so much holiday accrued they couldn't really object, and I've just completed a massive project I've been working on, so the timing was on my side. I need a bit of space to think, and it's easier to do that here rather than waste money on renting a hotel room while I try and find somewhere else to live.'

'Well I'm glad you're home for a bit. I've missed you.'

'I missed you too.'

It didn't escape Rick's attention that Liam hadn't said anything about being glad to be home.

* * *

Rick didn't get much of a chance to delve further into Liam's troubles that evening. Their parents were both thrilled to have him home, and although his mum seemed to have forgiven him, Rick was still very much on the outs with his dad. Not wanting to spoil his brother's homecoming, he'd made himself scarce. When he woke the next morning, Liam was already out and Rick was too busy down on the beach all day to think about anything other than keeping an eye on Ed as well as their customers. By the time he got home there wasn't much time to do more than jump in the shower and get changed ready for Ma's birthday party.

It didn't take long to walk to the restaurant and they arrived to find the rest of the family already there. They were sitting on the sea wall and rose to greet them. Rick stood back and let Liam enjoy the hugs and kisses and backslaps. It was so good to have him back, like a missing piece of their family puzzle had been found under the sofa and returned to the box where it belonged. Rick wasn't the only one who stayed back. Anya had remained seated on the wall, Freya on her lap. Rick raised a quick hand to her but kept his distance.

Harry appeared looking smart in his chef's whites, his thick curly hair tied back off his face with a blue and white bandana. 'Table's ready when you are,' he called. 'Where's the lady of the night?'

'Henry Penrose, did you just call your grandmother a sex worker?' their mother exclaimed as the rest of them laughed.

Ma sashayed up to the door. 'If you only knew the half of it.' She grinned up at Harry as she tapped her cheek.

Harry leaned down and planted a kiss. 'Hello, Ma, you're looking gorgeous as ever.'

Clearly enjoying her moment in the spotlight, she hooked her arm through his. 'That charm will get you into trouble one day.'

'Let's hope so! Come on, guys, let's get you all sat down.'

There was a bit of a faff as everyone tried to take charge of who was sitting where. To no one's surprise, Ed hadn't got around to his promised seating plan. Again Rick was happy to stand back and let them get on with it. As long as he wasn't sat next to his dad he'd be happy. Anya had taken Freya to the far end of the table where a waitress was waiting with a booster cushion for Freya to sit on. Anya got her settled and as she turned to take her own seat she caught Rick's eye. He was about to turn away, embarrassed at being caught staring like some lovesick puppy, when to his surprise Anya patted the seat next to her.

He hesitated with his hand on the back of the chair. 'Are you sure?'

She nodded. 'Yes. It's Ma's evening and I don't want her worrying that I'm still upset with you.'

'Thanks.' It was only after he'd sat and was placing his napkin across his lap that Rick realised she hadn't said she wasn't still upset with him, only that she didn't want to give Ma that impression. He glanced across the table to where Davy was sitting further up on the other side, between Chloe and Helen. 'How's things at the hotel?'

'Fine, thanks. It's been a busy couple of weeks as we're at capacity, but nothing I can't handle.'

'That's great to hear.'

There was a stilted silence for a moment. 'How's things with The Hire Hut?'

'Same, same. Busy, I mean, but Ed's been helping me out, which takes the pressure off.'

'That's good. And it must be nice to have Liam home.'

'Yeah, it is.' Rick didn't think it would be a good time to mention Liam and Caroline splitting up. He was also regretting accepting Anya's offer to sit by her. If the choice was between her ignoring him and this tortured, awkward politeness, he'd take the former. More for something to do than anything else, Rick reached for the basket of bread and offered it to her. Their eyes met and he was instantly back on their first date when she'd been so worried about eating too much, as if he was the kind of man who cared about anything other than the woman he was with feeling content and well-fed. *I will always want you to eat the bread*, he'd told her, and damn it, he'd meant every word.

Anya stared down at the basket then back up at him. Was he fooling himself that he saw the same regret he was feeling? With a stiff smile, she shook her head and looked away. Rick set the bread down and swallowed a sigh. How had they gone from so much promise to this painful awkwardness in just a few short weeks?

Things improved a little once Ed and Matt came and sat opposite them. The pair kept up a steady stream of chatter with Anya. The waitress arrived with an activity pack to keep Freya occupied and the next minute Matt was rearranging the chairs and Freya was knelt up between him and Ed, playing spot the difference.

'It's about their intellectual level,' Rick muttered to Anya from behind his hand and was pleased when she properly met his eyes for the first time and laughed. After that things felt a bit easier between them and the noise level around the table ramped up as one plateful of delicious food after another was placed in front of him and glasses were topped up for a second and then a third time.

'Can you pour me some water, please?' Anya asked him, gesturing up the table to a large jug.

'Of course.' He retrieved the jug and poured them both a glass.

'Thank you.' She took a long drink, her lashes fluttering down to shade her eyes, and she let out a little sigh as she set down her glass. 'That's better.' Her cheeks bore a rosy glow. It was warm in the restaurant, even with the door open, but he thought perhaps it might be something to do with Ed's generous pouring hand. Even flushed and with her hair rumpled from where she'd pushed it off her forehead, she'd never looked more beautiful. Regret flooded through him that he'd messed everything up between them and he had to look away before he did something unconscionably stupid like fall on his knees and beg for her forgiveness. *God, Harry better be right about this.*

Instead of dessert, Harry appeared from the kitchen bearing an enormous three-tiered chocolate cake with a pair of gold sparklers sticking out the top of it. They sang 'Happy Birthday', the rest of the guests who were in for dinner joining with both the singing and the round of applause afterwards.

'Speech! Speech!' Ed called out and, to more applause, Ma stood, beaming from ear to ear.

'I'd like to thank you all for making such a lovely fuss of me,' she started.

'It's no more than you deserve,' Ryan interrupted, and they all cheered in agreement.

'We love you, Ma!' Chloe said, after the cheers had died down.

'I love you too, dearest. I love you all.' Clasping her hands together, she looked around the table. 'The most important people in my life are all sat here with me tonight. Especially you.' She reached out a hand to Pa, who was sitting to her right. 'From the day I first set eyes on you, I knew you were the one, Ron Penrose. You've made every day since a delight.'

'And you mine, my love,' Ron replied.

Rick wasn't the only one who had to have a gulp of their drink as Pa took her hand and kissed the back of it. He couldn't resist stealing a quick glance at Anya. She was looking back, her eyes shining.

That could be us, one day. He longed to give voice to the ache in his heart, the desire to put things right almost overwhelming his vow to give her the space he knew she needed.

A chair scraped loudly, breaking the moment, and they both looked around to see Davy rising to his feet. 'I don't want to distract you from tonight's celebrations, but I can't let the chance to apologise to you all pass me by. I don't know what to say other than I was scared and I was selfish and I'm sorry that I've put you all through so much unnecessary worry.' He looked along the table and met Rick's eyes. 'I'm especially sorry for the position I put you in, Rick, and I don't want anyone here taking out what was my decision on this boy a moment longer.' Davy's gaze rested on Jago for a long moment until Rick's dad nodded. 'Good, now that's sorted, there's just one more thing I need to do.' He reached into his jacket pocket and pulled out an envelope. Rick assumed it was a birthday card for Ma until Davy tossed it over the table to land in front of Liam.

'What's this?'

'Best open it and find out,' Davy said with a wink. 'Now if you'll excuse me, I've got somewhere else to be.' He pushed back his chair and walked towards the door, one hand held out and a broad smile on his face.

They all turned to see Maud step out of the shadows, her neat bob dyed a fetching shade of lilac and her jeans so tight they looked sprayed on. Davy leaned over to peck a kiss on her cheek then tucked her hand into the crook of his arm and the pair of them walked out. The table was silent for a moment before they all began to talk at once. Rick turned to Anya, who was smiling to herself. 'Did you know about that?'

She shook her head. 'I had no idea, but good for them.'

Rick wondered if it was such a good idea given what Davy might be facing, but then decided that it didn't matter what he thought about it. 'Yes, good for them.'

'I can almost hear your brain whirring from here, Rick.'

He gave her a sheepish grin. 'I'm trying, okay.'

Ed leaned across the table and Rick had to reach out and grab a half-empty wine bottle before his brother sent it flying. 'Come on, Liam, the suspense is killing me. What's in the envelope?'

Clearly uncomfortable at suddenly being the centre of attention, Liam pulled up the flap and slid a thick wedge of documents out. He scanned it over, his frown deepening, before he eventually handed it to their father.

'What is it?' Ed demanded again.

Looking completely dumbfounded, their eldest brother sat back in his chair. 'It's the deeds to the hotel.'

As uproar broke out around the table, Rick heard Anya murmur, 'Oh, Davy, what are you playing at now?'

34

The evening broke up soon after Davy's spectacular walkout. While the others fussed around, dividing up the birthday cake while Ryan and Jago argued jovially over who was paying the bill, Anya busied herself packing up Freya's things. She'd already worked out what their food had cost and she'd sort it out with whoever ended up winning in the next couple of days. 'Come on, poppet, time to go,' she said to Freya in her best encouraging voice.

'I'm tired, Mummy.' Freya held up her arms, refusing to stand.

Seeing she was on the edge of being too tired that could easily tip over into tears, Anya crouched and picked her up. 'Oof, you're getting too big to be carried,' she said as she braced Freya on her hip. 'Let's give Ma her card and present, then it's home to bed for us, young lady.'

Anya fumbled with the handbag hanging over her opposite shoulder, trying to keep hold of Freya with one hand.

'Here, let me.' The strain in her arm disappeared as Rick lifted Freya up like she weighed nothing.

'Thanks, I won't be a sec.'

She quickly worked her way around the table and handed Ma her card and the apron she'd made for her. 'Thank you so much for inviting us,' she said, pressing a kiss to Ma's cheek.

'Thank you for coming.' She unfolded the apron and held it up. 'Oh, this is beautiful, thank you. Did you have a nice time?'

'It was great. I'm going to dash though, because it's way past Freya's bedtime.'

Ma laughed. 'She's not the only one! We can catch up in the morning when you drop her off. Go on, get that poor child home to bed.'

Though she'd only been gone a couple of minutes, Freya was fast asleep on Rick's shoulder, her arms clasped around his neck. Anya held out her hands to take her. 'I don't mind carrying her,' he said, quietly. 'I know you don't need my help, Anya, but I really don't mind.'

She stared up at him for a long minute. Was she really going to risk waking Freya up on a point of principle? Yes, she could manage to carry her home, but it would be bloody hard work. 'Thank you.' She glanced around but everyone else was still chatting and didn't look like they would be on the move anytime soon. 'I don't think we should wait for the others, if you don't mind?'

'Whatever you need is fine with me.' Rick gestured towards the door before laying a large, protective hand on Freya's back to hold her safe. *She'd always be safe with him.*

The truth of it burned deep into Anya's bones as they strolled along the seafront in silence. Yes, he'd lied to her, but Rick was nothing like Drew. Everything he did was for other people's benefit, whereas Drew had only ever been out for himself.

I don't think anyone has ever stopped to ask him what he needs.

Anya realised she had no idea because they had never taken the time to actually get to know each other. Not really.

The sun was setting, turning the horizon where the sky met the sea into a molten river of fire. It was so beautiful, Anya had to stop and watch as orange turned to red, to shades of violet and indigo and finally to the soft grey of a dove's wing.

'I never get tired of that,' Rick said with a sigh as they began to walk again.

'Do you like living here?'

She could sense him glance down at her but she kept her eyes fixed on the path. 'In the Quay? Sure, I mean it's the only place I've ever known, but yeah, I'm happy here.'

'And it's never bothered you, that you didn't get to move to London like Liam did?'

Rick was quiet for a moment as though considering the question. 'I think I was jealous now and then when I was younger, but I'm not sure living there has done Liam much good in the long run.'

'And what about working for your parents?'

Rick's chuckle was soft. 'What's with all the questions?'

She stopped and looked up at him. 'I'm just interested. I've known you all my life and yet somehow I feel like I don't know you at all.'

'I thought we'd got to know each other very well.' Rick's voice was husky and she was glad the sun had set and she couldn't really make out his expression.

'Yes, we did, and maybe that's part of the problem. We went about things all the wrong way, rushed ahead before either of us was ready.'

He was silent for a long time before he finally nodded. 'I... I think I was so caught up in the idea of you that I never really saw you beyond what you've always meant to me, and I'm sorry about that.'

Anya sighed. 'And having someone to take care of me again was too tempting. I know now that what I really need is to learn to take care of myself.'

'You seem to be doing a pretty good job of that.'

Warmth spread through her at the clear admiration in his tone. 'I'm not so sure. Call me a work in progress.'

'Is that all I'll ever be able to call you?'

Reaching up, she dashed a tear from her lashes, grateful again that it was almost dark. 'I'd like it one day if we could call each other friends.'

'Friends sounds good.'

It did sound good. And some day perhaps they'd be able to call each other more than that. 'Maybe we could start again. Forget the past couple of months and try and get things right this time.'

'Is that what you want?' The hope in his voice was a match for the delicate flame of it glowing inside her.

'What about what you want?'

'I want you. I want Freya. I want all three of us to be a family one day. I want it to be you and me sitting at a table in fifty years' time surrounded by our children and grandchildren as we celebrate a life well lived together.'

Wetness soaked her cheeks. 'I want that too, but I don't think I'm in the right place for that just yet.'

Rick's warm hand circled her shoulder, pulling her against his side, but oh so carefully so they didn't disturb Freya. He pressed a kiss on her hair. 'The best things in life are worth waiting for, Anya. We've got time.'

She curled her arms around his waist and leaned in to the comforting strength of his body. For a moment she was tempted to throw caution to the wind and say to hell with waiting. But Rick deserved her at her best. She didn't want someone to look after her. She wanted someone she could look after too. A partnership. A foundation solid enough they could build a happy life together on it. 'I promise it'll be worth waiting for.'

Rick tilted his head and rested it on top of hers. 'I'll wait as long as you need and next time it'll be perfect.'

Anya shook her head. 'No, it'll be better than perfect; it'll be the real thing.' She'd learned the hard way that perfection was an illusion, and she'd never make that mistake again. When the time was right, she wanted everything with Rick: the good, the bad and all the wonderful messy in-between bits. Because those were the foundations they could build a life on. Build a love on that would carry them through the years to come. This was just the beginning of their story.

* * *

MORE FROM SARAH BENNETT

Another book from Sarah Bennett, *Where We Belong*, is available to order now here:

https://mybook.to/WhereWeBelongBackAd

ACKNOWLEDGEMENTS

It's always so exciting (and a little bit scary) plunging head first into a new series but here we are! I had so much fun building a new setting and community and I hope you will enjoy spending time in this pretty little coastal village as much as I am. Though writing feels like a solitary effort sometimes, I couldn't possibly do it without the help and support of lots of wonderful people.

Top of the pops has to be Sarah Ritherdon, who is simply the best editor any writer could wish for. xx

A special mention to Niamh Wallace, who supports all my books with innovative publicity campaigns. It's a joy to work with you. Thank you so much for all your hard work. xx

Thanks to Candida Bradford and Helen Woodhouse for helping me with edits. You really made this book shine.

As ever, Amanda Ridout and the team at Boldwood Books are second to none. It's so inspiring to work with such a dedicated and creative publisher.

Thanks to Alice Moore for my beautiful cover.

Loads of love to all the authors who make up #TeamBoldwood. You are simply the best. x

To my wonderful writer friends, Phillipa Ashley, Jules Wake, Bella Osborne and Rachel Griffiths, Donna Ashcroft, Rachel Burton, Jessica Redland and Portia MacIntosh. Simply brilliant storytellers and always there when I need them in good times and bad. xxx

As always, I couldn't do this without the love and support of my husband. Thanks, Bun. xxx

ABOUT THE AUTHOR

Sarah Bennett is the bestselling author of several romantic fiction trilogies. Born and raised in a military family she is happily married to her own Officer and when not reading or writing enjoys sailing the high seas.

Halfmoon Quay awaits! Sign up to Sarah Bennett's newsletter for an exclusive first read of the first chapter of her brand new book Just the Beginning!

Visit Sarah's website: https://sarahbennettauthor. wordpress.com/

Follow Sarah on social media:

- facebook.com/SarahBennettAuthor
- x.com/Sarahlou_writes
- bookbub.com/authors/sarah-bennett-b4a48ebb-a5c3-4c39-b59a-09aa91dc7cfa
- instagram.com/sarah_bennettauthor

ALSO BY SARAH BENNETT

Mermaids Point

Summer Kisses at Mermaids Point

Second Chances at Mermaids Point

Christmas Surprises at Mermaids Point

Love Blooms at Mermaids Point

Happy Endings at Mermaids Point

Juniper Meadows

Where We Belong

In From the Cold

Come Rain or Shine

Snow is Falling

Halfmoon Quay

Just the Beginning

Boldwood